MRS. HENRY WOOD

The Foggy Night at Offord

Martyn Ware's Temptation

The Night-Walk Over the Mill Stream

Elibron Classics
www.elibron.com

Elibron Classics series.

© 2005 Adamant Media Corporation.

ISBN 1-4021-8692-4 (paperback)
ISBN 1-4021-1713-2 (hardcover)

This Elibron Classics Replica Edition is an unabridged facsimile of the edition published in 1872 by Bernhard Tauchnitz, London.

Elibron and Elibron Classics are trademarks of Adamant Media Corporation. All rights reserved.

This book is an accurate reproduction of the original. Any marks, names, colophons, imprints, logos or other symbols or identifiers that appear on or in this book, except for those of Adamant Media Corporation and BookSurge, LLC, are used only for historical reference and accuracy and are not meant to designate origin or imply any sponsorship by or license from any third party.

COLLECTION
OF
BRITISH AUTHORS

TAUCHNITZ EDITION.

VOL. 1217.

THE FOGGY NIGHT AT OFFORD;
MARTYN WARE'S TEMPTATION; THE NIGHT-WALK OVER
THE MILL STREAM.

BY

MRS. HENRY WOOD.

IN ONE VOLUME.

TAUCHNITZ EDITION.
By the same Author,

EAST LYNNE	3 vols.
THE CHANNINGS	2 vols.
MRS. HALLIBURTON'S TROUBLES	2 vols.
VERNER'S PRIDE	3 vols.
THE SHADOW OF ASHLYDYAT	3 vols.
TREVLYN HOLD	2 vols.
LORD OAKBURN'S DAUGHTERS	2 vols.
OSWALD CRAY	2 vols.
MILDRED ARKELL	2 vols.
ST. MARTIN'S EVE	2 vols.
ELSTER'S FOLLY	2 vols.
LADY ADELAIDE'S OATH	2 vols.
ORVILLE COLLEGE	1 vol.
A LIFE'S SECRET	1 vol.
THE RED COURT FARM	2 vols.
ANNE HEREFORD	2 vols.
ROLAND YORKE	2 vols.
GEORGE CANTERBURY'S WILL	2 vols.
BESSY RANE	2 vols.
DENE HOLLOW	2 vols.

THE
FOGGY NIGHT AT OFFORD;

MARTYN WARE'S TEMPTATION;

THE NIGHT-WALK OVER THE MILL STREAM.

BY

MRS. HENRY WOOD,

AUTHOR OF "EAST LYNNE," "DENE HOLLOW," ETC.

COPYRIGHT EDITION.

LEIPZIG

BERNHARD TAUCHNITZ

1872.

The Right of Translation is reserved.

CONTENTS.

	PAGE
THE FOGGY NIGHT AT OFFORD	9
MARTYN WARE'S TEMPTATION	187
THE NIGHT-WALK OVER THE MILL STREAM	259

THE

FOGGY NIGHT AT OFFORD.

THE FOGGY NIGHT AT OFFORD.

CHAPTER I.

Verner Raby.

It was the height of the London season—not now, but years ago—and a drawing-room, all sun, and light, and heat, looked out on a fashionable square in an exceedingly fashionable locality. At the extreme end of the room, away from the sun's rays, a yet young and very lovely lady reclined in an easy-chair; a feverish flush was on her cheeks, but otherwise her features were white as the pillow on which they rested. The house was the residence of Mr. Verner Raby: this lady was his wife, and she was dying.

It was said of spinal complaint—of general debility—of a sort of decline: friends and doctors equally differed as to the exact malady. None hinted that care, disappointment, crushed feelings, could have anything to do with her sinking: yet it is probable they had more, by far, than all the other ailments ascribed to her. Somewhat of remorse may have been added also.

Once, when very young, she was engaged to be

married to a Mr. Mair. She thought she liked him; she did like him; but one, higher in the world's favour, came across her path. His dashing appearance dazzled her eyes, as the baron dazzled fair Imogene's, in the old song; his position dazzled her judgment; and Maria Raby would have discarded Arthur Mair for him. Her parents said No; common justice said No; but Mr. Verner exerted his powers of persuasion, and Maria yielded to her own will, and clandestinely left her father's house to become his wife. The private union was followed by a grand marriage, solemnised openly; and the bridegroom took his wife's name with her fortune, and became Verner Raby. Very, very soon was her illusion dissolved, and she found she had thrown away the substance to grasp the shadow. Mr. Raby speedily tired of his new toy, and she lapsed into a neglected, almost a deserted wife. He lived a wild life; dissipating his fortune, dissipating hers, tinging his character, wasting his talents. Meanwhile, the despised Arthur Mair, through the unexpected death of a man younger than himself, had risen to affluence and rank, and was winning his way to the approbation of good men. He had probably forgotten Maria Raby. It is certain that his marriage had speedily followed upon her own: perhaps he wished to prove to the world that her inexcusable conduct had not told irremediably upon him. Thus, Mrs. Raby had lived for many years, bearing her wrongs in silence, and battling with her remorseful feelings. But nature gave way at last, and her health left her: a few months of resigned suffering, and the grave drew very near. She was conscious of it; more conscious this afternoon than she had yet been. Her first child, a girl, had died at its birth; several years afterwards a boy was born. She was lying now, sadly thinking of him, when her husband entered. He had come home to dress for an early dinner engagement.

"How hot you look!" was his remark, his eye carelessly noting the unusual hectic on her cheeks.

"Things are troubling me," she answered, her breathing more laboured than common. "Alfred, I want to talk to you."

"Make haste, then," he replied, impatiently pulling out his watch. "I have not much time to waste."

To waste! On his dying wife!

"Oh yes, you have if you like, Alfred. And, if not, you must make it. Other engagements may give way to me to-day, for I think it will be my last."

"Nonsense, Maria! You are nervous. Shake it off. What have you to say?"

"I think it will be," she repeated. "At any rate, it can be but a question of a few days now; a week or two at the most. Alfred, do you believe you could ever break an oath?"

"Break an oath!" he echoed in surprise.

"You are careless as to keeping your word; promises you forget as soon as made; but an oath imposes a solemn obligation, and must be binding on the conscience. I want you to take one."

"That I will not marry again," he responded, in a tone of suppressed mockery. "Calm yourself: it is not my intention to do so."

"Not so," she sadly uttered; "that would be an obligation I have no right to lay upon you: my death will leave you free. I want you to undertake to be a good father to the child."

"And you would impose such obligation by oath!" cried Mr. Raby. "It is scarcely necessary. Of course I shall be good to him. What is running in your head, Maria?—that I shall beat him, or turn him adrift? The boy shall go to Eton, and thence to college."

She put out her fevered hands, and clasped his, with the excitable, earnest emotion of a dying spirit.

"O Alfred! when you are as near death as I am, you will know that there are other and higher interests than even the better interests of this world. If the knowledge never comes to you before, it will too surely come then. It is for those I wish you to train him."

"My dear," he rejoined, the mocking tone returning to his voice, and this time it was not disguised,

"I will engage a curate at a yearly stipend, and he shall cram Raby with religion."

A cloud of pain passed across her brow; then she looked pleadingly up again to urge her wish.

"There is no earthly interest can be compared with that: we live here for a moment, in eternity for ever. I want you to undertake that he shall be trained for it."

"So far as my will is good, he is welcome to grow up an angel," observed Mr. Raby; "but as to taking an oath that he shall, you must excuse me. We will leave the topic; it is one that we shall do no good at together. The boy will do well enough; what is there to hinder it? And do you get out of this desponding fit, Maria, and let me find you better when I come home at night."

"Stay!" she implored. "I lie here alone with all my pain and trouble; and wild thoughts intrude themselves into my mind, something like they come to us in a dream. It *was* a wild thought—an improbable one—the speaking to you of an oath; perhaps it was a wrong one. Will you pass your word to me, Alfred, that Raby shall be reared to good, not to evil? And you surely will hold sacred your word to the dying!"

"I promise you that the best shall be done for the boy in all ways, Maria, so far as I can do it."

He turned impatiently as he spoke, and left the

room. She did not call again. And just then her little boy peeped in. He had been christened Raby.

"You may come, dear."

Raby Verner, a child of seven, who had inherited his mother's beauty, drew towards her on tiptoe. He was too intelligent for his years, too sensitive, too thoughtful. His large and brilliant brown eyes were raised to hers with a sweet, sad expression of inquiry. Then the long, dark eyelashes fell over them, and he laid his head on her bosom, and threw up his arms lovingly to clasp her neck.

"Raby, I was just thinking of you. I must tell you something."

As if he had a dread presentiment of what was coming, he did not speak, but bent his face where she could not see it, and slightly shivered.

"Raby, darling, do you know that I am going to leave you—that I am going to heaven?"

The child had known it some time, for he had been alive to the gossiping of the servants, but, true to his shy and sensitive nature, he had buried the knowledge and the misery within his poor little heart. True to it now, he would not give vent to his emotion, but his mother felt that he shivered from head to foot, as his clasp tightened upon her.

"I read a pretty book, Raby, once. It told of the creed of some people, far, far away from our own land, who believe that when they die—if they die in

God's love—they are permitted to become ministering spirits to those whom they leave here; to hover invisibly round them, and direct their thoughts and steps away from harm. My dearest, how I should like to find this to be really the case! I would come and watch over you."

His sobs could no longer be suppressed, though he strove for it still. They broke out in a wail.

"Raby, dear, you have heard that this is a world of care. All people find it so: though some more than others. When it shall fall upon you hereafter—as it is sure to do—remember God sends it only to fit you for a better land."

The child looked up, his large eyes swimming. "Mamma, have you had much care?"

"A great deal; more than many have. But, Raby, that care has taken me home; it has shewn me the way to get there. It will shew you. I shall be there waiting for you. Carry always with you, through life, the hope to come there, and you will be sure to come."

What more she would have said is uncertain. Probably much. The child was not like a child of seven; he was more like one of fourteen, and he understood well. It was Mr. Raby who interrupted them.

"Raby! crying, sir! What for? Has your mamma been talking gloomy stuff to you, or saying that she fears that she is worse? It is not true, boy, either of it. Dry up that face of yours. Maria, you are *not* worse: if you were, I should see it. Run away into the nursery, sir."

The boy drew away choking, and Mr. Raby continued—

"It is not judicious of you, Maria, to alarm the boy. I cannot think what has put these ideas into your head. He will be in tears for the rest of the day."

"He is so sensitive," she whispered. "Alfred, something seems to tell me he will be destined to sorrow. It is an impression I have always felt, but never so forcibly as now. Shield him from it wherever you can. Oh that I could take him with me!"

"You are growing fanciful," answered Mr. Raby. "Destined to sorrow, indeed! Is there nothing else you fancy him destined to? Whence draw you your deduction?"

"I do not know. But a timid, sensitive, refined nature, such as his, with its unusual gift of genius, is generally destined to what the world looks upon as adverse fate. It may be deep sorrow, or it may be an early death."

"All mothers think their child a genius," interrupted Mr. Raby, in his slighting tone.

"Well, if he lives, time will prove," she panted. "I fear you will find my words true. When the mind is about to separate from the body, I believe it sees with unusual clearness—that it can sometimes read the future, almost with a spirit of prophecy."

"I am not given to metaphysics, Maria," remarked Mr. Raby, as he again escaped from the room.

Mrs. Verner Raby died. Raby, in due course, went to Eton, and afterwards to college. A shy, proud young man: at least, his reserved manners and his refined appearance and habits gave a stranger the idea that he was proud. He kept one term at Oxford, and had returned to keep a second, when a telegraphic despatch summoned him to London. Mr. Verner Raby had died a sudden death.

When Raby went back to Oxford, it was only to take his name off the college books, for his father had eaten up all he possessed, had died in debt, and Raby must no longer be a gentleman. A *rentier*, the French would say, which is a much more suitable term: we have no word that answers to it. Mr. Raby, after the death of his wife, had plunged into worse expense than before; he had lived a life of boundless extravagance, and his affairs proved to be in a sad state. He had afforded Raby a home; he had educated him in accordance with his presumed rank; but he had done no more. He had given him no profession; he had squandered his mother's money, as well as his own; he had bequeathed him no means to live, or even to complete his education; he left him to struggle with the world as he best could. And that was how he fulfilled his promise to his dead wife!

Yes; Raby must struggle now with the world— fight with it for a living. How was he able to do it? His mother said he possessed genius, and he undoubtedly did—a genius for painting. He had loved the art all his life, but his father had been against his pursuing it, even as an amateur—had obstinately set his face and interposed his veto against it. Raby determined to turn to it with a will now.

CHAPTER II.

Dreams of Fame.

A GENTLEMAN stood one morning in the studio of a far-famed painter, the great Coram, as the world called him. The visitor was Sir Arthur Saxonbury, one of those warm patrons of art all too few in England. Rich, liberal, and enthusiastic, his name was a welcome sound, not only to the successful, but to the struggling artist. The painter was out; but, in a second room, seated before an easel, underneath the softened light of the green blind, was a young man, working assiduously. Sir Arthur took little notice of him at first; he supposed him to be a humble assistant, or colour-mixer of the great man's; but, upon drawing nearer, he was struck with the exceeding and rare beauty of the face that was raised to look at him. But for the remarkable intellect of the high, broad brow, and the flashing light of the luminous eye, the face, in its sweet and delicate symmetry, in its transparency of complexion, might have been taken for a woman's. Sir Arthur, a passionate admirer of beauty, wherever he saw it, forgot the pictures of still life around him, and gazed at the living one: gazed until he heard the painter enter.

"Who is that in the other room?" inquired Sir Arthur, when greetings were over.

"Ah, poor fellow, his is a sad history. A very common one, though. When did you return to England, Sir Arthur?"

"But last week. Lady Saxonbury is tired of France and Germany, and her health seems to get no better. I must look at your new works, Coram; I suppose you have many to shew me, finished or unfinished."

"Ay. It must be three years since you were here, Sir Arthur."

"Nearly."

They proceeded round the rooms, when Sir Arthur's eye once more fell on the young man.

"He has genius, that young fellow, has he not?" he whispered.

"Very great genius."

"I could have told it," returned Sir Arthur. "What

a countenance it is! Transformed to canvas, its beauty alone would render the painter immortal. His face seems strangely familiar to me. Where can I have seen it?"

Mr. Coram had his eyes bent close to one of his paintings. He saw a speck on it which had no business there. The baronet's remark remained unanswered.

"I presume he is an aspirant for fame," continued Sir Arthur. "Will he get on?"

"No," said Mr. Coram.

Sir Arthur Saxonbury looked surprised.

"It is the old tale," proceeded the painter. "Poverty, friendlessness, and overwhelming talent."

"Talent has struggled through mountains before now, Coram," significantly observed the baronet.

"Yes. But Raby's enemy lies *here*," touching his own breast. "He is inclined to consumption, and these ultra-refined natures cannot battle against bodily weakness. His sensitiveness is something marvellous. A rude blow to his feelings would do for him."

Sir Arthur had looked up at the sound of the name. "What did you call him? Raby?"

"Raby Verner Raby is his name. The son of spendthrift Verner and Maria Raby the heiress."

Raby Verner Raby! Middle-aged though he was, years though it was ago, now, since his dream of love with Maria Raby had come to an abrupt ending, Sir

Arthur Saxonbury, once Arthur Mair, positively felt his cheeks blush through his gray whiskers. He glanced eagerly at Raby's face, and memory carried him back to its spring-time, for those were her very eyes, with their sweet, melancholy expression, and those were her chiselled features.

"I saw Verner Raby's death in the papers," said Sir Arthur, rousing himself, "two—three years ago, it seems to me. What is the son doing here?"

"Raby left nothing behind him but debts. The son sold off all, and paid them, leaving himself, I believe, about half sufficient for the bare necessaries of life. So he turned to what he loved best, painting, and has been working hard ever since. He expects to make a good thing of it. I let him come here to copy, for he has no convenience at his lodgings! Poor fellow! better that he had been a painter of coach panels."

"Why do you say that, Coram?"

"A man whose genius goes no higher than coach-painting can bear rubs and crosses. We can't. And Raby is so sanguine! Thinks he is going to be a second Claude Lorraine. He *is* great in landscapes."

At that moment they were interrupted by Raby. He came across the room in search of something wanted in his work, and Sir Arthur Saxonbury saw that the beauty of the face did not extend to the form. Not more than the middle height, and slender, his long arms and legs looked too long for his body. He stooped in the shoulders, he had a sensitive look of physical weakness, and his gait was uncertain and timid. Coram laid his hand on his shoulder.

"This is Sir Arthur Saxonbury, of whom you have heard so much," he said.

Raby was unacquainted with the episode in his mother's early life, therefore the flush that rose to, and dyed his face, was caused only by the greeting of a stranger; with these sensitive natures, it is sure to do so, whether they be man or woman. The bright colour only served to render him more like Maria Raby, and Sir Arthur, in spite of the sore feeling her treatment had left, felt his heart warm to her son. A wish half crossed his mind that that son was his—his heir; he had no son, only daughters. Raby was astonished at the warmth of his greeting. Sir Arthur clasped and held his hand; he turned with him to inspect the painting he was engaged on. It was a self-created landscape, betraying great imaginative power and genius; but genius, as yet, only half cultivated.

"You have your work cut out for you," observed Sir Arthur, who was an excellent judge of art, and its indispensable toil.

"I know it, Sir Arthur. I ought to have begun the study earlier; but during my father's lifetime the opportunity was not afforded me. It is all I have to depend on now, for with him died my wealth and my prospects."

"He had great wealth once. How could he have been so reprehensible as to dissipate it all, knowing there was one to come after him?" involuntarily spoke Sir Arthur.

"These are thoughts that I avoid," replied Raby. "He was my father."

"Do you remember much of your mother?"

"I remember her very well indeed. She died when I was seven years old. All the good that is in me I owe to her. I have never forgotten her early lessons or her early love. I seem to see her face as plainly as I saw it then. I see it often in my dreams."

"It was a face that the world does not see too often," said Sir Arthur, whose thoughts were buried in the past. "Your own is like it," he added, rousing himself.

"Did you know my mother, Sir Arthur?"

"Once: when she was Miss Raby," answered the baronet, in an indifferent tone, as he turned again to the painting. "Where do you live?" he suddenly asked.

"I give my address here," answered the young man. "Mr. Coram allows me to do so: though indeed it is never asked for. I have only a room in an obscure neighbourhood. I cannot afford anything better."

Sir Arthur Saxonbury smiled. "You are not like most people," he said: "they generally strive to hide their fallen fortunes: you make no secret of yours."

Raby shook his head, and a strangely painful flush rose to his face. His poverty was a sore point with him, the sense of disgrace it brought eating into his very heartstrings.

"My fallen fortunes have been a world's talk," he answered. "I could not keep them secret if I would."

"Have you retained your former friends?" asked Sir Arthur.

"Not one. Perhaps it is, in some degree, my own fault, for my entire time is given to painting. Few would care to know or recognise me now: Raby Verner Raby, the son and heir of the rich and luxurious Verner Raby, who made some noise in the London world, and Raby, the poor art-student, are two people. None have sought me since the change. Not one has addressed me with the kindness and sympathy that you have now, Sir Arthur."

"I shall see you again," remarked Sir Arthur, as he shook him by the hand, and turned away to the great artist and his paintings.

In the evening, Raby returned to his home—if the garret he occupied could be called such. Coram had spoken accurately: not half sufficient for what would generally be called the bare necessaries of life, remained from the wreck of his father's property. But it was made to suffice for his wants. It would seem that surely his clothes must take it all, and none could conjecture how he contrived to eke it out. He was often cold, often hungry, always weary; yet his hopeful spirit buoyed him up, and pictured visions of future greatness. He never for one moment doubted that he was destined to become a world's fame: those who possess true genius are invariably conscious of it in their inmost heart: and he would repeat over and over again to himself the words he felt must some time be applied to him — "The great painter — the painter Raby."

He sat down that evening to his dinner-supper of bread and cheese. It tasted less dry than usual, for his thoughts were absorbed by the chief event of the day, the meeting Sir Arthur Saxonbury. He attributed, in his unconsciousness, the interest which Sir Arthur had betrayed in him, to admiration of his genius: he knew how warm a supporter of rising artists Sir Arthur was, and he deemed the introduction the very happiest circumstance that could have befallen him. Could he but have foreseen what that introduction was to bring forth!

CHAPTER III.

Maria Saxonbury.

THE golden light of the setting sun was falling on a golden room. It is scarcely wrong to call it such, for the colour prevailing in it was that of gold. Gold-coloured satin curtains and cushioned chairs, gilt cornices, mirrors in gilded frames, gilded consoles whose slabs of the richest lapis lazuli shone with costly toys, paintings in rich enclosures, and golden ornaments. Altogether the room looked a blaze of gold. The large window opened upon a wide terrace, on which rose an ornamental fountain, its glittering spray dancing in the sunlight: and beyond that terrace was a fair domain, stretched out far and wide; the domain of Sir Arthur Saxonbury.

Swinging her pretty foot to and fro, and leaning back in one of the gay chairs, was a lovely girl budding into womanhood, with bright features and a laughing eye, the youngest, the most indulged, and the vainest daughter of Sir Arthur. She was in a white lace evening dress, and wore a pearl necklace and pearl bracelets on her fair neck and arms. They had recently come home after the short London season, which had been half over when they returned from the Continent, and were as yet free from visitors. Lady Saxonbury was in ill health, and Mrs. Ashton, the eldest married daughter, was staying with them while her husband was abroad.

In a chair, a little behind Miss Saxonbury, as if conscious of the difference between them—for there *was* a distance—sat Raby Raby. It was said the house was free from visitors, but he was scarcely regarded as such. Sir Arthur, in the plenitude of his heart, had invited him to come and stay a couple of months at Saxonbury; the country air would renovate him; he could have the run of the picture-gallery, and copy some of its *chefs d'œuvre*. And Raby came. Sir Arthur's early secret was safe with himself, and he could only explain that his interest in Raby Raby was but that which he would take in any rising artist. So the family, even the servants, looked upon him with a patronising eye, as one who had "come to paint." Raby had accepted Sir Arthur's invitation with a glow of gratification—the far-famed Saxonbury gallery was anticipation enough for him. He forgot to think where the funds could come from to make a suitable appearance as Sir Arthur Saxonbury's guest; but these the painter Coram delicately furnished. "It is but a loan," said he: "you can repay me with the first proceeds that your pencil shall receive."

Thus Raby went to Saxonbury. And there had he been now for half his allotted time, drinking in the wondrous beauties of the place and scenery—and other wondrous beauties which it had been as well that he had not drunk in. The elegance that surrounded him, and to which he had been latterly a stranger,—the charms of the society he was thrown amongst once again, as an equal for the time being, —the gratification of the eye and mind, and the pomp and pride of courtly life; all this was but too congenial to the exalted taste of Raby Raby, and he was in danger of forgetting the stern realities of life, to become lost in a false Elysium.

He was thrown much with Maria Saxonbury—far more than he need have been. The fault was hers. A great admirer of beauty, like her father, and possessing a high reverence for genius, the exquisite face of Raby Raby attracted her admiration as it had never yet been attracted; whilst his eager aspirations, and love for the fine arts, were perfectly consonant to her own mind. His companionship soon grew excessively pleasing, and she gave her days up to it without restraint, absorbed in the pleasure of the moment. Nothing more: of all people in the world, Maria Saxonbury was the last to think seriously of one beneath her. So, leaving consequences to take care of themselves, or be remedied by time, she dwelt only on the present. She would flit about when he was at work in the picture-gallery, she would linger by his side in the gardens, one or other of the little Ashtons generally being their companion: in short, it seemed that the object of Maria's life, just now, was to be with the artist-visitor.

Even this night, when her father and sister had gone out to dinner, she had excused herself: she would stay at home with her mother, she said: but Lady Saxonbury was in her chamber, and Maria remained in the drawing-room with Mr. Raby. It is probable that Lady Saxonbury, if she thought of him at all, believed him to be painting then. Was it in remembrance of some one else that Sir Arthur had named his youngest child "Maria?" But they sometimes called her by her other name, Elizabeth.

"Do you admire this purse?" she suddenly inquired, holding out one of grass-green silk, with gold beads, tassels, and slides; a marvel of prettiness.

Raby rose and took it from her, and turned it about in his white and slender hands. Those remarkable hands! feeble to look at, elegant in structure, always restless; so strongly characteristic of genius, as well as of delicacy of constitution.

"It is quite a gem," he said, in answer.

"You may have it in place of your ugly one," continued Miss Saxonbury: "that frightful portemonnaie, of grim leather, I saw you with, the other day. I made this for somebody else, who does not seem in a hurry to come for it; so I will give it to you."

A rush of suspicious emotion flew to his face, and her eyes fell beneath the eloquent gaze of his. "How shall I thank you?" was all he said. "It shall be to me an everlasting remembrance."

"That's in return for the pretty sketch you gave me yesterday," she went on. "One you took at Rome, and filled in from memory."

"You mistake, Miss Saxonbury. I said I drew it from description. I have never been to Rome. That is a pleasure to come."

"As it is for me," observed Maria. "I was there once, when a little girl, but I remember nothing of it. A cross woman, half governess, half maid, who was hired to talk Italian to us, is all my recollection of the place. Last year and the year before, when we were wasting our time in Paris and at the baths of Germany, doing mamma more harm than good, I urged them to go on to Rome, but nobody listened to me. I have an idea that I shall be disappointed whenever I do go: we always are, when we expect so much."

"Always, always," murmured Raby.

"I long to see some of those features I am familiar with from paintings," added Miss Saxonbury. "The remains of the Cæsars' palaces—the real grand St. Peter's—the beautiful Alban Hills—and all Rome's other glories. I grow impatient sometimes, and tell papa there will be nothing left for me to see: that Sallust's garden will be a heap of stinging nettles— I dare say it *is* nothing else; and Cecilia Metella's tomb destroyed."

And thus they conversed till it grew dark, and the

servants came in to light the chandeliers. Miss Saxonbury remembered her mother then, and rose to go to her, to see why she had not come down.

When Maria returned, the room was empty, and she stood in the bow of the window and looked out. It was the custom at Saxonbury House to leave the curtains of this window open on a favourable night; for the moonlight landscape, outside, was indeed fair to look upon. Mr. Raby was then walking on the terrace; his step was firm and self-possessed, his head raised: it was only in the presence of his fellow-creatures that Raby Raby was a shy and awkward man. He saw her, and approached the window.

"I have been studying the Folly all this time," he said; "fancying it must look like those ruined Roman temples we have been speaking of; as they must look in the light and shade of the moonlight."

"Does it?" she answered, laughingly. "I will go and look, too."

Miss Saxonbury stepped on to the terrace, and he gave her his arm. Did she feel the violent beating of his heart, as her bracelet lay against it? They walked, in the shade cast by the house, to the railings at the end of the terrace, and there came in view of the fanciful building in question, "Lady Saxonbury's Folly." It rose, high and white, on the opposite hills, amidst a grove of dark trees.

"I do not like the building by day," he observed;

"but, as it looks now, I cannot fancy anything more classically beautiful in the Eternal City, even when it was in its zenith."

"It does look beautiful," she mused. "And the landscape, as it lies around, is equally so: look at its different points shewing out. You have not seen many scenes more gratifying to the imaginative eye than this, Mr. Raby."

"I shall never see a second Saxonbury," was the impulsive answer. "Take it for all in all, I shall never see——but look at this side," he abruptly broke off, turning in the opposite direction.

"Oh, I don't care to look there. It is all dark. I only like the bright side of things."

"Has it never struck you that these two aspects, the light and the dark of a moonlight night, are a type of human fortunes? While some favoured spirits bask in brightness, others must be cast, and remain, in the depths of shade."

"No. I never thought about it. My life has been all brightness."

"May it ever remain so!" he whispered with a deep sigh: but Miss Saxonbury turned to the pleasant side again.

"What a fine painting this view would make!" she exclaimed. "I wonder papa has never had it done. One of *your* favourite scenes, Mr. Raby, all poetry and moonlight, interspersed with a dash of melancholy.

Some of you artists are too fond of depicting melancholy scenes."

"We depict scenes as we find them. You know the eye sees with its own hue. There may be a gangrene over the gladdest sunshine."

"Artists ought to be always glad: living, as they do, amidst ideal beauties: nay, creating them."

"Ideal! That was a fitting word, Miss Saxonbury. We live in the toil and drudgery of the work; others, who but see the picture when it is completed, in the ideal. When you stand and admire some favourite painting, do you ever cast a thought to the weary hours of labour which created it?"

"No doubt the pursuit of art has its inconveniences, but you great painters must bear within you your own recompense."

"In a degree, yes," answered Raby; the expression "you great painters" echoing joyfully on his ear. "The consciousness of possessing that rare gift, genius, is ample recompense—save in moments of despondency."

"And yet you talk of melancholy and gangrene, Mr. Raby, and such like unpleasant topics!"

"The lives of great men are frequently marked by unhappiness," observed Raby. "In saying 'great men,' I mean men inwardly great, men of genius, of imaginative intellect. Look at some of our dead poets—at what is said of them."

The Foggy Night at Offord, etc.

"I think their fault lay in looking at the dark side of things, instead of the bright," laughed Maria. "Like yourself at present. You will keep turning to that gloomy point, where the scenery is all obscure, nothing bright but the great moon itself; and that shines right in your face."

"They could not look otherwise than they did," he argued, his own tone sounding melancholy enough.

"Well, well, I suppose it is the fate of genius," returned Maria. "I was reading lately, in a French work, some account of the life of Leonardo da Vinci. He was not a happy man."

"He was called Da Vinci the Unhappy. How many of his brethren might have been called so!"

"Were I you, I should not make up my mind to be one of them; I should be just the contrary," said Maria, gaily. "Fancy goes a great way in this life. And so," she added, after a pause, "you think some of the queer old temples in Italy must look like that?" pointing to the Folly. "How I wish I could see them!"

"How I wish *we* could see them!" he murmured —"that we could see them together!"

Perhaps he wondered whether he had said too much. She did not check him,—only turned, and began to move back towards the drawing-room, her arm within his.

"We may see them together," she said, at length. "You will, of necessity, visit Italy; I, of inclination, and we may meet there. I hope we shall know you in after life, Mr. Raby; but of that there will be little doubt. Everybody will know you, for you will be one of England's famous painters."

They reached the window, and he took her hand in his, though there was no necessity, to assist her over the low step; he kept it longer than he need have done. Not for the first time, by several, had he thus clasped it in the little courtesies of life. Oh, Raby Raby! can you not see that it had been better for you to clasp some poisonous old serpent? He did not enter, but turned away.

Lady Saxonbury was in the room then, in her easy-chair, which had its back to the window. The tea was on the table, and Miss Saxonbury began to pour it out.

"My dear," cried Lady Saxonbury, a simple-hearted, kind woman, "where's that poor painter? I daresay he would like some tea."

"He was on the terrace just now," replied Maria.

"He must feel very dull," resumed Lady Saxonbury. "I fear, child, we neglect him. Send one of the servants to ask him to come in."

The "poor painter," lost in anticipations of the time when he should be a rich one, was leaning against the railings, whence he had stood and gazed abroad with Miss Saxonbury,—the purse she had given him lying in his bosom. In the last few weeks his whole existence had changed, for he had learnt to love Maria Saxonbury with a wild, passionate love. To be near her was bliss, even to agitation; to hear her speak set his frame trembling; to touch her hand sent his heart's blood thrilling through his veins. It is only these imaginative, unearthly natures, too sensitive and refined for the uses of common life, that can tell of this intense, pure, etherealised passion, which certainly partakes more of heaven than of earth. He stood there, indulging a vision of hope—a deceitful, glowing vision. He saw not himself as he was, but as he should be—the glorious painter, to whose genius the whole world would bow. Surely there was no such impassable barrier between that worshipped painter and the daughter of Sir Arthur Saxonbury!

Alas for the improbable dream he was suffering himself to nourish! alas for its fatal ending! Three or four weeks more of its sweet delusion, and then it was rudely broken. Mr. Yorke, a relative of Sir Arthur's, and the heir presumptive to a portion of his estates, arrived at Saxonbury. He had been named Arthur Mair, after Sir Arthur. Raby Verner recognised him, for they had been at Christ Church together, but he had not recalled him to his memory since, and had never known him as the relative of Sir Arthur Saxonbury. He was a tall, strong, handsome young fellow; but ere he had been two days at Saxonbury, a rumour, or suspicion, (in the agitation of Raby's feelings he hardly knew which,) reached the artist that his visit was to Maria, that she was intended for her cousin's wife. The same evening, calm and lovely as the one when they had looked forth together at the Folly, the truth became clear to Raby.

They were seated in the drawing-room, all the family, when Maria stepped on to the terrace, and the artist followed her. Presently Arthur Yorke saw them pacing it together, Raby having given her his arm. Mr. Yorke drew down the corners of his lips, and stalked out.

"Thank you," he said to Raby, with freezing politeness, as he authoritatively drew away Maria's arm and placed it within his own, "I will take charge of Miss Saxonbury if she wishes to walk."

He strode away with her, and Raby, with a drooping head and sinking heart, descended the middle steps of the terrace. He stole along under cover of its high wall—anywhere to hide himself and his outraged feelings. That action, those words of Mr. Yorke's, had but too surely betrayed his interest in Maria. He came to the end of the terrace, and found they had halted there, right above him. He was to hear worse words now, and he could not help himself.

"Then you had no business to do it—you had no

right to do it," Maria was saying, in a petulant tone. "He was not going to eat me, if I did walk with him."

"Excuse me, Maria, I am the best judge. Raby was in the position of a gentleman once, but things have changed with him."

"Rubbish!" retorted Miss Saxonbury. "He is papa's guest; and he is as good as you. A gentleman once, a gentleman always."

"I am not saying he is not a gentleman. But he is no longer in the position of one."

"He was born and reared one; he will always be one; quite as much as you are," persisted Maria, in her tantalising spirit.

"Well, I don't care, then, to put my objection on that score. But it is not agreeable to me to see you walking and talking so familiarly with him."

"Just say you are jealous at once, Arthur. If you think to control me, I can tell you"———

"Hallo, Arthur! Step here a moment."

The voice was Sir Arthur Saxonbury's. Maria paused in her speech, and Mr. Yorke unwillingly retired towards the drawing-room. Raby, in the frenzy of the moment, darted up the end steps, startling her by his sudden appearance.

"Miss Saxonbury! will you answer me?—Forgive me," he panted, as he laid his hand upon her arm, in his painful eagerness—"forgive me that I must ask the question! Has Arthur Yorke a *right* to take you from me, as he did but now?"

"Of course he has not, Mr. Raby. How can he have?"

"I mean—pray forgive me—the right of more than cousinship?"

She was half terrified at his parted lips, his laboured breathing, his ghastly face, from which suspense took every vestige of colour, and she saw that she might not dare to tamper with him; that the kinder course, now, was to set his ambitious dream at rest.

"Well, then," she whispered, "though of course he had not the right to interfere, and it was very bad taste, and I will not submit to his whims, yet, yet— the time may come when he will be to me more than a cousin."

His hand unloosed its clasp of her arm, and Maria Saxonbury hastened towards the drawing-room. He watched her in, and then, when no human eye or ear was near, his head sunk upon the cold railings, and a low wail of anguish went forth on the quiet evening air. Too surely, though Maria Saxonbury might never know it, had the iron entered into his soul.

CHAPTER IV.

The Blow telling Home.

In December, business took Sir Arthur Saxonbury to London. He paid a visit to the artist Coram, but he did not see Raby. His easel and chair were there, but the former had no work in its frame, and the chair was empty.

"Has he abjured the art, or found another studio?" inquired Sir Arthur.

The great painter shook his head. "He has not abjured it. A different art—or power—is claiming him now; one to which we must all succumb—Death."

"Death!" echoed Sir Arthur.

"He has gone off very rapidly; in a decline, or something of that sort. I saw him two days ago, and I did not think, then, he would last until now. I wonder I have not heard of his death."

"What can be the cause of its coming on so suddenly? He was remarkably well when at Saxonbury. I saw no symptom of decline or any other illness about him then."

"Do you remember my telling you, Sir Arthur, that a blow to the feelings would kill him?"

Sir Arthur considered. "I think I do."

"He has had it, unless I am mistaken. He got it at Saxonbury."

"What do you mean?" inquired the baronet.

"I do not understand it,—and indeed it is no business of mine,—but when he came up from Saxonbury, he had certainly received his death-blow. A suspicion has crossed me whether your lovely daughter had anything to do with it. Pardon me, Sir Arthur, we are old friends—it is a thought only mentioned to you."

"I should like to see him," said Sir Arthur. "Will you go with me?"

They went. Raby was still alive, but it was getting towards his last day of life. He lay panting on his humble bed, alone. A hectic flush, even then, lighted up his wasted cheek at sight of *her* father. Sir Arthur, inexpressibly shocked, sat down by him, and took his poor damp hand.

"What can you have been doing to yourself," he asked, "to get into this state?"

"I think it was inherent," murmured Raby. "My mother died in a decline."

"You have had the best advice, I hope?"

Raby made a movement of dissent. "A medical student, whom I know, comes in sometimes. I could not call in good advice, for I had not the means to pay for it."

"Oh, my boy!" uttered Sir Arthur, in a tone of anguish, as he leaned over him, "why did you not let me know this? Half my purse should have been yours, for your mother's sake."

"All the skill in England would not have availed me," he earnestly said. "Sir Arthur, it is best as it is, for I am going to her. She has been waiting for me all these years. She told me my lot would not be a happy one. But it will soon be over now," he added, his voice growing fainter; "earthly pain of all kinds has nearly passed away."

Curious thoughts were perplexing Sir Arthur Saxonbury as he quitted the scene. If a rude blow to his feelings had indeed caused Raby to sink into bodily illness, and thence to death, and that blow had been dealt by Maria Saxonbury, how very like it was to retribution for the blow Maria Raby had dealt out to him! He was a strong man, and had weathered it, but it had left more permanent traces on his heart than he had suffered the world to know. Sir Arthur lost himself in these thoughts, and then shook them off as a disagreeable and unsatisfactory theme.

On Christmas-eve he returned to Saxonbury. After dinner, his two daughters only being at table, he told them of the expected death of the artist Raby. Mrs. Ashton expressed sorrow and surprise. Maria said nothing, but her face drooped, and a burning colour overspread it. Sir Arthur looked sternly at her. Her head only drooped the lower.

"It has been hinted to me that you tampered with

his feelings," he said, in a severely reproachful tone.
"Let me tell you, Maria, that the vain habit of
encouraging admiration whence it cannot legally be
received, always tends to ill. No right-minded girl
would condescend to it."

"I thought Maria talked a great deal with young
Raby," remarked Mrs. Ashton. "Had he been of our
own order, I should have interfered; but I knew she
could not be serious. He was only a painter."

"She killed him," was the significant answer of Sir
Arthur. And Maria Saxonbury burst into tears.

Sir Arthur said no more. He may have thought
it was the province of women to inflict such wounds,
and of men to bear them. He knew not how far
Raby's own impressionable nature might have been in
fault, or whether Maria, in the exercise of coquetry,
of vanity, had unwarrantably drawn him on. It
booted not to inquire now; the past could not be
undone; neither could Raby be brought back to life.
One thing was indisputable, that beautiful as Maria
Raby had been in the old days, beautiful was Maria
Saxonbury now. It is impossible for some men to be
near such beauty and not suffer from it once in their
lives.

Maria, vexed and angry with herself for the outburst of feeling, had dried away her tears as hastily
as they came, and was going on with her dinner with
what appetite she might. Sir Arthur went on with

his, glancing at her now and then between his eyelashes.

"When did Mr. Raby die?" asked Mrs. Ashton.

"I do not know yet that he is dead," replied Sir Arthur. "He was alive when I quitted London, a week ago; but it was certain he could not last long."

"Did you see him, papa?" continued Mrs. Ashton.

"I saw him several times. I"——

"You seemed to be very much interested in that young man, papa," was Mrs. Ashton's interruption.

"I was so," quietly replied Sir Arthur. "I looked up to him as one of a superior order."

"Superior!" somewhat slightingly remarked Mrs. Ashton.

"Yes; in my opinion. I bow to genius; I respect misfortune: Raby Raby was rich in both. Had he lived, I should have done something for him: as it is, all I could do was to render his deathbed a little more comfortable than it might otherwise have been."

"Does he suffer much?"

"I hope not. The doubt was, that he might towards the last. I invited Mr. Janson to come down for a day or two when all was over, and bring the account of his last hours."

"Who is Mr. Janson, papa?"

"A friend of Mr. Raby's. A young surgeon who has been much with him in his illness; very kind and attentive to him. A gay, gentlemanly, pleasant young fellow as ever I came across," somewhat warmly added Sir Arthur.

"Papa, I think you evince a great liking for young men!"

"Possibly I do, Louisa. The having no sons of my own may have induced it. It is not often, though, one meets with so charming a young man as Mr. Janson."

"Is he a gentleman?"

"By birth do you mean? I never asked him the question. He is one in mind and manners, and that is sufficient for me. You were always overfastidious, Louisa."

Maria, meanwhile, said not a word. After the rebuff administered by her father, she could but shew some sense of it: though, indeed, her thoughts were too busy to admit of her joining lightly in the conversation. Heartily sorry was she to hear of the death of Raby Raby; and certain qualms of conscience were reproaching her. In the midst of all her vanity and her flirting, her laying her charms out for admiration, and her lingering interviews with Mr. Raby, she had not lost her heart to him. In point of fact, that vulnerable portion of the human frame was as yet intact in Maria Saxonbury. But she had liked him much. She had admired his beauty of face; she had reverenced his great gift, genius; she had sat most complacently to listen to his softly-breathed words, and their scarcely-disguised theme, love. It had been very reprehensible. Maria had conveniently ignored that fact at the time; but she was feeling it deeply now. Putting aside her vanity, her consciousness of beauty, her love of admiration, she was a noble-hearted girl; and she was wishing just now that she could recall Raby Raby to life, almost at the sacrifice of her own. That she had wrecked his happiness, she had had some cause to believe; but to have wrecked his life—Maria turned all over in a hot glow, and wondered whether she might yet dare to ask God to forgive her.

"Why should some people's nature be so sensitive?" she somewhat peevishly asked herself. "They are not fit to be in the world."

No, they are not. And many a one has had cause to know that truth besides Maria Saxonbury.

She sat in her dainty dress of white, the jewels shining on her fair neck and arms—sat in her old favourite attitude, after she went into the drawing-room—leaning back in a fauteuil, her black satin slipper tapping petulantly the carpet. Not so much in petulance, possibly, as in sorrow, was that pretty foot moving. Life seemed to her particularly gloomy that evening: as if it were to have no future.

For one thing, she had been vexed by the non-arrival of Arthur Yorke. He was to have spent Christmas at Saxonbury, to have been with them that day, but a letter, telling of the serious illness of his mother, had come instead. Maria liked Arthur Yorke very well; quite sufficiently well to be grieved at his non-arrival, and to feel it as a disappointment. And yet she did not love him. She did not love Arthur Yorke any more than she had loved Mr. Raby. It is a capricious passion, one that will not come for the bidding; and, perhaps, the very fact of Maria's having gathered hints that she was destined to be Mr. Yorke's wife, had kept the love away.

Sir Arthur Saxonbury had never said to Maria, "All going well, I wish you to be the wife of Arthur Yorke." Lady Saxonbury had never said it. More than all, Mr. Yorke himself had never said it. And yet, that Maria knew such was her projected destiny, was certain. Sir Arthur Saxonbury wished it; there was not the slightest doubt that Mr. Yorke wished it; but neither of them had spoken directly to Maria. She was very young, and Sir Arthur, who would not for the world have pushed on such a project against her inclination, had desired of Mr. Yorke that he should not speak at present. "Give her time to get a liking for you first," he said. And the advice was good. But the project had, in some way, oozed out, and Maria knew it as well as they did. In fact, there was a tacit understanding that she did, between herself and Mr. Yorke. She was contented to contemplate the prospect, and to believe that some time or other she should be Mrs. Yorke. At present she was pleased to shew off her caprices and her coquetries to him, as she did to others, secure in her own power.

Lady Saxonbury, a confirmed invalid, suffering under an inward complaint, reclined in a fauteuil opposite Maria. Mrs. Ashton, who had always some work in hand for one or other of her children, sat at the table between them, doing something to the lace of a little cap, and grumbling at her unconscious nursemaids for having allowed it to get torn. "Have you heard the news about Mr. Raby, mamma?" she suddenly asked.

"Your papa told me," replied Lady Saxonbury. "What a sad thing that consumption is! But it must have attacked Mr. Raby suddenly. He was not ill when he was here."

"Very suddenly," returned Mrs. Ashton, in a marked tone, made tart for the benefit of Maria.

"He never looked strong," resumed Lady Saxonbury. "He had a remarkably fragile appearance. I used to say so to Maria. Who can that be?"

The "Who can that be?" referred to the signs of an arrival. Wheels had sounded on the gravel, and the hall bell was now ringing. But no one appeared, and the occurrence passed from their minds.

The time went on to tea-time, and the tea waited on the table for Sir Arthur. Never given to take much wine, Lady Saxonbury openly wondered what could be keeping him in the dining-room.

"It is possible that, tired with his journey, he may have dropped asleep," she suddenly said. "Go and see, Maria."

Maria rose listlessly, and proceeded to the dining-room, speaking as she entered it:—

"Papa, you don't come to tea. We have been wondering"——

And there she stopped. Seated by Sir Arthur was a gentleman, a stranger to Maria. He rose as she spoke, and stood facing her, a beaming smile on his countenance. A gentlemanly-looking man, young, with a remarkably winning expression of face, and frank manners. Sir Arthur rose also.

"My daughter, Mr. Janson, Miss Saxonbury."

Maria remembered the name Janson in connexion with Raby Raby; and not possessing a perfectly easy conscience on that score altogether, left the room again as quickly as she could. Sir Arthur followed her, bringing his guest to the drawing-room.

Raby had died the day following the departure of Sir Arthur Saxonbury from London. He, Sir Arthur, had paid a visit of nearly a week upon the road. Mr. Janson waited to bury his friend, and then availed himself of the invitation to Saxonbury.

"Did he die hard—in much pain?" inquired Lady

Saxonbury, when they had been speaking of him some little time.

"Quite easy in all ways," replied Mr. Janson. "He appeared to think he was going to his rest."

CHAPTER V.

Rivals at Saxonbury.

A WEEK passed over; a fortnight passed over; a month passed over; and still Mr. Janson was located at Saxonbury. It may appear curious that the stranger, come down for only a day or two's visit, should remain so long, but the explanation is easy. A medical student, nearly qualified, and clever in his profession, Lady Saxonbury, who felt a liking for him the first moment she saw him, naturally confided to him her ailments. Mr. Janson took quite a new view of her case, and recommended remedies which had never been tried. It may be, that they did not do her any permanent good; indeed, he acknowledged the doubt himself; but they considerably alleviated her daily sufferings, and it rendered her unwilling to part with him. She besought him to remain with almost impassioned fervour; she pressed Sir Arthur to keep him. Mr. Janson frankly assured Lady Saxonbury that he did not require pressing; that he would remain as long as she liked, in reason. His course of studies in London was over for the present; he was about to pass some months in Paris, and pursue them there; and, whether he went a few weeks later or earlier, was of no consequence.

So he stayed on. Indispensable to Lady Saxonbury, winning every day on the esteem of Sir Arthur, rendering himself agreeable to Mrs. Ashton, and— falling in love with Maria.

It was the old story over again of Raby Raby. With one exception. There were morning meetings in the picture-gallery, and afternoon roamings in the fair grounds of Saxonbury, and evening lingerings in the deep bay-windows, gazing out on the Folly, on the lovely scenery by moonlight. Just as it had been in Raby's time. But, what Raby had not done with all his poetry and passion, had been effected by the less poetical, far less impassioned Mr. Janson—he had gained the heart of Maria Saxonbury.

Does a woman ever love a man of a timid nature? Poor Raby, with his innate refinement, his sensitive reticence, his consciousness of his present fallen fortunes, contrived to impart to Maria a knowledge of his self-conscious inferiority. Mr. Janson, whose birth was far inferior to Raby's, whose position and prospects in point of fact, were little, if any, better than Raby's fallen ones, gave to her an idea of his being superior. Not purposely: few men thought less about setting forth his own merits, or making himself appear what he was not, than Edward Janson. His frank, open words, his thoroughly easy and gentlemanly bearing, his somewhat off-hand manner to the servants, contributed to the impression. Who or what he was, Maria Saxonbury did not ask; she had never been in the habit of troubling herself with such questions where a companion was attractive: she gave herself up to the full charm of the intercourse, and—before she was aware of it, before she had cast so much as a thought to the danger, she had learnt to love Mr. Janson.

Not before he had learnt to love her. Every tone of his voice, every glance of his eye, every pressure of his hand, given in common intercourse, told of the secret. Not a word was spoken between them; not a word perhaps would be spoken; but the heart has a language of its own, unneedful of common words, and they had found the way to use it.

Did either give a thought to the future? Probably not. The present happiness was all-sufficient for the present hour. Had Mr. Janson soberly set himself to contemplate that inevitable future, it would have looked unpromising enough. To imagine a union with Miss Saxonbury would have been in the highest degree preposterous: and on Miss Saxonbury's part, she would have deemed it a great calamity—nay, a disgrace—to wed one so far beneath her. So the love, though it had come, was but an unsatisfactory good, take it for all in all.

And the pleasant intercourse was soon to have an ending. They were in the picture-gallery one wet day in February, Louisa and Fanny Ashton making a great noise with a ball at the other end of it. Maria sat on one of the crimson benches, and Mr. Janson stood near her. She was toying with the blue ribbons that tied her lace sleeve at the wrist, her eyes and eyelids drooping.

"Why need you go so soon?" she asked, in reply to a remark from him that the end of the week would see his departure.

"So soon!" echoed Mr. Janson. "I came here for less than one week, and I have stayed more than six. I *wish* I could stay," he added in a lower and more impassioned tone. "I wish I could stay on for ever."

"You have been able to do mamma so much good," returned Maria, after a pause.

"Could I have done her permanent good, I should be better satisfied, Miss Saxonbury."

"Do you think, as others do, that the illness will last for years—that she may never, even, get well?"

"I have given my opinion to Sir Arthur," was Mr. Janson's reply, after an almost imperceptible hesitation. He could not say to Maria, "Far from getting well, I fear that a very few weeks will see the ending."

"It will be a marked change, my hard work in Paris after this delightful time of—of idleness," he resumed.

Maria played more abstractedly than ever with her blue ribbons. "Do you go on to Paris direct, on leaving Saxonbury?"

"I shall stay a week on the road with my mother."

Maria lifted her eyes. "Your mother? I don't think I have heard you mention her. Where does she live?"

"On the coast of France. One of the quiet seaport towns in direct steam communication with England. She has lived there since my father died. Being a Roman Catholic, and her income small, the place suits her."

The words somewhat surprised Maria. "You are not a Roman Catholic?" she said, recalling the fac that he had attended church with them on Sundays.

"No, I was reared in my father's faith. Had there been daughters, they would have been brought up in my mother's."

"Your father was a soldier, I have heard you say?"

"A soldier and a gentleman," somewhat pointedly replied Mr. Janson. "But a poor one, and one of whom promotion seemed shy. He had not so much as gained his majority when he was killed."

"Why did you not go into the army?"

"My mother set her face against it: scared, no doubt, by my father's fate."

"I think I would have been anything, rather than

a doctor," remarked Maria, pulling more vehemently at her ribbons.

"Would you? I like it. I chose it. My mother wished me to read for the bar, but I did not fall in with the idea. I have neither talent nor liking that way."

"I would have chosen it," said Maria. "Look at the honours open to a barrister."

"Some few in our profession attain to honour also," he said; "to honour and to fame. I may: though I do not think I am very ambitious. The chances are," he added, laughing, "that I shall settle down into a jog-trot country surgeon, keeping my one-horse gig, and doctoring the parish."

"There; it's untied now!"

Miss Saxonbury had pulled the ribbons of her sleeve a little too far: a slight accident, and one scarcely sufficient to account for her tone of vexation. She began to twist the ribbons impatiently round her wrist.

"Will you accept of my clumsy tying?"

She laughed, and held out her arm towards him. He was in the act of tying the bow, his eyes fixed on her face at the same time, as he whispered some gallant nonsense connected with the occasion, and Maria was listening with a half-raised face and a self-conscious flush, when some one moved towards them from the entrance of the gallery.

It was Mr. Yorke. And he had time to take in full view of signs and appearances before they saw him. The bent head of the handsome man, and his whispered words; the employment, bringing their hands into so close a contact; and the crimson cheeks, the downcast lashes of Maria. Something very like an ill word burst from his lips.

They looked round; and Maria, scarlet now, but not losing self-possession, advanced a few steps to welcome him. He came on, and the gentlemen stood face to face.

Rivals from that moment; and they both saw it. Never destined to be open ones, perhaps; but rivals beyond dispute in their secret hearts.

"Mr. Janson, Mr. Yorke."

A gaze from the one to the other went out as Miss Saxonbury spoke. Mr. Janson saw a tall, powerful man, whose very height and strength gave him beauty. A fine countenance, too; though, when angered, he had a habit of shewing too much of his white teeth. Mr. Yorke, on his part, saw a frank, open, generous-looking man, whose personal attractions, if brought into play, might render him a dangerous rival.

"How you have surprised me!" began Maria. "Have you seen papa?"

"Not yet," he gravely answered. "White thought Sir Arthur was in the picture-gallery, and I came on here. But I do not see him, Maria."

"I saw Sir Arthur walk across the grounds in the rain an hour ago," interposed Mr. Janson in a clear, ringing tone. "He has not come in, probably."

A haughty bow in return for the information, and Mr. Yorke fairly turned his back upon the speaker. Mr. Janson walked away to the end window, with the good-natured intention of looking out for Sir Arthur.

"Who *is* that man, Maria?"

"I told you—Mr. Janson," she answered; resentment against his haughty air, his assumption of authority, seating itself within her there and then, and peeping out in her tone. "He is a medical student, and a friend of papa's. He was the deathbed friend of poor Raby Raby," she added in her spirit of bravado. "He has been here since Christmas, and papa likes him very much. We all do."

Mr. Yorke's lip curled. A medical student! Taking the hand of Maria, he placed it within his arm to lead her away. "Let me conduct you to Lady Saxonbury, Maria. I suppose she is visible."

What rebellion she might have offered, whether any or none, it is impossible to know, for at that moment Sir Arthur entered. The little girls, too, becoming aware of Mr. Yorke's presence for the first time, came running from the upper end of the gallery. Maria seized the opportunity to escape.

Changes came to Saxonbury ere the week was over.

Mr. Janson took a cordial farewell of all, and departed, as he had planned to do. Mr. Yorke also departed; but not until he had had a serious quarrel with Maria. Without their tacit engagement having been mentioned or alluded to, it was understood between them that it was at an end, that they had parted; and though the name of Mr. Janson was not breathed, each knew that but for his having come to Saxonbury that parting had not taken place.

CHAPTER VI.

The Voyage of the "Rushing Water."

It is eminently suggestive of our uncertain life here, to mark how time works its changes. Sometimes, in an incredibly short period, changes of the most unexpected and startling nature will take place. Thus it was with the family at Saxonbury. But three years have elapsed since you last saw them; and yet the changes which that time has wrought seem to have been sufficient for the marking of half a century.

Lady Saxonbury died of her malady. A twelvemonth afterwards Sir Arthur married the widow of Colonel Yorke, an uncle of Mr. Yorke's. Mrs. Yorke was notable for little, save a somewhat fractious spirit, and for her overweening indulgence of her boy, the son and heir of the late Colonel Yorke. Six months subsequent to his second marriage, Sir Arthur died, and

Mr. Yorke succeeded to Saxonbury. The second Lady Saxonbury—often called Mrs. Yorke still by the friends of her old days—removed to London with her establishment and her step-daughter Maria. With intervals of travelling, they had chiefly resided in London since. One year they had gone to pass the autumn at a comparatively little known French watering-place on the north coast—the very town which Mr. Janson had spoken of as being the residence of his mother. Some friends of Lady Saxonbury's were there for a sojourn, and that induced *her* to go. Once there, she became impressed with the idea that a little French schooling would prove of incalculable benefit to her son in regard to the acquiring of the language, and she placed him at the college as an *externe*, and prolonged her stay through the winter. But the young gentleman appeared to be more apt at picking up the Flemish *patois* he heard in the streets, than at the good French drilled into him in the school.

Maria stayed on, nothing loath, for—Mr. Janson was there. They had met once or twice temporarily since that visit of his to Saxonbury, and now they were in the habit of meeting daily—at least they had met daily until within the last few days. But the crisis had come and gone, and they had parted.

It was Mr. Janson himself who invoked it. Led on to believe (and there was every excuse for him that Maria's manner could afford) that she would regard his suit favourably, he at length spoke out, telling her how deeply he loved her; how, if she could but reconcile herself to become a surgeon's wife, there was a good practice waiting for him in England. The terms of purchase were arranged, and his mother was ready to supply the funds. It startled Maria beyond everything. It brought her to her senses. She, Maria Saxonbury, sink down into an obscure surgeon's wife, one who had yet his way to make! Her brow grew red at the thought, and she told him quietly that it could never be.

"Why have you led me on, then?" he inquired, his tone one of strangely acute anguish.

Why, indeed! Maria could not answer. She could not tell him that she had loved as passionately as he did, or that the anguish at her own heart was great as his.

And so they parted. Nothing more could be said or done. The dream of romance was over, and each must make the best of the future.

About a week went on after this final interview, and the last day of March came in. The harbour of this fine old fishing town was alive with bustle. On the following day, the first of April, the Iceland fishing-boats were to go out with the morning's tide. A whole fleet of vessels, some large, some small; some with their complement of ten or twelve men and boys on board, some with but four or five, who were making ready to depart on their annual voyage to the North fishery, praying for success.

Yes, *praying*. The streets were crowded with promenaders, going to or returning from the beautiful little chapel of the port, a chapel especially consecrated to fishermen. For three days had that small chapel been besieged, so that it was difficult to push a way in or out. It was a small building, little larger than a fair-sized room; models of ships were suspended in it, and it was tastefully decorated with landscape pictures, with gilding, and flowers, and ornaments, after the manner of the favourite chapels of the Roman Catholics. Some marine views in particular were attractively painted. They lined the walls of the porch, five or six of them, in glittering frames, and represented the vicissitudes of a sea-life. One portrayed a calm sea, on which glided a large ship with her white sails set, a scene of peace; another view shewed her rocking and tossing in all the perils of a storm, apparently about to succumb to its fury. Here was a small picture, representing a fishing-boat sinking, sinking hopelessly, beyond possibility of hope or succour, its mariners' hands and their beseeching countenances outstretched to heaven. The frame above it contained a view of another fishing-vessel approaching its harbour in safety. The chances and dangers of its past voyage were surmounted, and home faces were collected on the beach to welcome it in.

The chapel was dark; dark even in the daytime. The windows were sombre with their stained glass; and the ornaments, cases of relics, images, and pictures, raised against them, further obstructed the light. It never was wholly dark, for the high candles on the altar were kept continually burning, and numberless collections of miniature tapers were lighted up by the kneeling women. From sunrise till late at night the chapel was receiving and pouring forth its crowds. The sailor men and boys would come in, sink on their knees before one or other of the images, St. Andrew, or St. Peter, or the Virgin, and remain there, still as death, for a couple of minutes, praying to the saint. Then they crossed themselves and passed out, and the short prayer would last most of them until their return, when they would go into the same chapel and offer as brief thanks. The women remained kneeling longer: their prayers were chiefly for a *bon voyage* and safe return; the men's, for a good haul of cod. Not half the people who crowded there on the few evenings preceding the boats' departure could get an entrance into the chapel; therefore many were content to kneel outside, on the enclosed space of waste ground around it, and there pray. They all managed to steal a look through the open door at whichever image they patronised, bowed to it, made the sign of the cross, and so departed in peace.

There glided a lady into the chapel this evening

at the dusk hour. She looked of superior class, and was handsomely but quietly dressed. She drew aside to the remotest obscurity of the chapel entrance, and leaned against the bar that was placed there to guard the paintings, waiting till her turn should come to push in with the stream. She was a middle-aged woman, and must once have been beautiful, but her features looked clouded with care. A young woman followed her in the neat dress of a French domestic servant, wearing the universal dark cloth cloak, and close snow-white cap. The lady was anxious to pray, and soon passed on; the maid was more anxious to look about her and to gossip, so she stopped at the entrance. Presently an acquaintance came up, another woman-servant, who accosted her:—

"Hey, Thérèse, is it you? Who have you come to pray for? I thought your brother was not going this year."

"I am attending madame."

"Madame Janson! What does she do here? She has nothing to do with the cod-fishery."

"I can tell you that she has, though," was the reply of Thérèse, "and a fine way the house has been in, through it. You know her son?"

"Who does not? A rackety blade."

"Rackety! Well, he may be a little. Everybody likes him, though."

"Well, what of him?"

"He is going out with the cod-boats to Iceland."

"With the cod-boats! That young Englishman! Why, what on earth—— it can't be."

Thérèse nodded her head several times in succession. "Some whim of his. He goes for pleasure, he says."

"Stuff, Thérèse! Such a thing was never heard of as going out with the cod-boats for pleasure. It's a precious hard voyage and hard life. Besides, the crew don't want a fine gentleman on board."

"Oh, what do they care? He has made it all right with Messrs. Vandersphinks, the owners."

"Vandersphinks! Which is he going out in, then?"

"The *Rushing Water*."

"Well, he has got a taste! To go out in a dirty cod-boat to that cold barren Iceland, a handsome young fellow like that! Will he share the sailors' fare?"

"Not he: any more than he'll share their labour. There's some tins of preserved meat gone on board for him, and a big hamper of prime Bordeaux wine."

"And that brings his mother here—to pray for his safe return! Thérèse, it's a lucky thing she is not a heretic, though she is one of them English, or she couldn't have come here to pray for it—at least, with any chance of St. Peter listening to her. But, I say, he is a heretic, isn't he?"

Thérèse nudged her companion for silence. And the woman, looking round, saw close to her a party of "heretics;" two English ladies and a child, who had come, full of British curiosity, to witness the praying in the chapel.

"You shouldn't call 'em so to their faces," whispered the tolerant Thérèse. "They are as good as we are, for all I see, and"——

Thérèse broke off suddenly, and dropped upon her knees. Her mistress was coming out again, after her short prayer.

"Thérèse, have you not been in?" demanded Mrs. Janson, in very good French, her tone betraying reproach and surprise.

"Couldn't get in, madame," answered Thérèse, without thinking it necessary to add that she had not tried.

It took some time to get out. Several were pushing out, as well as themselves, but they were obstructed by the numbers pushing in. Immediately following Mrs. Janson, were the two English ladies mentioned, the younger one, who was an elegant girl of remarkable beauty, remonstrating at their leaving so soon.

"Henry is so troublesome," replied her companion. "I could scarcely hold him still, do all I would. He wanted to run inside, amidst the mass kneeling there."

"I told you it would be so, mamma. You should have left him at home."

The Foggy Night at Offord, etc.

"Oh, of course," observed the elder lady, in a sharp accent. "I know he is an eyesore to you, Elizabeth."

"Mamma, you know that he is nothing of the sort. But he is the most troublesome boy that ever existed, especially to take anywhere."

Miss Saxonbury was right; for it was no other. Never was there so troublesome a child as Henry Yorke. He was a slender boy of ten, fair and delicate, with well-formed features and long wavy hair, the combing out of which every morning by his mother, and the coaxing into curls, kept the house in an uproar for an hour. He was one of those precocious, clever children, who, to use a familiar phrase, are "awake to everything," restless, mischievous, and wilful. Yet the boy had admirable qualities, had they been allowed fair play, but his mother pursued a system of ruinous indulgence. He was the pride and delight of her life, and the torment of every one else's. A whim had taken him lately to call his half-sister (if she might be termed such) by her second name, Elizabeth. He detected that she did not like it, and therefore he did it, for mischief's sake. Lady Saxonbury fell sometimes into the same name. Maria felt convinced that it was done to please Henry and vex herself.

No sooner were they outside than Henry managed to emancipate himself from his mother's grasp, and she had the satisfaction of seeing him rush back again, twist himself amidst the blockade at the entrance, and disappear.

"There!" uttered Lady Saxonbury, "he is gone —just like an eel! What am I to do to get at him? Wait here, Maria."

"Thérèse," said Mrs. Janson, who had seen and heard this bit of byplay, "go home fast and get supper ready. If Mr. Edward should be at home, tell him I shall soon be in."

Thérèse went off, picking her way through the lines of kneelers on the earth, and turning her head and her drooping gold earrings from side to side, in search of a gossip to walk with. Miss Saxonbury, who had drawn aside to be out of the way of passers-by, found herself suddenly addressed.

"You are Maria Elizabeth Saxonbury?"

"Yes," she replied, wondering at the stranger's familiarity.

"I knew you by intuition. I heard Miss Saxonbury was of rare beauty, and I have not often witnessed beauty to match what I now see in you. If it shall prove the blight to others that it has to me, better for you that you had been a model of deformity."

"I do not understand you," haughtily spoke Miss Saxonbury. "I do not know you."

"I have given you no opportunity to know me. I

am Edward Janson's mother. I have lived in this place many years, holding myself aloof from my countrymen, who flock here to make it their few years' residence, or their few weeks' sojourn. I am too poor to compete with some of their ostentatious purses. I am saving for my son; and I am too proud to risk familiarity with doubtful characters—as many of them are. Therefore your family and I have never met. I wish I could say that you had never met my son. You have played your beauty off upon him, flirted with him, courted him—yes, you have, Miss Saxonbury!—and drawn him on to love you. When that love had reached a height that it could no longer be suppressed within the bounds of prudence, and he told it to you, you rejected him. It may be, with scorn, because he was poor and you were rich: I know not: from him I have learnt nothing. He has kept his own counsel and your secret; but I have watched closely, and know the day that brought to him this despair. In blighting his happiness you have blighted mine."

Maria Saxonbury's glowing features had turned to paleness, and now they were glowing again. The words told home. She appeared too confused to answer, and Mrs. Janson continued—

"He came over here to pass a few weeks with me before he should settle in his profession, in his own country. Those weeks have been passed with you, rather than with me, and now he is going out with these wretched cod-fishers, and may never return."

"Going out with the cod-fishers!" mechanically interrupted Maria.

"Yes, he is," replied Mrs. Janson. "When he came home, two days ago, and told me his intention, I thought my heart would have broken; and in my haste I wished that you had been dead—dead, young lady—before you had lured my boy on to love you, and then treated him so, that he must go this hard voyage to forget you and strive for peace. I have pity for misfortune," added Mrs. Janson, "but I have none for wilful fault, for the sinful indulgence of vanity. I do not wish you ill, Maria Saxonbury; I trust I have too much Christian charity deliberately to wish it to any one; but I cannot help feeling that, should your existence become as bitter to you as you have made mine, it will only be a just retribution."

Without another word, she turned away, leaving Miss Saxonbury rooted to the spot, and miserably conscious. All that Mrs. Janson had reproached her with was, in the main, only too just. In the old days at Saxonbury she had first flirted with Edward Janson for love of admiration's sake. Now that the love which supervened had been spoken, she meant to bury hers within her own breast, to stifle it, to extinguish it; and she had turned him adrift to do the same.

"I was obliged to hold up a five-franc piece to bribe him to come out," said Lady Saxonbury, emerging from the chapel, hot and red, the truant a fast prisoner in her grasp. "And glad enough to get him out on terms so easy: he had got close up to that lighted altar at the other end."

Miss Saxonbury took hold of the boy's other hand, and away they went; Harry delighted at his five-franc piece, and kicking up clouds of dust as he walked between them.

The morning rose bright and clear. The tide served at eight o'clock, but long before that hour the port was taken possession of. Half the town was there to witness the departure, thronging the piers and the heights. It was a stirring sight. Vessel after vessel, hoisting its sails, came smoothly down the harbour, each receiving an animated, hearty cheer of hope from hundreds of voices. Wives, mothers, sisters, and little children, leaned over the nearly unprotected sides of the piers, to wish good luck to the several crews, and utter the last farewell in their familiar *patois*.

One vessel in particular came gaily down, a trim-built craft of middling size. A sunburnt boy, in a fishing-cap, and red flannel shirt, was in the bows, grinning. "Here comes the *Rushing Water*," cried a spectator. "So, she is taking out young Paul!" he added, as he caught sight of the boy's face. "The crew of the *Fleur de Marie* would not take him."

"Why not?" inquired those around.

"He has been in three different vessels, three years running, has that monkey, and they all had enough of him. A worse boy never sailed than that young Paul; he is made up of ill-nature and mischief. The *Rushing Water* must have been hard up for hands to take him."

"The *Rushing Water* is taking out a hand or two short," chimed in an old fishwife. "Some gentleman took a whim to go out in her, and he wouldn't be crowded, he said. They took this young shaver aboard last night: he can be put anywhere."

Leaning over the side of the pier with Henry Yorke, and attended by a maid and footman, was Miss Saxonbury. The *Rushing Water* came gliding past, and her cheeks expressed plainly their consciousness of it. Standing upright in the boat, in a jaunty sailor's costume, was Mr. Janson, handsomer than ever. He looked at her with a face schooled to impassiveness, and gravely raised his hat in token of adieu. She forgot her resolution for a moment: her eyes were strained yearningly on him, and the tears shone in them, as she waved her handkerchief in answer. Another grave bow ere he resumed his glazed hat, and the *Rushing Water* glided down the harbour.

A gentleman stood at Miss Saxonbury's side, somewhat behind her. He had seen the signs of her emotion, and his lips parted with a defiant expression. He was a tall, powerfully-built man of near thirty, with remarkably white teeth, which he shewed too much. Without perceiving him, Miss Saxonbury turned to pursue her way to the top of the crowded pier. It was a work of difficulty, and Henry Yorke exercised his feet and his elbows.

"Harry, if you behave so rudély, if you push the people unnecessarily, I will send John home with you."

"That you won't. I would jump over the pier first, and go home ducked, on purpose to get you into a row with mamma. You know you are not to dictate to me."

"Hush! Be a good boy."

"I say, Elizabeth, don't you wish you were going out with Mr. Janson?"

It was a telling question, innocently put. And he who was following close behind, saw that her very neck was in a glow.

"I do," continued Harry. "It is so nice to sail over the sea. I'll be a sailor when I grow up."

"Nice to sail over the sea!" cried Miss Saxonbury. "Don't you remember how ill you were, only crossing here from London?"

"It was the nasty steamer made me ill. I do mean to be a sailor, Maria, and I'll bring you lots of things home from foreign countries. Mamma thinks I only say it to tease her, when I want anything that she won't give me. I'll bring you a monkey from Africa."

Every inch of ground, towards the extremity of the pier, was contested for, that being the best gazing place. The sea was calm and lovely, the light wind, which served to spread the sails, scarcely ruffling it; more than thirty boats were already out, studding the marine landscape, and the morning sun shone brightly on their canvas, as they skimmed over the water. Miss Saxonbury was struggling on, when a crash and shouting below, and a worse press than ever to the side of the pier, suggested that some untoward accident had occurred. The *Rushing Water*, in going out of harbour, had, by some mishap or mismanagement, which none on board could account for, struck against the end of the pier. The boy, Paul, had been left for a single moment near the rudder: could he have mischievously altered the boat's course?

"What damage is done?" inquired Miss Saxonbury of a bystander, a fisherman, when the excitement was abating.

"Not much—as far as I can see. They will have to put back, though, till the evening's tide, and give her a haul over."

"Good morning, Miss Saxonbury. You are out early."

She turned sharply round at the voice, to encounter Mr. Yorke. He was staying in the French town also, herself, no doubt, his motive-power. Perhaps he was waiting the opportunity to say to her what he had thought to say years ago.

"We came to see the boats go out," she said, giving him her hand.

"I should scarcely have thought a fleet of paltry fishing-boats would be a sufficient attraction to call a young lady from her bed."

"Oh, Mr. Yorke! Look at the numbers of English around: nearly every one we know is here. It is a sight which has the charm of novelty for many of us."

"I see your friend young Janson's courage has not failed him at the last," he said, mockingly. "We shall be rid of him for a time."

"For good, probably," she replied with the utmost apparent indifference. "Before he returns, we shall no doubt have left for home."

"I hope so. I wonder at Lady Saxonbury's having brought you here at all. I wonder that she should remain here! These continental towns are not places for Miss Saxonbury."

"She remains for Henry's improvement in French," said Maria.

"And, that he may gain facility in speaking it, she sends him to the college, where he mixes with a dozen other English boys," said Mr. Yorke. "And they abuse each other all day in genuine Queen's English."

"We are not going to associate with those pigs of French beggars," interposed Master Yorke, shaking back his pretty curls in token of scorn.

"Pigs!" echoed the gentleman. "You are polite, sir."

"At any rate it is what they are always calling us," retorted the lad. "*Gros cochons Anglais.*"

In returning down the crowded pier, they got separated from Mr. Yorke, also from the servants. As Maria and Henry were passing through the old fortified gates of the port, three or four lads, all older than himself, came up to hold a conference with Harry. It appeared to be productive of some pleasurable excitement, for he turned to his sister with sparkling eyes and an eager face.

"Maria, may I go out fishing?"

"Fishing, no! You would send mamma into a fever. You know she never allows you to go near the water."

"There's no danger, Miss Saxonbury," spoke up one of the inviters, a boy of fifteen or sixteen. "We are going up the canal in a boat for a mile or two, and then shall land and fish. He can't come to any harm: we are accustomed to the management of a boat, and we shall take our provisions with us. We mean to make a day of it."

"It is impossible that I can allow him to go," replied Maria. "He can ask his mamma if he likes; but I am sure it will be useless."

"It's a shame then!" exclaimed Henry. "I can never do anything that I like. Won't I when I get bigger!"

He walked sullenly by his sister's side until they reached the streets. As they were passing the college, one or two boys were going in at the scholars' entrance, and the old church clock, further off, chimed out nine.

"I shall go into school now," said Henry.

"Nonsense," returned Maria. "You have not had your breakfast."

"I don't want any. I don't want to be marked late. It's your fault for stopping so long upon the pier. So good-bye, Elizabeth."

"Good-bye," she repeated, scarcely heeding his departure or what she said, for at that moment Edward Janson appeared, crossing the street, having landed from the *Rushing Water*. The sight made her oblivious to everything else.

At six o'clock, when they assembled to dinner, Henry was missing. Lady Saxonbury supposed he was kept in at school, not an unfrequent occurrence, and began dinner with a very bad grace. She inquired of John what time he went back to school after luncheon: she and Maria having been out in the middle of the day.

"Master Henry did not come home to luncheon, ma'am."

Lady Saxonbury was indignant. "No breakfast, and keep him from two meals besides!" she uttered. "It is enough to throw him into a consumption. The master must be a bear. Go at once and bring the child home, John; bring him home by force if they object, and threaten them with the police. I'll summons that master before the Criminal Tribunal."

The footman went leisurely enough to the college; but he ran back again at full speed. Master Yorke had not been into class that day, and he was to be punished for it on the morrow.

"Not into class!" repeated the alarmed mother. "Elizabeth, you told me you left him at the college."

"So I did. I saw him run to the gates. I—I think—I saw him enter," she added, more hesitatingly, trying to remember whether she did or not.

"You think! What do you mean by that?" demanded Lady Saxonbury, who really cared nothing for anybody except her son. "You saw him, or you did not."

"He never can have gone off with those boys!" suddenly exclaimed Maria, in alarm, remembering the fishing expedition.

"What boys? Why don't you speak plain?"

"Jones and Anson, and a few more English lads, were going up the canal in a boat to fish, and they wanted Harry to go with them," explained Maria. "I refused, of course."

"Then he is sure to be gone! and if he is drowned you will have been the cause!" screamed Lady Saxonbury, in agitation. "After such a thing as that put into his head, you ought to have brought him home, and kept him here. You know what he is."

There was no further peace. Lady Saxonbury not only sent about the town, but went herself, to the houses of the boys' parents, and to every place where there was a possibility of hearing of him. The other parents were alarmed now. With some difficulty they discovered which canal the young gentlemen had favoured with their company, and bent their steps to it in a body, Mr. Jones carrying a lantern, for it was dark then. They had not proceeded along its banks many minutes when they encountered a small army of half-a-dozen, looking like drowned rats. It proved to be the young gentlemen themselves, who had all been in the water, through the upsetting of the boat.

"Where is Henry?" asked Lady Saxonbury, trembling so that she could scarcely put the question. "Has he been with you?"

"Yes, he has been with us."

"Where is he? Oh, where is he?"

"He was in the boat when it capsized. We can't make out where he is. I'm sure he scrambled out."

Maria was very pale. "How are you sure?" she asked, in a dread tone.

"I am positive I saw him," cried Philip Anson, "and I spoke to him. I said to him, 'That was a splash and a near touch, wasn't it, Hal?' and he answered, 'By Jove, if it wasn't!'"

"No, it was me answered you that, Phil," interposed a little fellow about Henry's age.

"Well, I'm positive he is out," rejoined Phil Anson, "for I know I saw him, and his hair had got the curl out of it, and was hanging down straight."

"Did any of the rest of you see him?" inquired Maria, in painful suspense.

All the boys began talking together. The result to be gathered was, that they could not be sure whether he was out or not; it was all a scramble at the time, and nearly dark.

"Oh, mamma, do not despair!" implored Maria. But Lady Saxonbury had fainted away, and was lying on the towing-path.

CHAPTER VII.

A Lost Boy.

IT was a terrible misfortune. Apart from Lady Saxonbury's almost insane grief for the child himself, it was a great misfortune in a pecuniary point of view. With her son's death a considerable portion of her income passed from her; her resources as the widow of Sir Arthur Saxonbury not being large. Just enough was left her to starve upon, she groaned, taking an exaggerated view of things, as she was apt to do. Her grief was, indeed, pitiable. She persisted in attributing all the blame of the boy's death to Maria. She commenced a system of unkind treatment, could not endure the sight of her; and when she did see her, it was only to break out into sobs and harsh reproaches.

"I should not bear it," observed Mr. Yorke, one day, to Maria.

"Is it just?" returned Maria, in a passionate tone of appeal. "When I saw him to the door of the college, how could I imagine that he pretended to go in only to blind me—that he would disobediently run to the canal the moment I was out of sight? Is it just of Lady Saxonbury?"

"No. Very unjust. I say I should emancipate myself."

"I cannot live this life. It makes me so wretched that I sometimes begin to doubt whether I am not really guilty. I will go away rather than bear it."

"Let me emancipate you, Maria," said Mr. Yorke.

She cast at him a rapid glance. The hour was come that she had expected; sometimes doubted, if she had not dreaded.

"You cannot be ignorant of my intentions," he resumed, "or why I have stayed here in this place, which I hate. You must know that I love you passionately; far more passionately than he did, Maria."

"Than who did?" she exclaimed, with a rush of conscious colour.

"Janson. As if you did not know."

"Why do you bring up Janson?" she said. "What is Janson to me?"

"Maria, you will be my wife? Do not refuse," he impetuously added. "I have sworn that if you are not mine you shall never be another's."

"Mr. Yorke!"

"I cannot live without you. I love you too passionately for my own peace. You must be mine, Maria. It was your father's wish."

What was she to answer? She did not know. A conflict was at work within her. She liked Mr. Yorke, but—she loved Edward Janson. Edward Janson, however, she could never hope to marry, and her days were passed in striving to forget him. With Mr.

The Foggy Night at Offord, etc.

Yorke she should go back to the dear old home at Saxonbury.

"Give me until to-morrow, and you shall have an answer," she said to him. "This has come upon me suddenly."

"Very well. Remember, Maria, that during the suspense I shall neither eat nor sleep; I shall have neither peace nor rest. Be my wife, and your days shall be a dream of love."

"A dream of love!" she bitterly repeated, as he left her. "For him, perhaps: not for me!"

She remained in her room until evening, communing with herself, and then she sought Lady Saxonbury, saying she wished to consult her.

"I am not worth consulting now," was the querulous answer. "My spirits are gone, my heart is broken."

"Mr. Yorke wants me to marry him."

"Mr. Yorke!" returned her stepmother, somewhat aroused. "Has he asked you?"

"Yes; to-day."

"Then you are more lucky than you deserve."

"I do not know whether to accept or reject him."

"Reject him!" fiercely interposed Lady Saxonbury. "You are out of your senses. With his fine fortune, his position, his amiability"——

"*Is* he amiable?" asked Maria. "He puzzles me at times."

"What puzzles you?"

"His words. I don't understand them. And the expression of his countenance."

"Had you not better set up for a phrenologist— or whatever they call the charlatans who pretend to read faces?" sarcastically retorted Lady Saxonbury.

"Mamma, listen. If I do accept him, it will be because I am unhappy with you."

"Pray, why should there be an 'if' in the matter at all? Why should you hesitate, or think of rejecting him?"

"Because I do not love him," answered Maria, in a low tone. "I like Mr. Yorke, but it requires more than liking to marry a man: or ought to require it."

"Oh, if you are going to run on about romance and sentiment, I do not understand it," returned Lady Saxonbury. "I never did more than 'like' my two husbands, yet I was happy with them. My love was wasted on somebody else; when I was almost a child."

"Was it?" cried Maria, eagerly.

"It was. It was over and done with before I married, and I did not make the less good wife. It is so with ninety-nine women out of every hundred; and rely upon it, their wedded lives are all the happier for their early romance being over. Romance and reality do not work well together, Maria. You are inexperienced, child."

Maria was beginning to think so.

"I give you my advice, Maria, and I give it for your happiness. Marry Mr. Yorke, and be thankful. Reject him, and pass your after-life in repining, in self-reproach at your own folly."

Mr. Yorke received the answer he wished for. They were to be married in England, in autumn, but preparations were at once commenced. It was only to be expected that Lady Saxonbury would now go home immediately, but she declined to do so. In spite of the somewhat cynical remonstrances of Mr. Yorke, she flatly refused. She would go home for the wedding in September, she said, and she would not go before. Perhaps some vague hope of recovering, even yet, the body of the child from the canal, chained her to the place. So Mr. Yorke remained on perforce in the despised town, feeling that he and they were alike out of place in it.

CHAPTER VIII.

The Return of the "Rushing Water."

AUGUST came in, and the fishing-boats began to return from Iceland, laden with their spoil: by ones, by twos, by threes, by little fleets of them. At length all were in, save two, the *Belle Hélène* and the *Rushing Water*. These two delayed much, and a report got about, nobody knew how, for it was certainly without foundation, that the *Rushing Water* was wrecked. Miss Saxonbury, in spite of herself and her betrothal, heard the evil fear with a sickening heart, and looked out for it in secret more yearningly than any one.

Or than any, save one. For, if her anxiety was great, what was it compared with that of poor Mrs. Janson? One day, it was on a Friday, Thérèse had gone to the fish-market to purchase the usual fast-day's dinner, when in the midst of her squally bargaining with the fish-vendor, news flew about the market that one of the two missing boats was signalled—it was thought to be the *Rushing Water*. Dashing the disputed fish back on the woman's board, away went Thérèse to her mistress, and without circumlocution announced that the *Rushing Water* was making the harbour.

Mrs. Janson went down to the port. The boat was then in, and being moored to the side: *La Belle Hélène*. She asked the crew news of the *Rushing Water*, but they had not seen her on their passage home. Yet the *Rushing Water* had been one of the first boats to leave Iceland.

Disheartening news. As Mrs. Janson went back again, with a heavy step, she encountered Miss Saxonbury.

"Young lady, go home and pray," she said, in her abrupt, stern manner; "pray that you may not have caused his death, as well as his misery. Stay upon your knees until Heaven shall be pleased to hear you, as I am going to do. There is little hope now."

"I heard the *Rushing Water* had come in this morning," answered Miss Saxonbury, in a faltering tone.

"So did I. But it proves to be the *Hélène*. And the *Rushing Water* left Iceland days before her."

She passed on with her pale, severe face, and Maria Saxonbury continued her way.

The days went on, five or six of them. Lady and Miss Saxonbury were sitting in the twilight, the latter expecting Mr. Yorke, whom she was trying, with all her might and main, to like better, as a dutiful bride-elect should, when one of their French servants came in, and said a gentleman was asking to see her.

"Me! To see me?" returned Maria.

"A gentleman-sailor, mademoiselle. I think it is Mr. Janson. He says will you allow him a minute's conversation?"

"O mamma!" she uttered, "Mr. Janson! Then the *Rushing Water* must be safe in."

Lady Saxonbury made some indistinct reply. Her thoughts were buried in other things. What, to her, was the safety of the *Rushing Water?*

Maria passed through the ante-room and entered the one where he had been shewn. He was in sailor's attire, his glazed hat carelessly thrown off, looking, or Maria fancied so, handsomer than ever.

"Then you are in safety!" she exclaimed, grasping his hand in her agitated thankfulness, perhaps for his mother's sake, but forgetful, at the moment, of Mr. Yorke, of the whole world. "We have been counting you as amongst the lost."

"Our homeward voyage has been bad, perilous, unlucky altogether, save that we have ultimately arrived. Miss Saxonbury, I hear that you have been mourning Harry as dead."

"Yes, yes. Oh yes!"

"He is safe. He has been with us."

She did not scream, she suppressed it. Then she thought that he must be dreaming, or that she was.

"He got into some trouble, fell into the water, and was afraid to go home," proceeded Mr. Janson. "That mischievous imp, Paul, encountered him in his wet plight, persuaded him into making the voyage, brought him on board, coiled him up under some sails and rope, and four-and-twenty hours after we left port, Master Harry came out. I wished the captain to put back, but he laughed at me; so he had to go with us, and I have taken care of him. Paul says Harry bribed him with a five-franc piece; three francs for himself, and two to give to a messenger to take word to his mother where he had gone."

"No messenger came to us," eagerly interrupted Maria.

"As I find. When I landed an hour ago, I heard

that the boy had been mourned as dead. So I came on at once, after calling in upon my mother. I should not have presumed to ask for you," he pointedly added, "but that I assumed it might be better to acquaint you first with the news, ere it was broken to Lady Saxonbury."

"Oh! how shall we ever thank you?" said Maria, attributing all the good to Mr. Janson, in her confused feelings of joy. "Where is Harry?"

"Waiting just inside the café at the next door, until I send for him, and being made a lion of."

Maria went into the drawing-room, which was almost dark then, and knelt down beside Lady Saxonbury's chair.

"Mamma! mamma! I have some joyful news for you. You will not faint if I tell it?"

"What news will ever be joyful to me again, Maria? What is the matter with you, that you kneel in that manner? How you tremble!"

"Mamma—suppose I have news to tell you about Harry? That—he—is—found?"

"Is it? is it?" excitedly uttered Lady Saxonbury.

It! She was thinking of the dead Harry; not the living one.

"Not 'it,' mamma. He. Could you bear for me to tell you that he is in life—safe—well?'

"Maria, what do you mean?" faintly asked Lady Saxonbury.

"He is, he is. Dearest Lady Saxonbury, he has been out with Mr. Janson in the *Rushing Water.*"

She did not continue. For the door had opened, and a happy lad stood peeping in, in a nondescript attire, composed partly of his own things, partly of Paul's. He was browned with the sea air, taller than before, and his fair curls were wild and entangled. With a cry, he flew into his mother's arms, and she sobbed upon his neck and kissed his pretty face and his untidy hair, and strained him to her as if she could never let him go again.

"Lady Saxonbury, will you forgive my saying that I think you will find him a more dutiful boy than he used to be?" said Mr. Janson, who had followed him. "He has had to rough it, and he now knows the value of a happy home and a mother's love. I have taken upon myself to discipline him; I have kept him from the sailors, so far as was practicable, and read him lessons on his faults, and I believe you will find him changed for the better."

"Oh yes, indeed, mamma," sobbed the lad, "I know now how naughty I was, and I will try and never grieve you and Maria again."

"Mr. Janson," cried the mother, rising and speaking in impassioned tones, "how can I reward you for the joy that you have brought me this night? If you asked me for my life in repayment, I almost think it should be yours."

She left the room as she spoke, too much overcome to remain in it. Harry followed her. Miss Saxonbury was lost in thought.

"Philip Anson has held to it to this day, that Harry was saved," she said in a musing tone. "He persisted in declaring that he saw Harry after he scrambled out of the water."

"And now that my task is done, I have only to take my leave," observed Mr. Janson, holding out his hand. "This house was an interdicted place to me before I left; I conclude that it is so still."

Miss Saxonbury put her hand in his, and burst into tears.

He held it, and looked at her. "Maria, what do those tears mean? That you hate me, as you did before?"

"I never hated you," she answered, forgetting prudence in her tumultuously glad feelings! "It was the contrary. I am very miserable."

"I went this voyage," he whispered, "striving to forget, if not to hate you. I come from it, loving you more than ever. The child's being on board was against my project; how, when I constantly saw him, could I forget you? My dearest, why should we separate?" he added, straining her hand to his heart. "Let it be between us as it once was. Your mother has said she would give me a reward, even to her own life; let me ask her to give me you."

"It may not be," she gasped, struggling to release herself from him. "It"——

"Not just yet can I marry," he interrupted. "I threw up the prospect opening to me in the spring; and the only position I could at present offer would not"——

"Edward, pray hear me," she said, in a broken voice, as she drew away from him. "You know not what you ask. I am promised to another."

"To another!"

"And in less than a month I shall be his wife," she continued, too agitated to weigh her words, "and I love you, and not him. Do you wonder that I am miserable? There—now that you have the avowal, let us part for ever."

"Who is this? Mr. Yorke?"

"Mr. Yorke."

There was a gloomy pause. "*Must* you fulfil the contract? Can you not give him up for me?"

She shook her head. "I can only be plain with you. I am not fit to be a poor man's wife. No, I have deliberately entered upon it, and matters have been advanced too far to be broken off now. Forgive me, Edward—forgive me all. We must forget each other."

"O Maria! must this indeed be the ending?"

"Yes," she answered, the tears raining from her eyes, and her heart aching with pain. "I wish it had been different, but circumstances are against us. Farewell, Edward; if ever we meet again, it must be as strangers. Not so," she hastily added, as he drew her face to his for a last embrace, "it is not right to *him*. Do you not hear me say that in a little space I shall be his wife."

"For the last time," he murmured; and she made but a faint resistance. "He ought not to grudge it to us. Now—farewell for ever."

Mr. Janson turned to leave the room. He saw not that somebody drew away from the door, and stood bolt upright, in silence, against the wall of the dark ante-room, while he passed out—somebody with a revengeful face, and teeth that glistened like a tiger's. Not that Mr. Yorke was of a dishonourable nature, or had dishonourably set himself to listen. He had caught somewhat of the scene as he was entering from the ante-room, and surprise, doubt, and rage had chained him there to the end. He followed Mr. Janson from the house, and strode about the old streets of the town till morning; now standing under its high and ancient tower, as it sent forth its sweet chimes on the night air, now pacing under the portico of the church, now slouching round the railings of the famous statue in the Place, the town's pride; and now striding off to the port, there to surprise the sentinels. But he buried his wrongs within him—very great wrongs indeed they appeared to be to his heated brain—and told them not.

Little did Miss Saxonbury think, on the day of her wedding, when she gave her hand without her heart, that the bridegroom, kneeling by her side, knew just as well as she did that she had no heart to give. At the best it was an inauspicious beginning of life. She felt that it was. She felt, too, that should her future existence bring somewhat of retribution, she had only invoked it on herself: as Mrs. Janson had almost predicted that night, outside the little chapel, when she had been praying for the safety of the *Rushing Water*.

CHAPTER IX.

Alnwick Cottage.

A BLAZING hot day in August. More especially hot it felt at the railway station of Offord, a quiet country village; for it was a small, bare station, with not a tree and but little covering about it, to shade off the sun's hot glare. The two o'clock train came puffing up, stopped, deposited a few passengers and a good deal of luggage, and went screaming and puffing on again.

Nearly all who had alighted were of one party. Mr. and Mrs. Yorke, their two young children, and some servants. She was young and beautiful still, but her manner had grown colder. Little trace remained of the gay lightness of Maria Saxonbury.

From the love, incidental to Englishmen, of temporary change, of new scenes, Mr. Yorke had quitted Saxonbury, its comforts and its elegances, for a "shooting-box" in another county. All he knew of "Alnwick Cottage," he knew through an advertisement, except what he learnt by two or three letters from Mr. Maskell, who had the charge of letting it, furnished. Excellent fishing and shooting were promised, and Mr. Yorke had taken it for six months. It stood nearly a mile beyond the village.

No one was at the station to meet them, and Mr. Yorke, in his haughty spirit, was not pleased at the omission. He deemed that Mr. Maskell ought to have been there.

"It is a disrespect which he ought not to have shewn me," he remarked to his wife, when the bustle of their arrival at the cottage was over.

"I wonder he was not there," she answered. "But something may have prevented him, Arthur; we don't know."

"I think I shall take a stroll out, and have a look at the locality," resumed Mr. Yorke. "Do you want anything ordered in, Maria?"

"Not that I know of," she answered. "The servants can see about all that."

Mr. Yorke departed, taking the direction of Offord.

When he reached the village, one of the first houses he saw was Mr. Maskell's, as the door-plate announced: "Mr. Maskell, Lawyer and Conveyancer." He rang, and was admitted.

"I am so sorry not to have met you at the station," began Mr. Maskell, when he learnt who his visitor was. "I was called suddenly out of Offord this morning to make a gentleman's will, and have not been home half-an-hour. I have despatched my clerk to Alnwick Cottage with the inventory. Sir, I hope you will like Offord."

"It seems a very poor place," remarked Mr. Yorke.

"The village can't boast much, but the neighbourhood is superior: a small society, but excellent. Capital shooting, too!"

"Have you good medical advice?"

"He is a very nice young fellow, our doctor. We have but one: the place would not support more. Not but what he makes a good thing of it."

Mr. Yorke's lip curled. He had not been thinking of "nice young fellows," but of superior medical skill. "I asked you about the doctor before I decided on the cottage, and you wrote me word there was an excellent one," said he, in a dissatisfied tone. "It is most essential, where there's a family, to be near a clever medical man."

"We all think him very clever," replied the lawyer. "He bought the practice three years ago: our surgeon had died, and I negotiated its sale with this gentleman. He has attended us ever since, and is a great favourite. He was in London for two years before that, qualified assistant to a large medical practitioner. Plenty of experience he had there: it was a large hospital practice. He was smoking his cigar with me yesterday evening; he often runs in, does Janson; and was saying"——

"What is his name?" interrupted Mr. Yorke, his accent shrill and unnatural.

"Janson."

"What?"

The lawyer wondered whether Mr. Yorke was attacked with sudden deafness, and why his eyes glared, and his teeth shone out, so like fangs.

"Janson," he repeated—"Edward Janson. Do you know him?"

Mr. Yorke's mouth closed again, and his manner calmed down. "It is a curious name," said he. "Is it English?"

"Of Dutch origin, I suppose. Janson is an Englishman."

"Does he live in the village?"

"A few doors lower down. It is the corner house as you come to Rye Lane: the garden door at the back opens on the lane. I assure you, sir, you may call in this gentleman with every confidence, should you or your family require medical advice."

Meanwhile, during this walk of Mr. Yorke's, everybody was busy at Alnwick Cottage, as is the case when going into a fresh residence. Finch, the nurse, a confidential servant, who had been Mrs. Yorke's maid before her marriage, was deputed to go through the house with the lawyer's clerk and the inventory. The eldest child, a boy of four years, chose, and he had a will of his own, to attend on Finch: Finch submitting to the companionship, failing in some coaxing attempts to get rid of him. But after a while he grew tired of the process of looking at chairs and tables and cups and saucers, and quitted her to go down-stairs.

"Go to Charlotte, Leo dear," said Finch. "I shall soon have done. Charlotte," she called out, over the balustrades, "see to Master Leo."

When Finch and the clerk had finished the inventory, the former proceeded to the small room on the ground floor, which had been appropriated as the nursery. In the list it was set down as "butler's pantry." Charlotte, the under-nurse, sat there, with the youngest child asleep on her lap.

"Where's Master Leo?" asked Finch, abbreviating, as she usually did, his name, "Leopold." "I sent him here, and ordered you to see after him."

"He didn't come," was Charlotte's answer, "and the little one was just dropping off to sleep. Master

The Foggy Night at Offord, etc.

Leo wouldn't come here to me, if he could go to his mamma."

"You'd let him be with his mamma for ever, you would, if it saved yourself a little trouble," cried Finch, who of course domineered over Charlotte, upper-nurse fashion. "I hate this moving, I do! such a bother! nothing to be got at, and one's regular meals and hours upset. I'm as tired as a poor jaded horse. And you sitting here doing nothing, with that child on your lap! you might have laid him down, and got a cup of tea for us."

"Am I to lay him on the floor?" retorted Charlotte. "I don't know which is to be the children's bed."

Finch flung out of the room in search of Leo: her labours that day, and the discomfort around, made her cross. He was not to be found in-doors, and she went to the garden. Very soon a shriek of fright and horror arose from her. It drew her mistress out: and the lawyer's clerk, who had been departing, heard it, and ran back in its direction.

Leopold Yorke had met with a ladder, reared against the side of the house, and had climbed up it, in all a boy's adventurous spirit. He had fallen off, poor child, it was impossible to say from what height, and now lay insensible on the gravel, with an ugly gash in his forehead, from which the blood was oozing.

Finch stopped her groans and lamentations, and

stooped to pick him up. But Mrs. Yorke snatched him from her, and crouched down on the earth, with one knee raised, and laid him upon it. She looked with a hopeless, helpless expression at the lawyer's clerk. The words, which came from her white lips, were scarcely audible.

"A doctor: where does one live?"

"I'll fetch him, ma'am; I'll run every step of the way; I don't mind the heat," cried the sympathising clerk.

He did not wait another moment, but sped away. Leopold was conveyed in-doors; and, before the surgeon got there—who also seemed to have come on the run—the child had recovered consciousness, and Finch had washed the wound, which now seemed disarmed of three parts of its terrors. Mr. Janson, handsome, frank, attractive as he used to be, wanting yet a year or so of thirty, bound it up, ordered the boy to be kept quiet, and said he would send in a little calming medicine.

"May I dare to shake hands with you?" he asked, with a frank, pleasant smile, but with a somewhat heightened colour, when he and Mrs. Yorke were left alone.

She placed her hand within his, quite as frankly, though the glow was far deeper on her face than on his. "How strange that we should meet here!"

she exclaimed. "I recognised you the moment you came in."

"As I did you," he returned. "But I was prepared. It was a matter of speculation in my mind, whether the Mr. and Mrs. Yorke who were coming to Alnwick Cottage, could be you and your husband, until Maskell set it at rest by saying it was Mr. Yorke of Saxonbury. I have been settled at Offord these three years."

"May I ask if you are"—— Mrs. Yorke hesitated, but probably thought she must finish her question as she had begun it—"married?"

"To my profession I am. In no other way. My thoughts and hopes have been wholly given to it since —since I fully entered upon it."

"Will the child do well?" she inquired.

"Oh yes. It is but a slight affair. I was prepared for something worse, by the account of Mr. Maskell's clerk. A little blood, especially on the head and face, frightens those not accustomed to it. These accidents will happen where there are children. He is your eldest?"

"Yes. I have but two."

"I will send up the medicine I spoke of, and call again in the morning," said Mr. Janson, rising. "Make my compliments to Mr. Yorke."

Mr. Janson departed, and Mrs. Yorke looked after him. As he turned to close the iron gate, he saw her standing at the window and politely raised his hat, and Mrs. Yorke politely bowed in return. Politely: the word is put advisedly: it best expresses the feeling each wished to shew to the other. Whatever there may have been of love or romance between them a few years ago, it was over now. Whatever sentimental reminiscence each had hitherto retained of the other, whether any or none, they knew that from that afternoon henceforth, they subsided into their proper and respective positions,—Mrs. Yorke as another's wife, and Mr. Janson but as a friend of hers and her husband's; as honourable, right-minded persons, in similar cases, ought, and would, and do subside.

Mr. Yorke, after exploring as far as he thought necessary that day, turned back to his new home. His thoughts ran not on the features of the village, or on the lovely scenery around, or on the fishing or the shooting; they dwelt exclusively on the few words of Mr. Maskell which had reference to the surgeon. Mr. Yorke hated that surgeon with a deep and nourished hate; and he would infinitely have preferred to find he had visited a locality where poison grew rank in the fields, like weeds, than one containing Edward Janson.

He was drawing pretty near to his own gate when he saw a gentleman emerge from it. A shudder, strange and cold, passed through Mr. Yorke's veins. Was it sent as a warning—the precursor of what was to come? Surely that was the man of his thoughts? It was! Janson, and no other! What! had he already found out the way to his home? *to his wife?* Mr. Yorke's lips opened in their usual ugly fashion, when displeased.

Mr. Janson did not observe him. He walked straight across the road, got over a stile, and was lost behind the hedge. "He may well try to avoid my observation," thought Mr. Yorke, in his prejudice. Had he been told the real facts—that Mr. Janson did not see him, and being in a hurry, was taking the short way through the fields to his home—he would have refused his belief.

Matters were not mended when Mr. Yorke turned in at his gate. There stood his wife at the window, her eyes unmistakably fixed on the path taken by Mr. Janson. She looked flushed and excited, which indeed was the effect of her late fright about the child. But Mr. Yorke set it down to a different cause.

"I am glad you have come home," she exclaimed, when he entered. "An unfortunate thing has happened?"

"I know," burst forth Mr. Yorke. "No need to tell me."

Maria supposed he had seen the lawyer's clerk. What else could she suppose?

"It will not end badly," she continued, fearing he was angry at its having happened—"Mr. Janson says so. Only think! he is the doctor here. You must have seen him leaving the house?"

"Yes, I did see him," retorted Mr. Yorke, nearly choking with his efforts to keep down his anger. "What brought him here?"

"I sent for him. At least, I sent"——

"And how dared you send for him, or admit him to my house? How could you seize the moment my back was turned, to fetch him to your side? Was the meeting, may I ask, a repetition of the parting?"

"What can you be talking of?" uttered Mrs. Yorke, petrified at the outburst. "What do you mean?"

"I mean Janson," hissed Mr. Yorke—"Janson, your former favoured lover. Have I been so distasteful a husband to you, that you must haste indecently to fetch *him* here in the first hour of your arrival? Who told you that he lived at Offord? How did you ferret it out? Or have you known it all along, and concealed the knowledge from me?"

Maria sank back in her chair, awed and bewildered. "I do think you are out of your mind," she gasped.

"No; I leave that to you: you are far more out of your mind than I am. Listen: I have a warning to give you," he added, nearly unconscious what he said in his passion. "Get Janson to visit you clandestinely again, and I will shoot him."

Maria rose majestically. "I do not understand the word 'clandestine,'" she haughtily said. "It can never apply to me. When the accident happened to Leopold —and I truly thought he was dead, and so did Finch, and so did the young man who had been going over the inventory—and I begged the young man to run for the nearest surgeon, I no more knew that it was Mr. Janson who would come, than did the senseless child. But it did prove to be Mr. Janson, and he dressed the wound of the child, and he is coming again to him to-morrow morning. He came here professionally, to attend your child, sir; not to see me. Clandestine!"

She swept out of the room, her face flashing with indignation, and Mr. Yorke strode up-stairs to Leopold's bedroom, and learnt what had happened. It cannot be said that it appeased him in any great degree, for he was blindly prejudiced, and jealousy and suspicion had turned his mind to gangrene. They had been smouldering there for years: perhaps the consciousness had been upon him throughout, that they would sometime burst into a flame. On the whole, his had been a happy wedded life, and his wife had not made him the less good wife because she had once loved Edward Janson.

On the following morning Mr. Janson came, according to his promise. Mr. and Mrs. Yorke were at breakfast. He shook hands with Mrs. Yorke, then turned, with his honest, open countenance, and held out his hand to Mr. Yorke. Mr. Yorke did not choose to see it, but he did move his own to indicate a chair.

"Thank you, I am pressed for time," replied Mr. Janson, laying his hand on the back of the chair, but not taking it. "This is my hour for visiting Lady Rich, who is a great invalid. She lives a little past you, up the road. How is my young patient?"

"He seems much better," answered Mrs. Yorke. "He is asking to get up."

"A most disgraceful piece of carelessness, to have suffered it to happen," interposed Mr. Yorke. "I have told the head nurse that should she ever be guilty of such again, she quits Mrs. Yorke's service. It might have killed him."

"Yes, it might," assented Mr. Janson. "Can I go to his room?"

Mrs. Yorke rose. "The one on the right, on the second floor," she said. "I will follow you directly. Finch is there."

Mr. Janson passed from the room and ascended the stairs; Mrs. Yorke stopped to speak to her husband.

"I must hear his opinion of the child, and shall go up. Would you like to accompany me?" she added, not wholly able to conceal the contempt of her tone.

"No." Mr. Yorke felt angry with himself.

They came down shortly, both Mr. Janson and Mrs. Yorke. "He is so much better that the difficulty will be to keep him quiet," said the surgeon. "He must be still for a day or two."

"You are sure there is no danger?" asked Mr. Yorke, who was now standing at the open window.

"Oh, none in the world. I will look in again to-morrow. Good morning, sir; good morning, Mrs. Yorke."

Mr. Yorke had thawed very much: perhaps the matter-of-fact, straightforward manner of Mr. Janson reassured him. "It is a hot day again," said he, as Mr. Janson passed the window.

"Very. By the way, Mrs. Yorke," added the surgeon, halting for a moment, "you must not suffer the boy to stir outside. The sun might affect his head."

"Of course not," she answered.

However, Leopold did get outside, he and his white-bandaged forehead, and tore about, boy-like, the sun's rays streaming full on his uncovered head. In some twenty minutes he was discovered; the bandage off, and he as scarlet as a red-hot engine boiler. Suddenly he began to scream out, "My head aches! my head aches!" Finch said it was "temper," at being fetched in, and crossly assured him if his head did ache, which she didn't believe, for he never had a headache, it had come as a punishment for stealing out in disobedience.

But at night the child was so ill and uneasy that Mr. Yorke himself sent for the surgeon. Leopold's face had not paled, and he still moaned out the same cry, "My head, my head!"

"He has been out," exclaimed Mr. Janson. "Why was I disobeyed? This is a sun-stroke."

The boy's self-will was alone to blame. Mrs. Yorke had coaxed him into lying on the sofa in the drawing-room "for a nice mid-day sleep," and went into the nursery, leaving him, as she believed, safe. Up jumped Master Leopold the instant he found himself at liberty, and dropped down from the low window, which stood so temptingly open. That was how it had happened. His heart was set upon getting into the garden, simply because it was denied to him.

CHAPTER X.

Jealous Doubts.

A FEW days, and Leopold Yorke was so far recovered, that an intermittent fever alone remained. Mr. Yorke, in spite of his jealous prejudices, had been obliged to submit to Mr. Janson's frequent visits, for there was no other doctor within miles, and the safety of his son and heir was paramount.

108 THE FOGGY NIGHT AT OFFORD.

The neighbourhood had hastened to make acquaintance with Mr. and Mrs. Yorke, and an early invitation arrived for them to take a quiet dinner at Squire Hipgrave's. It was accepted by both, for Leopold's intermittent fever was subsiding, and they were no longer under alarm for him.

On the appointed evening, they found a small party of seven at the squire's, themselves included. The eighth seat had been meant for Mr. Janson, but he had been called out unexpectedly, and was unable to come. The gentlemen's conversation turned chiefly upon out-door sports, and after dinner, when coffee was over, they went out, that Mr. Yorke might see a pond on the grounds, where the fish was being preserved, leaving the ladies alone.

Soon after, Mr. Janson came in. But scarcely had he had time to explain the cause of his absence at dinner, when a servant appeared, and told him he was wanted.

"How tiresome!" exclaimed Mrs. Hipgrave.

"A doctor's time is never his own," he remarked, good-humouredly. "Is it my surgery boy?" he inquired of the servant.

"No, sir. It is a footman from Alnwick Cottage. He says your boy sent him on here."

This excited the alarm of Mrs. Yorke. "Leopold must be worse!" she exclaimed.

As it proved to be. Master Leopold was took

worse, the man said, a-talking nonsense, and not knowing a word of it, and hotter than ever. Finch was frightened, and had sent him for Mr. Janson.

Mrs. Yorke grew frightened also, and said she must go home immediately. They tried to keep her, and to soothe her fears. Mr. Janson said he would make haste to the Cottage, and return to report to her. It was of no use: her mother fears were painfully aroused. Neither would she wait until Mr. Yorke came in. She loved her children passionately.

"Then, if you must go, I will be your escort, if you will allow me," said Mr. Janson.

"Indeed, I shall be much obliged to you," she answered. And hurriedly putting on her shawl, she departed with him, one of the ladies lending her a black silk hood for her head. She had anticipated returning in the carriage. It was a beautiful night in September, nearly as light as day, for the harvest moon was high, just the night poets are fond of consecrating to lovers; but Mr. Janson and Mrs. Yorke walked along, fast, and in sedate composure, neither remembering—at least, so far as was suffered to appear—that they had ever been more to each other than they were now.

The three gentlemen were strolling along the banks of the fish-pond, smoking their cigars, and talking. Suddenly one of them espied a couple walking arm-in-arm on the path in the higher ground, some distance off.

"It looks like Janson," said Squire Hipgrave. "That's just his walk; and that's the way he flourishes his cane, too. Who is the lady, I wonder? So ho, Master Janson! a good excuse for not joining us: you are more agreeably employed."

Mr. Yorke smiled grimly; his eye, keen as it was, had failed to recognise his wife, for the hood disguised her. They smoked out their cigars, and returned to the house.

"Have we not got a joke against Janson!" cried Squire Hipgrave. "I'll rate him for not coming. He's walking about in the moonlight with some damsel on his arm, as snug as may be."

"Is he, now?" returned one of the ladies, humouring the joke. "Who can it be?"

"Oh, some of our village beauties. Maybe Lucy Maskell. Master Janson has got an eye for a pretty girl, I know, quiet as he seems. He's making love to her hard enough, I'll be bound."

"Then you had better look out, Mr. Yorke," said Mrs. Hipgrave, with a laugh. "The lady is your own wife."

She had spoken innocently, never for a moment dreaming that her words could bear any interpretation but that of a joke to the ear of Mr. Yorke. And happily she did not see the livid look, the strange expression which arose to his face. He had turned it to the window, as if he would look out on the pleasant moonlight.

"How comes it to be Mrs. Yorke?" demanded the squire. And his wife explained: telling of the summons to Mr. Janson, the fever of the child.

Still Mr. Yorke did not speak. One of the party advanced, and stood at his side.

"A fine prospect from this window, is it not?"

"Very."

"Will you cut in for whist? How unfortunate to have our tables broken up! We cannot make two, now. Janson rarely plays at cards, but I meant to have pressed him into the service to-night."

"I am going home," said Mr. Yorke.

"Nonsense!" said Mrs. Hipgrave. "The child will do very well. Mr. Janson did not seem to anticipate danger. He said nurses were easily alarmed."

"I expect he did not," drily remarked Mr. Yorke. "Thank you, not to-night," he added, turning from the cards spread out to him. "Another time."

"Yorke's in a fever over that child," remarked the squire, knowingly, as his guest departed. "I can read it in his queer manner. Did you notice how it altered? What a nuisance children must be! Glad we have got none."

Mr. Yorke was not in a fever over the child; but Mr. Yorke was in a fever over something else. He was positively believing, in spite of improbabilities, that the story of the illness had been a got-up excuse, got up between his wife and Mr. Janson, to indulge in this night-walk of a mile and a half. And he clenched his hands, and gnashed his teeth, and strode fiercely along in his foaming jealousy. It is a passion which has turned many a sensible man to madness.

He stole in at his own gate and reconnoitered the house. The drawing-room was in darkness, its window open; they were not there. A light shone upstairs in Leopold's chamber, and one also in his wife's bedroom.

He stole up-stairs, stealthily still, and entered the bedroom; his own, jointly with hers. The housemaid was turning down the bed.

"Is your mistress come home?" asked he, speaking, perhaps unconsciously to himself, in a whisper.

"Yes, sir; she came in with Mr. Janson. They are with Master Leopold."

Up higher yet, but quietly still, till he reached Leopold's room. His wife stood there, at the foot of the bed, her shawl still on, and the hood fallen back from her head, and Mr. Janson was seated on a chair at its side, leaning over Leopold, his watch in one hand, the child's wrist in the other. He lay on his back, his little face a transparent white, as it had been lately, and his cheeks and lips a most lovely pink crimson. His eyes were wide open, and looked very bright.

"Papa!" said he, half raising his hand, when Mr. Yorke entered.

"I don't know why Finch should have been so frightened," said Mrs. Yorke to her husband. "He is quite rational now, and seems but little worse than he usually does when the fever is upon him."

"What do you mean by having thus sent to alarm us?" demanded Mr. Yorke, in a sharply irritable tone, as Finch entered the room with a night-light, which she had been down to get. "Frightened, indeed! *Did* you send?"

"I never knew any child change so," returned she, almost as irritably as her master. "He was burning with fever, as bad as ever he had been days ago, and delirious again. It alarmed me, sir, and I sent off for Mr. Janson: I didn't send for you and my mistress. No sooner had the man gone than he dropped asleep, and has now woke up calm—almost as much as to insinuate that I am telling stories."

"This class of fevers will fluctuate," interposed Mr. Janson. "One hour the patient seems at death's door, and the next scarcely ill at all. Something has certainly increased it to-night, but he will do well."

"If ever I saw any human body so changed as the master is, since we came here!" uttered Finch to Charlotte, that same evening. "Formerly he used to be pleasant enough in the house, unless any great thing crossed him, but now he's as growling and snappish as a bull put up for baiting. I wonder my mistress doesn't give him a bit of her mind! I wish he'd go off to Scotland, as he did last year."

Mr. Janson departed. Mrs. Yorke remained in the boy's chamber, but quitted it for her own at the usual hour for retiring. Before she had begun to undress, her husband followed her to the room, locked the door, and put the key in his pocket. Maria was surprised: they never slept with their door locked.

"Why have you done that?" she asked.

"Because I choose to do it. You can't sail out of the room now, with your tragedy air, and refuse to hear me. Now, Mrs. Yorke, who concocted this moonlight walk to-night? How far did your love-making go in it? I *will* know."

Mrs. Yorke did glance at the door, for it had become a custom with her to leave her husband to himself when the dark, jealous mood was on him, but she knew that she glanced in vain. She was caged.

"I will not bear it," she said, bursting into tears. "Why do you treat me so? If this is to continue, I will summon Lady Saxonbury here, and have a separation arranged. I have been to you a true and faithful wife; you know I have: what mania has come upon you that you should level these reproaches at me?"

"You have; I give you credit for it. I never doubted

you until we came here, and you renewed your intimacy and friendship with your old lover."

"He was no lover of mine," she replied, disdaining not to use evasion in such a case. "Were you not both before me in those old days, you and he, and I chose you? Which was the most favoured?"

"Janson," coolly repeated Mr. Yorke.

"He was not. You speak in the face of facts, Arthur. I married *you*."

"Loving him. But I was rich, and he was poor. Do you remember your last parting with him, the evening he returned from that absurd voyage, where I wish he had been wrecked?"

"What parting?" rejoined Maria; but her cheeks burned and her voice faltered.

"*What parting!* Shall I repeat it, though you know every word better than I? Ay, you do! When you told him, with tears and wails and sobs, that you were miserable, for you had bound yourself to marry me, and you loved him: when you lay passively in his arms, and welcomed his embrace, with a welcome you had never given to mine! I speak of that parting. I witnessed it."

Maria breathed hurriedly. She could not speak.

"You did not deceive me, Maria, though you thought you did, for I buried my injuries within me. Had I not loved you so passionately, I should have left you to him: and I knew that you pronounced your marriage vows to me with Janson's kisses not cold upon your lips."

She raised her head as if to speak, but no words came.

"It was not a pleasant knowledge for me, your bridegroom; but I never visited it upon you. You are aware I never did, Maria; my love for you was too great. I have loved you," he added, his tone changing to softness, "with a love passing that of man. I was forbearing, and never visited it upon you, save by deeper and deeper tenderness: I forced myself to think of it as a piece of girlish folly, and I was beginning to forget it: I had nearly forgotten it, Maria, when we came here."

"And so had I forgotten it," she spoke up, abruptly; "forgotten Janson, and all connected with him. I lived but for my children, for you, for my own natural ties and interests, and I never shall live for anything else. Janson! what is he to me now? For shame, Mr. Yorke! I am an English gentlewoman; your wife, and your children's mother."

"We have been here a month—more. Not a day, from the first afternoon we came, but he has been here, in your society. Sometimes twice a day."

"Could I help that? Circumstances have compelled it. The child cannot be left without medical attendance. You are frequently at home when Mr. Janson comes, and you know that his visits are limited to the child.

He rarely accepts the offer of sitting down with us, even for a minute, whether you are here, or whether you are away."

"And this night! for you to have walked home with him in the moonlight, resting on his arm; you and he, of all people in the world! And I following on your steps later, picturing what that walk had been to you both, in my jealous torment! Maria, I was mad this night as I came along, if ever man was; and Janson may be thankful that I did not meet him, for I might have sprung upon him in my anger."

"For shame, Arthur! again I say it," she reiterated, indignation rendering her speech firm. "I have never forgotten, by word or look, my own self-respect, since this our meeting with Mr. Janson. Neither has he. I have been to him as your wife, as my children's mother, secure in my position; and he has been to me, as to you, the plain family attendant. Do you doubt me still? Will you have me swear to it? I can. Arthur, Arthur! I think you *are* mad. Let us leave this place if your mania is to continue, and go where we can have other medical advice."

Was Mr. Yorke mad? He was certainly unhinged. He fell into a storm of sobs and tears, and clasping his wife to him, reiterated how passionately he loved her.

Maria grew alarmed. She had never seen him like this. Resentment for his groundless suspicions would have prompted her to turn scornfully from him: but she did not dare. She only repeated, in as conciliatory a tone as she could bring her angry mind to allow, that she had no unworthy thought connected with Mr. Janson. And she spoke truth.

He seemed to believe her. He did believe her. A better spirit came over him; and in the morning, when Mr. Janson paid his visit to the child, Mr. Yorke spoke cordially to him, and offered him his hand, a mark of favour he had never condescended to vouchsafe before.

But who can put away at will the pangs of jealousy? There is not an earthly passion that is less under control. As the days went on, it returned in full force to the unhappy Mr. Yorke, throwing its own jaundice over his sight and hearing. The most innocent movement of his wife or Mr. Janson, wore to him but one interpretation; the common courtesy of hand-shaking would excite him almost past repression. He said nothing more to his wife: he watched; and though he saw no tangible thing that even jealousy could take hold of, he grew only the more convinced that they were playing a part to deceive and blind him. If you ever felt the absurd passion of jealousy in its extreme force, you will understand and recognise Mr. Yorke's self-torments. They really did border on insanity.

CHAPTER XI.

Lost in the Fog.

THE child grew better; he was getting well; and Mr. Janson's visits were now paid but occasionally. At length the day came that he took leave. His task was done, he good-humouredly observed, for Master Leo was upon his legs again. Mrs. Yorke mentioned this to her husband in the evening, as an indifferent topic of conversation; glad, no doubt, for the sake of peace, to be able to do it.

"Left for good, has he?" repeated Mr. Yorke.

"Yes. I requested him to send in his account."

This was on a Monday. The next day, Tuesday, Mr. Yorke went out for a whole day's shooting, a thing he had not yet done. True, he had gone out shooting several times since the season came in, but only by fits and starts. Out for an hour or two, and back home again; out again for another hour, and back again. Maria understood it all, and thoroughly despised him in her indignant heart. But on Tuesday he went out in the morning, and came home at night, just in time for dinner. He was in good spirits, talked pleasantly with his wife, and played with Leopold. Wednesday was spent in precisely the same way, and on Thursday he also went out with his gun as soon as breakfast was over. On this day a Miss Hardisty, a relative of Mrs. Yorke's, arrived on a visit: somewhat unexpectedly, for they had not looked for her for a day or two. A hard-featured maiden she, of some five-and-forty years.

The afternoon of Thursday turned out wretchedly. It did not rain, but a dense fog, or sort of Scotch mist, overhung the atmosphere. Offord could remember nothing like it. Twilight set in, and Mrs. Yorke stirred her good fire into a roaring blaze, and wondered where her husband was. Her guest, fatigued with her railway journey, was in her chamber, lying down, and had requested not to be called until tea-time.

"Oh, here he is," cried Maria, as an indistinct form passed the window. "I wonder how many he has bagged? He will be surprised to hear that Olivia is come."

"Mr. Janson," said a servant, opening the door.

Mr. Janson entered. And as he took his seat, inquired after Leopold.

"He remains quite well," replied Mrs. Yorke. "I thought I understood you, last Monday, that you should not come again to him," she added, feeling uncomfortable lest her husband should return home and find him there—after her having stated that his attendance had ceased.

"This is not a professional visit," said Mr. Janson. "I have been to see Lady Rich, and thought I would call in as I passed your house to say, 'How d'ye do?'

and hear that Leopold continued all right. What a strange fog it is!"

"Thank you," answered Mrs. Yorke, in a rather constrained manner. For when jealous suspicions, entirely unfounded, are entertained by a husband, they must and do make the manners of the best of women constrained and embarrassed.

Mr. Janson drew his chair near to Mrs. Yorke's; not to be nearer her, but to enjoy the genial blaze of the fire. Unfortunately he had no idea of Mr. Yorke's fears; he only thought him an abrupt, haughty, uncertain man, different from what he used to be. When Maria Saxonbury became Mr. Yorke's wife, Mr. Janson had put her from his mind, as it was right to do. Mrs. Yorke rose to ring the bell. "You shall see Leopold," she said.

"Not yet; let me speak a word to you; pray sit down again," said Mr. Janson, interrupting her movement. "I want to consult some one, and I have—as you must know—a very high opinion of your discernment and good sense, so I wish to ask your advice. I shall value it more than that of any one else. You know Miss Maskell?"

"Yes. I have seen much of her since we came here," replied Mrs. Yorke.

"Do you believe she would make a good wife?"

"I think her a very amiable, nice girl, quite a lady.

Yes, I am sure she would. Who is going to marry her?"

"I don't know yet whether any one is," he answered, with a smile. "But—people tell me I must marry, or lose my practice, for my patients say they will have a family man to attend them, not a bachelor. So I have been looking round about me, and begin to think that Lucy Maskell would be suitable."

Mrs. Yorke laughed. "Oh, Mr. Janson! How coolly you speak! As coolly as you might if you were only going to take on a new surgery boy. These affairs should always be cased round with romance."

He shook his head. "Romance died out for me years ago." For one moment their eyes met; perhaps unwittingly; and then both looked determinedly at the fire again.

"I like Lucy Maskell much," he resumed; "so far as liking goes. And—I believe"—a smile hovered on his lips—"that she likes me."

"Let it take place, then, Mr. Janson. And I earnestly hope you will be happy. Believe me, you shall both have my best prayers and wishes for it," was Mrs. Yorke's answer. She was pleased that Mr. Janson was going to be happy at last, for she knew that she had once tried his heart severely. In the earnestness of her content, she put her hand into his, as she spoke —put it as a single-hearted, honest woman would.

And Mr. Janson clasped it, and leaned over towards her and thanked her kindly.

What dark shadow was that outside the window, with its face pressed against the pane? A face whose expression, just then, was as the face of a demon, whose eyes glared, and whose teeth glistened. *They* saw it not; but, as their hands met, and Mr. Janson leaned nearer to his companion, a noise, half savage growl, half shriek of defiance, escaped it. They heard that.

"What is that sound?" exclaimed Mrs. Yorke, turning towards the window. Nothing was there then.

"Somebody in the road come to grief in the fog," suggested Mr. Janson. "Or a night-bird, probably. Shall I see Leopold now?"

Mrs. Yorke opened the room door and called to the child, who came running in. Then Mr. Janson left. "I hope I shall get home," said he, jokingly.

Maria kept Leopold with her, and the time passed more swiftly than she thought. By and by, one of the servants came in to know if he should serve dinner.

"Why, what time is it?" inquired his mistress.

"Ever so much past six, ma'am."

"I had no idea it was so late."

"It was striking five when Mr. Janson left," said the man.

Mrs. Yorke chose to wait; but when it grew near

seven, she ordered the dinner to be served. She thought her husband had stopped to dine with some sporting acquaintance, or had lost his way in the fog. Scarcely had she sat down to it when she heard him enter, and go straight up-stairs; his step, as she fancied, unusually quiet.

"What can he want there without a candle?" she wondered. "Perhaps he thinks he can wash his hands in the dark, and would not wait for one."

"Maria," called out Mr. Yorke, his loud tones echoing through the house.

She rose and went to the door. "Yes."

"Bring me up a light, will you. Bring it yourself."

"What fad now?" thought Mrs. Yorke. "*I* take it up!" But she lighted a chamber candle, and went up-stairs with it, the servants, who were waiting at table, wondering. Her husband was standing inside their bedroom door, which was all but closed; nothing to be seen of him but his one hand stretched out for the light.

"Where have you been so late? Did the fog cause you to miss your way?"

He did not reply, only took the light from her. She pushed the door, wishing to enter, but it resisted her efforts. "Let me come in," she said; "I have some news for you. Olivia Hardisty's come."

Not a word of reply was vouchsafed to her. Only

the door banged to in her face, and the key of it turned.

"He is sulky again," thought Maria. "How fortunate he did not happen to come home while Mr. Janson was here! Make haste," she condescended to call out, as she retreated, "I have begun dinner."

Mr. Yorke soon came down, dressed. A mark of attention given to Miss Hardisty, Maria supposed: or, so late as that, he would scarcely have troubled to dress. He did not speak, and did not eat; but he drank freely. He seemed also to have been drinking previously. A failing he was not given to.

"I asked you why you were so late," said Maria.

"You answered yourself," was the reply—"That I lost my way. The fog was dense."

"The fog seems to have taken away your appetite; and to have made you thirsty."

"Luncheon did both. The meat was salt."

"Where did you take luncheon?"

"At Squire Hipgrave's."

"Have you had good sport?"

"Middling. Who can shoot in a fog?"

"You have brought no birds home?"

"I left them at Hipgrave's."

"Pheasants, I suppose?"

"Yes. I wish you would not keep up this running fire of questions, Maria. My head aches."

Mrs. Yorke ceased, and eat her dinner. As the

cloth was being removed, her guest came in. Also Leopold. Mr. Yorke was compelled to exert himself a little then, but he had partaken too freely of wine, and Mrs. Yorke was vexed, for she believed it must be apparent to Miss Hardisty.

"How well Leopold looks, considering his long illness!" remarked Miss Hardisty.

"He is wonderful," said Mrs. Yorke. "You would not think, to see him now, that he had been so very ill."

"Papa," cried Leopold, "Mr. Janson says I am got well soon because I was good, and took the physic without crying."

"Ah!" said Mr. Yorke. "When did he say that?"

"To-night, when he was here with mamma, and they called me in."

Mr. Yorke turned his eyes upon his wife, fixedly, steadily. "Was Janson here to-night?"

"This afternoon, between four and five. It seemed like night, it was so dark," she answered, equably, but in spite of herself she could not prevent a vivid flush rising to her cheeks.

"You told me he had given over coming."

"As he had. I remarked to him that I understood him to say so, and he replied that he did not call to-day professionally, but just dropped in, as he was passing, to inquire how Leopold continued. He told me a little bit of news, too, about himself," added

Maria to her husband, affecting to speak gaily. "I will repeat it to you by and by."

When the child's bedtime arrived, instead of Finch coming for him, it was Charlotte.

"Where's Finch?" demanded Mrs. Yorke.

"She's gone as far as the village, ma'am. She wanted to buy some ribbon at the shop."

"Why did she choose such a night as this?" returned Mrs. Yorke. "How stupid she must be! she will lose her way."

"She took a lantern, ma'am," answered Charlotte. "She said she did not care for fogs. She won't be long."

Charlotte went off with Leopold, and Miss Hardisty smiled. "Servants are sadly wanting in common sense, many of them."

"I suppose Finch had previously fixed on to-night to go out, and of course she could not bear to disappoint herself, but must go, fog or no fog. It's just like them."

Mr. Yorke lay back in the easy-chair, and seemed to sleep. His wife apologised to Miss Hardisty, saying that he had had a hard morning's shooting, and seemed "done up."

About nine o'clock Finch came bursting into the room—her things on, just as she had entered the house. She was panting for breath.

"O ma'am, I don't know how I've got home, what

with the fog, and what with the fright! There has been such an awful murder!"

"Where?" asked Mrs. Yorke.

"Close on the other side the village. Some thieves set upon a farmer's son riding home from market, and shot him, and pulled him off his horse, and beat him about the head till he died, and then rifled his pockets of his watch and money, and then left him in a pool of blood," vehemently reiterated Finch, all in a breath. "He was found about five o'clock, and the village has been up in arms ever since. Everybody's out of their houses."

Mr. Yorke sat bolt upright in his chair. His eyes glittered upon Finch.

"A pretty tale!" said he to his wife and Miss Hardisty, as Finch flew off to impart the news to the household. "This is how stories get exaggerated. There was no horse in the affair, and no robbery, and it was not a farmer's son going home from market."

"You heard of it, then?" exclaimed Miss Hardisty.

"Yes," was Mr. Yorke's reply.

"And never to have told us!" remonstrated his wife. "You say it was not a farmer's son. Do you know who it is?"

"Janson. Murdered in his own garden as he was going in. Just inside the gate."

CHAPTER XII.

A Premature Disclosure.

HORROR rose to the countenance of Miss Hardisty. It is natural it should so rise when a woman hears of such a crime committed in her vicinity. But what was her look of horror, compared to that overspreading the face of Mrs. Yorke? A living, shrinking horror, which pervaded every line of her features, and turned them to the hue of the grave.

Strangely tumultuous thoughts were at work within her, flashing through her brain in quick confusion. "Janson! who had sat by her side that afternoon! *He* murdered! Who had done it?"

"Who is Janson?" inquired Miss Hardisty. "Did you know him?"

Mrs. Yorke seemed incapable of replying. Her husband spoke up volubly:—

"Janson was the village surgeon. You heard Leo say he was here to-night. He has been attending Leopold; but *I* thought had ceased his visits. A fine young fellow. Unmarried."

"Who can have been so wicked as to murder him?" wondered Miss Hardisty.

"Ah! Who indeed!"

"How did you come to know it?" interrupted Mrs. Yorke, lifting her white face to her husband.

"Ill news travels fast. As I reached home tonight, some people were passing the gate, apparently in excitement; I inquired what their trouble was, and they told me. It was the gardener and his wife, up above, returning home from the village."

"Finch said he was shot," observed Miss Hardisty.

"He was not shot. Beaten to death."

"Finch's account may be the correct one, instead of the gardener and his wife's," said Mrs. Yorke, in a low tone. "She said he was robbed. Shot and robbed."

"He was not robbed, I tell you, Maria," said Mr. Yorke. "Have it so, if you like, however. Shot and robbed; what matters it?"

Mr. Yorke went to sleep in his chair again, or appeared to go to sleep, and the ladies conversed in an under tone, Maria shivering visibly.

About half-past ten, they were startled by a sudden and violent knocking, which came to the house door. Startled! Olivia Hardisty, her mind and tongue full of robbers and murderers, gave vent to a faint scream, and Mr. Yorke sprung up from his chair with a start, as if he would leave the room, halted in indecision, and then sat down again. A deep silence succeeded, and again the knocking came, louder than before. They heard a servant hurry to answer it, they heard an entrance and the sound of voices, and then the footman threw open their room door.

"Master Henry Yorke."

A tall, fine lad, between fifteen and sixteen, leaped into the room, seized Mrs. Yorke, and gave her some kisses, and then turned to shake hands with her husband. He had not changed, save in growth: he was random and generous as when we last saw him.

"If I don't believe that's Olivia Hardisty!" cried he, holding out his hand to the lady. "What brings you here?"

"I think I may ask what brings you here?" returned Miss Hardisty.

"Ah! Are you not taken by surprise, Maria?" said he to Mrs. Yorke. "Didn't I knock! I thought you should hear it was somebody. Did you think it was the fire-engines?"

"Why did you not let us know you were coming?"

"How could I? My old tutor had news this morning of his father's death, and went off; so I told mamma I might as well spend the few days' holiday looking you up. And away I came, without waiting for her to say yes or no."

"Where's your portmanteau, Henry?"

"Didn't bring any. She'll send some shirts and things after me; sure to. What a precious slow railway station you have got here! Not a carriage or an omnibus waiting, or any conveyance to be had, for love or money. Mind, Maria, if I have not brought enough tin for myself, you must let me have some, and write to mamma to pay you back. I didn't stop to ask for any, for fear she'd put in a protest against my journey."

"How did you find our house?" asked Mr. Yorke.

"Oh, I got into the village, which seemed all in a hubbub, and tipped a boy with a torch, to shew me. This is not such a nice place as Saxonbury," added the lad, casting his eyes round the room.

"It is very well for a change," said Mr. Yorke. "I wanted some shooting and fishing."

"There's no accounting for taste," said the boy, shrugging his shoulders. "Maria, you don't look well."

"I should wonder if any of us could look well to-night," interposed Olivia Hardisty. "Your knocking nearly frightened us to death, too. We had just heard of such a dreadful murder."

"A murder! Where?"

"In the village. He lived quite in the middle of it, did he not, Mr. Yorke?"

"Then that accounts for the row," said Henry, before Mr. Yorke could reply. "The natives were standing about in groups, trying who could talk the fastest. I thought they were taking observations of the fog. In one place, at the corner of a street or lane, they had mustered so densely I had to administer some shoves to get through. Who has been murdered, Mr. Yorke? A poacher?"

"No. A doctor."

"That's worse."

"It is awful," shivered Miss Hardisty. "He had been attending Leo, Henry, and was here only this afternoon."

"What, the man who is murdered?"

"He was; this very afternoon; and but just before the deed was committed. It was five o'clock, I think you said, Mrs. Yorke, when Mr. Janson left you."

"Janson! a doctor!" interrupted the boy. "It was no relation to our Mr. Janson, was it, Maria?"

"Your Mr. Janson! What do you mean by your Mr. Janson?" demanded Miss Hardisty.

"Oh, Maria knows. A Mr. Janson we used to be intimate with abroad, when I was a youngster. Is it any relation?"

"It is the same man," said Mr. Yorke, in a curious tone.

Henry Yorke sprung up from his chair, and looked from his sister to Mr. Yorke in dismay and incredulity.

"The same man! The same Mr. Janson who took such care of me on that long voyage, when I went away in the *Rushing Water?*"

Mrs. Yorke inclined her head. "Yes, he had settled here," she said, in a low tone.

Sorrow rendered Henry's ideas confused. "Oh, I wish I had seen him! Why did you not write me word, Maria, that I might have come before he was murdered?"

"You stupid boy!" cried Olivia Hardisty. "Could your sister tell he was going to be murdered?"

"Well, I do wish I had seen him. I would have gone all over the country to meet Janson. He was the nicest fellow going."

"Was he?" asked Miss Hardisty, appealing to Mr. Yorke, who did not seem in a hurry to answer her.

"You had better ask Maria," retorted Henry, speaking with the random thoughtlessness of his age. "She'll tell you he was. Why, it was a near touch, I know, whether she became Mrs. Janson or Mrs. Yorke. Didn't she flirt away with him, sir, before she promised herself to you? She thought I was only a youngster and couldn't see; but I was as wide awake as she was. Don't be cross, Elizabeth."

"You always were wide awake, Harry," drily responded Mr. Yorke.

Olivia Hardisty, somewhat stunned and bewildered with the vista into past things opening to her, unclosed her lips to speak; but she thought better of it, and closed them again. So! this was the Mr. Janson she had heard of in past times, who had loved, it was said, Maria Saxonbury, and she him; whom Maria had rejected because he was poor.

Henry talked on, until they grew tired of answering him. Talked incessantly until his supper came in.

When they retired for the night, Finch was waiting in Miss Hardisty's room to assist her to undress. The two were old friends, so to speak, for Finch had lived at Saxonbury many years, maid to the first Lady Saxonbury.

"I'm glad you are come soon, ma'am," began Finch. "I can do nothing but think of that awful murder. And that sleepy Charlotte would go to bed and leave me. She cares for nobody but herself."

"I am pleased you did stop for me," returned Miss Hardisty, "for I feel nervous to-night. A common murder, though very distressing, does not affect the nerves like such a one as this. It must have happened, Finch, immediately after he left here."

"After who left here?" asked Finch, wondering what Miss Hardisty was talking of.

"The doctor. Mr. Janson. Oh, I forgot; you did not hear; you thought it was a farmer's son who was murdered. But it was not: it was Mr. Janson."

"Mr. Janson!" echoed Finch; "Mr. Janson who was murdered! Who says so?"

"Mr. Yorke. He heard of the murder as he came home to dinner."

Finch collected her ideas. "I wonder where master picked up that news," she said presently. "It's nothing of the sort, ma'am. It was a farmer's son going home from market, on horseback, in leather breeches and top-boots. Mr. Janson does not wear breeches and top-boots."

"Mr. Yorke said decidedly it was Mr. Janson, and that he was murdered in his own garden. He was very positive."

"He always is positive," retorted Finch. "But it was no more Mr. Janson than it was me. As if the village would have said it was a farmer's son, if it had been Mr. Janson! Why, ma'am, the man in the shop, where I was, had been to see the body, and he spoke particularly about the breeches and boots. I daresay Mr. Janson was fetched to the dead corpse, and that's how his name got mixed up in it. Mr. Janson, indeed! that would be a misfortune."

"So Henry Yorke seemed to think. He was talking of their former acquaintance with him abroad. The nicest fellow going, he said."

"Yes, everybody liked Mr. Janson. Except"——

"Except what?" asked Miss Hardisty, for Finch had stopped.

"Except master, I was going to say. He had used to be jealous of him in those old times, and I think—at least," added the woman, more hesitatingly, "I have once or twice thought lately whether he is not jealous again. Master's temper, since we have been here, has been quite strange, and I don't know what should make it so, unless it's that."

"Dear me!" uttered Miss Hardisty; "Mrs. Yorke. would not give cause"——

"No," indignantly interrupted Finch, "she would not give cause for that, or for any other wrong thing. I don't say that she was right to encourage both Mr. Janson and Mr. Yorke in the old days, as I believe she did, and let each think she might marry him; but, ma'am, young ladies will act so, just to shew their power; and her head was turned upside down with her beauty. However, all that nonsense was put away when she married, and a better wife nobody has ever had than Mr. Yorke. And if master *has* got a jealous crotchet in his head, he deserves to have it shook out of him. Mr. Janson has come here to attend Master Leo, but for nothing else."

"Did they ever meet after Mrs. Yorke's marriage until now, when they met here?" inquired Olivia Hardisty.

"No, never. I asked my mistress once—I think she had been married about two years then—if she knew where Mr. Janson was, and she had no idea. I don't much like this place, ma'am," added Finch, musingly. "I shall be glad when we get back home."

"It seems scarcely worth while my telling you now the news that Mr. Janson imparted to me," observed Maria to her husband, when they were left alone. "Dead! instead of—— It is so very dreadful!"

"It is dreadful enough," returned Mr. Yorke.

"He was going to be married," she continued. "But, of course, it will not do for us to speak of it abroad, after this shocking ending. He thought of marrying Miss Maskell."

"And giving up you?"

The taunt sounded most unseasonable. Maria, subdued by the events of the evening, turned meekly to her husband. "Arthur, let this unpleasantness end; it is time it did," she said, speaking firmly in her honest truth. "We may both have something to forgive each other. I was foolish, vain, careless in the old days; but I solemnly declare in the presence of Heaven, in the presence, it may be said, of that poor dead man, that never a thought has strayed from you since you became my husband. You have been bitter and angry with me lately, but it has been without cause; for not a wrong word, not a look that you could not approve, has passed between me and Mr. Janson. So help me Heaven!"

Mr. Yorke was silent. He had sat down, and seemed to be looking at his wife.

"When he called here this evening to ask after Leopold, he told me he thought of marrying Lucy Maskell. I wished the union God speed from my very heart."

Still Mr. Yorke did not speak. Maria passed into her dressing-room. She had said her say.

CHAPTER XIII.

The Gardener's Word against the Gentleman's.

MR. YORKE and Henry went out for an early walk the following morning. As Mrs. Yorke and Miss Hardisty were waiting breakfast for them, they were surprised by a visit from Squire Hipgrave.

"What a horrible thing this is!" he exclaimed to Mrs. Yorke, when the introduction to Miss Hardisty was over. "You have heard about poor Janson?"

"Yes," she faintly said. "Is he dead?"

"Dead! the wretches who murdered him took care of that. They left no life in him."

"Then it *is* Mr. Janson!" interposed Miss Hardisty. "Mr. Yorke said so, but one of the servants here insisted that it was a farmer."

"It's both," answered Squire Hipgrave. "A double murder. Never has this quiet neighbourhood been so stained. Young Louth was passing through the village on his way home from market, and, about a mile beyond it, he was shot from his horse and robbed. He had been selling stock, and had got a good round sum about him, which, as is supposed, was known. Janson's affair is different."

"He was going into his house by the back entrance, and was set upon just inside the garden door, and beaten to death, Mr. Yorke told us," said Miss Hardisty.

"That is correct. Poor young fellow!"

"It must have occurred soon after he left here," said Mrs. Yorke, speaking with an effort.

"Was he here last night?" asked Squire Hipgrave, eagerly.

"In the afternoon," replied Mrs. Yorke. "He called in as he was returning from his visit to Lady Rich, and saw Leopold. It was five o'clock when he left, but quite dark, the fog was so thick."

"Oh, that was hours before the murder. The precise time of its committal has not been ascertained. He was found about ten o'clock."

"That must be a mistake," said Miss Hardisty. "Mr. Yorke was home before seven."

"But he did not know of it then."

"Yes, he did."

"Impossible," said Squire Hipgrave. "Janson was not found until ten o'clock; not a soul knew of it previous to that. He was being hunted for all over the village, to go and examine young Louth, and nothing could be seen or heard of him, and it was only by the servant's going out to lock the back gate, which she always did at ten at night, that he was found. Did you ever see such a fog as it was."

"But indeed Mr. Yorke did tell us," persisted Miss Hardisty. "Certainly not immediately after he came in—I daresay he was willing to spare us so horrible a recital as long as was possible—but when Finch got home afterwards from the village, with the news that a farmer's son was killed, Mr. Yorke said it was not a farmer's son, but Janson. You see he had heard of the one murder, and the servant of the other."

"But Yorke could not have heard that Janson was murdered before he was murdered," obstinately protested Squire Hipgrave.

"And he could not have dreamt it beforehand," as obstinately returned the lady. "The fact must be, that he did know of the murder, though all might not."

"But it was not known at all to any one," reiterated the squire; "neither is it believed to have occurred at that time."

"You must perceive that Mr. Yorke *must* have known of it," coolly continued Miss Hardisty, suppressing the contempt she was acquiring for the squire's understanding. "It was not a mere vague rumour he had got hold of, but he described the facts, which you have just said were correct; that the unfortunate gentleman was killed in his own garden, close to the gate, and found beaten to death."

"It is very strange," debated Squire Hipgrave, struck at length with the points placed before him by his antagonist. "I wonder where Yorke heard it?"

"From a man and woman who were running by

this house as he came in," readily responded Miss Hardisty. "They told him Mr. Janson was murdered. And that was before seven o'clock."

"Good heavens! it may have been the very perpetrators themselves! Indeed, it must have been; no one else would have known it. We must find those people," continued the squire, in his most magisterial voice. "I wonder if Yorke would recognise them again?"

"It was the gardener and his wife at the cottage higher up, near to Lady Rich's," interposed Mrs. Yorke.

"Oh—they," said the magistrate, considerably disappointed when he found the presumed murderers subside into a quiet, inoffensive couple, long known. "I'll go up and ascertain where they heard it. I'd give twenty pounds out of my own pocket to pounce upon the guilty men, for Janson was a favourite of mine. Not to speak of the unpleasantness of having such crimes happen in the neighbourhood."

Away went Squire Hipgrave, and was back again directly. Mr. Yorke and Henry were then returning from their walk.

"Good morning, Yorke. How did you hear the report last night that Janson was murdered?"

"From the gardener, up there—what's his name? —Crane," replied Mr. Yorke. "From Crane and his wife."

"Well—it's your word against theirs," hesitatingly remarked Squire Hipgrave, in a puzzle. "They say they never told you anything about Janson; and, in fact, did not know themselves till this morning that anything had happened to him."

"If they choose to eat their words, that is no business of mine," said Mr. Yorke. "As I was turning in at this gate last night—it was late, for I lost my way in the fog after I left you, and did not get in till near seven—Crane and his wife were running by from the village in great excitement. They had a torch with them. I asked what was amiss, and they told me Janson was murdered. Nobody else could have told me," proceeded Mr. Yorke. "I saw nobody else, and spoke to nobody else."

"Then what do they mean by denying it?" asked Squire Hipgrave, sharply. "Upon my word, if they were not so well known, I should suspect they knew something about the murder. I wish you would let me confront Crane with you."

"You are quite welcome to do that," said Mr. Yorke.

Away went the squire again, and Mr. Yorke and Henry leaned over the gate, watched, and waited for him. Crane's cottage was within view, and he came back with the man. Maria and Miss Hardisty came out of the breakfast room.

"There seems some mistake about this here business, sir," said Crane, a civil, respectful man, "and Squire Hipgrave have fetched me down along of him, to set it right."

"The mistake is on your part, not on mine," haughtily returned Mr. Yorke. "You went by here with your wife last night; she seemed in a fright, and I inquired what was the matter."

"Yes, sir, my wife was frighted, fancying she saw thieves in the hedges; she haven't run so fast since her joints got stiff. When you stopped us, sir, and asked, I told you a poor gentleman had just been murdered."

Mr. Yorke looked at Squire Hipgrave. "You hear," said he. "Repeat what you did say to me," added he to the man.

"That my wife was frighted, and we was making haste home, for a poor gentleman had been found murdered, down yonder, beaten to death. Them was the words, sir, as near as I can remember."

"Exactly," said Mr. Yorke.

"But did you say it was Mr. Janson, Crane?" resumed Squire Hipgrave, looking at the man.

"Law no, sir. I couldn't say it, as I have just told you, for"——

"You did say it was Mr. Janson," interrupted Mr. Yorke.

"I beg your pardon, sir. I was just a-going to say to you last night that report went as it was a farmer, but you turned short away in-doors, and didn't wait to hear me; and I and my wife ran home. This morning, when the milk-woman came, she told us about Mr. Janson, that he was murdered, and my wife sat down on a chair—though we never believed it at first—and burst out a-crying; for he was more like a friend to us than a doctor, a-coming up at all weathers to her rheumatiz, and charging us next to nothing. I'm sure, sir, I speak the truth, when I say it was not till this morning we heard about poor Mr. Janson, and that there had been a double murder."

"A double murder!" echoed Mr. Yorke, his face a mixture of astonishment and perplexity.

"Why, did you not know it?" said Squire Hipgrave. "Young Louth was shot from his horse last evening, and rifled of all he had about him. That was what Crane wished to tell you of: Janson was not murdered—at least, not found—for hours afterwards."

"And Finch was right, after all, when she said it was a farmer's son," interrupted Olivia Hardisty; "though you"—looking at Mr. Yorke—"ridiculed it, and said it was Janson."

"Yorke, where *did* you hear about Janson?" demanded Squire Hipgrave. "At the time you appear to have spoken of it, it was not known. In fact, I don't believe it had happened."

There was a blank, distressing pause—an awful pause.

"Where did you hear about Janson, I ask?" continued Squire Hipgrave, in a voice that sounded strangely uncompromising and clear.

Still the same ominous pause. Mrs. Yorke struggled for composure, but her breath came gaspingly through her ashy lips. Henry stole round to her side, as if by an uncontrollable impulse, and Olivia Hardisty gazed in open dismay at Mr. Yorke.

"I heard it from Crane," said Mr. Yorke at length, rousing himself, and speaking in a firm, deliberate tone. "Though it appears to be his purpose to deny it now."

Crane shook his head and turned to Squire Hipgrave. "The gentleman's making a great mistake, sir," he quietly said. "I never mentioned Mr. Janson's name last night, for he never was in my thoughts; and if anybody had come and told me to guess who was murdered, (besides the farmer,) I should least of all have guessed Mr. Janson. I'm a-going back to my garden, ladies and gentlemen, and if you please to want me again, there I shall be."

The man, with a civil bow, turned away and went towards his home. Squire Hipgrave was the next to depart. A strange mantle of constraint seemed to have fallen upon them all.

CHAPTER XIV.
Awful Dread.

NEVER had the insignificant village of Offord been so full of stir, excitement, and dread. Two murders in one night! it was enough to put fear into the stoutest heart. At first it was universally assumed that the same parties had been guilty of both, but this impression wore away. Young Mr. Louth had evidently been molested for the purpose of robbery. Not so Mr. Janson. His watch and chain, his pocket-book and purse, each containing money, were all found upon his person, undisturbed—carrying out Mr. Yorke's assertion that there had been no robbery. *How did he know it?* began to ask Olivia Hardisty.

Mr. Janson had a habit of going in at the back door of his house, through the garden; it was the quicker mode of entrance, since at the front he had to ring: it was surmised that his assailant must have known of this; have got into the garden, and waited for him. He was probably struck down and stunned, at the moment of entering, and was again beaten about the head one or two blows. The medical men were asked with what sort of instrument. "Was it likely to be a gun?" spoke up somebody, while they were deliberating—the question probably being dictated by the remembrance of the shot which had destroyed the farmer. They replied that they did think it likely to be a gun, as likely, or more likely, than any other blunt weapon; but, if so, they added, the gun had probably been broken by the violence of the blows. The blow which had killed him was an unfortunate one, given underneath the left ear.

The woman-servant's testimony was as follows:— About six o'clock, (she thought it must have been,) while she was in her kitchen, waiting for her master to come in to tea, she heard a noise in the garden, to which the kitchen looked. This was followed by a groan, by more than one groan, she thought, and she got atop of the ironing board underneath the window, and looked out above the half shutter, but she could see nothing but mist. When asked to describe what sort of noise it was that she had heard, she replied it was a "sudden" noise, a "scuffling" noise. And that was the best explanation that could be obtained from her. There were often drunken folks about on a market night, she said, and she had supposed it might be some going by in the lane, quarrelling with one another; she "didn't think no worse." Everything was quiet after that, so far as she heard, except for people coming to the front door inquiring for her master. Five or six times they came; they wanted him to go and see the gentleman who was murdered, young Mr. Louth. At ten o'clock, she went out to lock the back gate, taking a lantern with her, for the lock was small and awkward; and then she came upon her master, lying in the path, dead. And when people flocked up, after she had given the alarm, and came to look at him, they said he must have been dead for some hours. Such was her testimony, given in a plain, straightforward way; she was a simple countrywoman of middle age, Mr. Janson's only maid-servant. By a somewhat curious coincidence, the surgery boy had had holiday given him that afternoon, and was away.

Squire Hipgrave propagated the unsatisfactory dispute between Mr. Yorke and Crane the gardener. The extraordinary fact that the murder should have been known to either of them at that early hour of the evening struck everybody: upon Mr. Maskell, a keen man of the law, it made a strong impression. Who could have known it, hours before he was found, save those concerned in the deed? argued Mr. Maskell. Very true, said the village, but Crane and his wife are above suspicion, and so—of course—is Mr. Yorke. This must be sifted, concluded Mr. Maskell, and I shall take care that all three are summoned before the coroner.

Ere the day, Friday, was over, the murderers of the farmer were in custody—two men, of whose guilt there was not a shadow of doubt. The spoil taken from Mr. Louth was found upon them, and there were other proofs, which need not be entered into, since that is not the murder with which we are most concerned. These two men had been seen lurking about the village in the afternoon with another suspicious character—a man named King. It was assumed that this third had also been in the mischief, but at present he could not be found. The murder of Mr. Louth and that of Mr. Janson must have taken place about the same time, rendering it next to an impossibility that the same parties were guilty of both. The inquest was fixed for Monday, the coroner being unable to hold it sooner, and poor Mr. Janson lay in his own house, the outside of which presented a scene of bustle, night and day, inasmuch as it was regularly besieged by crowds of the curious, who stood there for hours on the stretch, gazing at its closely-curtained windows. Towards evening, on the Saturday, their perseverance was gratifyingly rewarded by witnessing the arrival of Mr. Janson's mother, who had been summoned from a distance. She took up her abode at the sorrowful house, although several neighbourly offers to receive her were made, and the delighted crowd of stationary gazers was forthwith doubled.

Now the reader cannot fail to perceive that suspicion lay fearfully strong upon Mr. Yorke. His jealousy of his wife and Mr. Janson supplied the motive; a jealousy for which there was no foundation, save in his own distorted mind. Certain attendant circumstances, known to Mrs. Yorke, were fraught with suspicion. His staying out that night, saying he lost his way in the fog, his stealing up-stairs in the dark when he came home, and the complete changing of his clothes, would have been comparatively nothing; but there was his prematurely-proclaimed knowledge of the murder. Mrs. Yorke heard of the opinion, expressed by the surgeons, that a gun had probably been used to inflict the blows, and she shivered as she listened. Did her husband bring home his? She could not tell. Neither could she arrive at any satisfactory conclusion as to the clothes he wore, whether they were put away in concealment, or whether they were amongst those hanging openly in the closet; for Mr. Yorke was an extravagant man in the matter of wearing apparel, and possessed several suits for outdoor sports. The terrible suspicion was eating into her brain. And yet it appeared too monstrous a one to have real foundation.

On the Sunday morning, though Mrs. Yorke rose to breakfast, she excused herself from going to church. She said she was not sufficiently well; perhaps it was no false plea, for she looked very ill. Mr. Yorke went, accompanied by Miss Hardisty and Henry Yorke. When they were gone, Maria entered her bedroom and locked herself in. A desperate determination was on her face, the index to that which had settled on her mind; her dreadful fears, her uncertainties, were hard to bear, day and night they were as one living agony; and now that the house was free from interruption she would search and find, or not find, proofs. The gun. That was the point; had he thrown it away as he came home that night, stained with his crime, or had he brought it home with him and concealed it? A gun appeared as usual in the customary place; but—was it the gun he had taken out with him, or the other one, which he might have reached from his gun-case and put there? The gun-case was fast, and she had no means of ascertaining.

There was an old-fashioned piece of furniture, half bureau, half chest, in the bedroom, black with age, very long and narrow. Mr. Yorke had laughed when this caught his eye on their taking possession of the house. "Why, it's long enough," said he, in a joking way, "to put a coffin in." He had appropriated it to himself for his private use, and this was the plague-spot of dread to Mrs. Yorke; if the gun was in the house concealed, it was there.

She had been to the box of tools, and by dint of exertion she contrived to bring the bureau from the wall. Her intention was to break in the back, satisfy herself, and then replace the furniture. Knock, knock! hammer, hammer! Two servants were at home, the rest at church; Charlotte was in the nursery, the cook in the kitchen. Whether they heard the noise, or, hearing it, what they might think, Mrs. Yorke did not stop to inquire; her resolution was desperate. She persevered, and at length the wood was stove in. Not space enough yet, but she soon made it so.

Alas! she did not require a second glance. On the very top of all, quite at the back, lay the gun, *broken*. How many pieces she did not count, she could not have touched them for the whole world; they were wet, as if they had been soaked in water for the purpose of washing, and they lay on a suit of wet shooting-clothes; had he got into a pool, as he came home that night, to wash away traces? Probably. Mrs. Yorke staggered away and sat down, pale and sick. Beyond all doubt, her husband was Edward Janson's murderer.

Again she dragged up her shaking limbs, and, leaving everything as she found it, save for the great hole, pushed the bureau back to its place. The first time her husband opened it, he would see the hole, and detect what she had done. She cared not; henceforth, there was little that she would care for in life. She took up the heavy hammer and the chisel, and was concealing them under her black silk apron, lest she should be met going down-stairs on her way to the tool-box, when a quick knock came to the chamber door right in front of her. It startled her into a scream, which she could not have prevented had her life depended on it.

"Please, ma'am, it's only me," said the cook's

voice. And what Mrs. Yorke answered was a mystery to herself, but the servant rejoined—

"It's a stranger, ma'am, asking to see you directly, and won't take no denial."

With a ghastly face and a frame that shook from head to foot, Mrs. Yorke opened one of her drawers, and shut up the hammer and chisel. Then she unlocked the door, and the cook stepped inside.

"It's a strange lady who wants to see you; she —— Why, ma'am, what's the matter? Aren't you well?"

"One of my sick headaches," murmured Mrs. Yorke. "A visitor, did you say? I am not well enough to see any one. Go and say so."

"A few minutes' conversation only," interrupted a strange voice close at the door; and there stood the visitor, who must have silently followed the servant up-stairs. Her face, stern and pale, bore the remains of severe beauty; and Mrs. Yorke grew sick, as unto death, with undefined fears, for she recognised Mr. Janson's mother.

She utterly lost her self-possession. She did not say, "Walk down to the drawing-room," or, "Walk in here;" she only looked up with her ghastly face, the picture of terror and misery. Mrs. Janson stepped in, and closed the bedroom door, fixing her searching eyes full upon Mrs. Yorke.

"I have come to ask you who murdered my son."

Mrs. Yorke felt as if her brain were turning. There stood his mother, putting that startling question, and there, at her back, were the hidden pieces of—the—gun; there, in another spot, were the hammer and chisel. Ominous witnesses, all.

"Did *you* kill him?" proceeded Mrs. Janson.

Mrs. Yorke, in her perplexity and confusion, burst into tears. "I kill him!" she uttered—"*I* set on, and beat a man to death! it would be physically impossible. Why do you come here with so cruel a thought?"

"Ever since I heard the details of the crime yesterday," continued Mrs. Janson, "my thoughts have never quitted it, no, not for an hour, for my eyes last night were sleepless. I have sought in vain for its motives. All tell me that my son had no enemy here, that he was beloved and respected. To-day I heard that you were living here, and I said to myself, '*There* lies the clue.' You could not kill him yourself, you say; perhaps not: but you might get it done. Did you?"

Strange to say, Mrs. Yorke endured such words without indignation. Indignation from her!—when the wicked instrument of his death was within a few inches! She answered in a tone of humility, of pitiable depression:—

"You may spare yourself such thoughts. I would have given my own life to save his."

It may be that her words struck Mrs. Janson as being the words of truth, for her voice lost some of its harshness.

"Years ago you were my son's bane; you led him on to love you, and then left him for another: what wonder, then, amidst so complete a dearth of motive for others committing the crime, that my thoughts should turn to you?"

"If I did marry another, it was not that I disliked your son," answered Mrs. Yorke, in a low tone; "it was that circumstances were not favourable to my marrying him. Since we met again, on the occasion of my coming here, we have been excellent friends. Madam, I beg you to understand me—friends; the past was forgotten by both of us; it was never once recalled or alluded to by either; your son has attended my child, and brought him through a dangerous illness. Pray, put away these dreadful ideas," added Mrs. Yorke, with emotion. "Your son was the last person in the world whom I would have injured."

"What makes you look so ill?" demanded Mrs. Janson, abruptly. "It appears like mental illness, not bodily."

"I have no objection to tell you that I have felt ill ever since the news of the horrible crime was brought to our house—as I should do had its victim been any other friend. And to-day," she added, with a faint colour at her invention, "I have a sick headache, which kept me from church, and causes me to look as I do now. Believe me, I knew no more of the crime than you did, who were far away."

"Nor your husband?"

"My husband!" echoed Mrs. Yorke, with well-feigned astonishment. "What motive could my husband have in wishing him ill? Quite the contrary; had I not chosen him, when I could have chosen Mr. Janson?" Ah, poor thing! was it wrong that she should appear thus brave in his defence, guilty though she believed him in her breaking heart? He was her husband; he was the father of her children. Mrs. Janson's keen eyes were upon her. Could she bear them, and stand the ordeal?

"Mrs. Janson," said she, rising, and assuming a courageous, open tone, "you must search elsewhere for the guilty parties—not in our house."

Mrs. Janson probably thought so. She likewise rose.

"Years ago, Maria Saxonbury—I beg your pardon, Mrs. Yorke—I told you that should your future existence be one of retribution, you had richly earned it. Should it have been so, or should it ever become so, you may remember my words."

Ay, she did remember them; remembered them with an awful shudder. *Her future existence!* Mrs.

Janson walked to the threshold of the chamber, and turned her gaze full on Maria.

"Then, you can give me no information? No help—no clue?"

"Indeed I cannot. You might as well ask me after the murderers of Mr. Louth," she added, with desperate energy.

Mrs. Janson turned, and began to descend the stairs. Maria made no effort to shew her out, or to have her shewn out: the courtesies of life were as nothing to her then. She sat down and strove to keep herself from fainting. As she heard her go through the front door, some one appeared to enter it, and footsteps came up the stairs. Was it Mrs. Janson returning? A cold fear was turning Maria's heart to chillness, and something like a dull sound began to thump in her brain. Not Mrs. Janson. It was Miss Hardisty who entered.

"You!" exclaimed Mrs. Yorke, glancing sideways at the drawer which contained the hammer, and wishing it was safe in its place. "Church cannot be over!"

"No. I came out before the sermon. Maria, you look like death. Stay! let me speak to you: I came home to do so. I thought of doing so yesterday, but my courage failed me. What shadow is it that has fallen on the house?"

"Shadow?" she gasped.

"Ay, shadow. I have known you from a child, and I loved and reverenced Mr. Yorke's mother. I have liked him. For your sake and hers I have resolved to speak. As I went into church—Mr. Yorke was in advance, and I behind with Henry—some people stood in the churchyard. They did not know us, we were strangers, and they continued talking over the marvel of Mr. Yorke's knowing that the murder was committed before others could know it— for it seems that the neighbourhood trusts Crane, who has been in it all his life, in preference to Mr. Yorke. I spoke a few words to Henry, and we went in. In the commandments, when the clergyman repeated, 'Thou shalt do no murder,' and I remembered next to whom I was standing—Maria, don't scream: suspicion, above all things, must not be courted here, even from your servants. Well, I felt as if I *could not* remain there by his side, and when the clergyman went out to change his surplice, I left, and came back to you. Let me say to you what I have to say."

Mrs. Yorke only bowed her head. She could not speak.

"Understand, Maria. I assume no one's guilt or innocence; I ask not what led to that incautious revelation of your husband's, the premature knowledge of the murder and the manner of its committal; I would rather not know. But that avowal must be remedied."

"Remedied!" wailed the unhappy lady, in a tone of despair. "Oh, my children!"

"There is a remedy, Maria."

"How?"

"I and Henry Yorke must give false testimony," continued Miss Hardisty, in a slow, distinct whisper. "Your husband also; but to him the speaking falsely will probably be of no moment. Henry, as he came through the village on his way to us that night, saw the crowd gathered round Mr. Janson's house; and the murder, as we have heard since, *was* then discovered. He must have heard the details; must have mixed with the crowd and heard them; and he brought the news to us. Do you understand?"

"But he did not," said Mrs. Yorke, less quick of comprehension than she would have been at a more tranquil moment.

"No; but he must say he did; and swear to it, if necessary. I am also prepared to do so—that is, that I heard him tell the tale when he came in. I am not insensible to the disgrace and danger—let us not allude to the guilt—of taking a false oath," added Miss Hardisty, her voice growing harsh, and her brow contracting, "but it may save disgrace, the most frightful that can be inflicted on man, from falling on Mr. Yorke, and consequently upon you and your children. We must have been under a mistake you know: Mr. Yorke must have confounded the words spoken by Crane with the account afterwards brought in by Henry Yorke; and thus the mistake must be explained away. Do you not understand now, Maria?"

"Yes—yes," she replied. "O Olivia," she continued with a shudder, "this is a horrible affliction!"

"Do not speak of it to me," hastily interrupted Miss Hardisty. "I know that you are innocent, and I would rather not know more. I wish I could have saved you from it, more effectually than I am now trying to save you from its consequences."

"But about Henry?" whispered Mrs. Yorke.

"Henry will be found all right. The boy's doubts were excited before mine. Did you notice his countenance on Friday, when Crane and Squire Hipgrave were here? He is even more alive to the dread and the danger than I; and this plan is as much his as mine, for he met me half-way in it. There is no fear of Henry: deep feeling and sound sense lie under his random manner. Do you suggest this course to your husband, and be assured of us. Fortunately, *fortunately*, Mr. Yorke did not speak while Finch was in the room telling of Mr. Louth's murder, and none of the servants know but what Henry Yorke did bring the news of Mr. Janson's."

In the most intense pain, both of mind and body, —for the headache, only put forth as a plea in the morning, had come on with violence,—Mrs. Yorke had retired to bed before the family got home from church.

Not to her own bed: to a small curtainless bed in the room of Leopold, which had been placed there for a nurse's use temporarily, during the boy's illness. She cared not for the comments of the servants, but went up there. And yet her excuse to Finch proved that she *did* care; for when Finch, in surprise, volubly demanded why her mistress had not lain down in her own room, she answered that she was here more out of the way of hearing the noise of the house. Maria said the same to Mr. Yorke, when he came up and questioned her.

Miss Hardisty had said, "Suggest this course to your husband." How was she to do it? If ever woman shrunk from a topic, Maria shrunk from that. The very breathing of it to her husband seemed as if it would cost her her life.

All day she lay dwelling upon it. How should she speak? how let him know that her suspicions were awakened? In the dusk of the evening Mr. Yorke again came up.

"Are you no better, Maria?"

"I think I am worse," she answered.

"You would be more comfortable in your own bed."

"It is quieter here. Do not stay. It must be your dinner-time."

He bent to kiss her cheek. With a wail of pain,

she turned her head away, and buried it in the pillow. Mr. Yorke bent over her, whispering softly—

"What strange idea have you been getting into your head? *It is a wrong one.*"

Speaking the words with marked emphasis, he quitted the room. Maria, in the course of the evening, called for Miss Hardisty.

"You must speak to him yourself, Olivia," she said. "You must arrange all with him. I *cannot.*"

"It may be better that I should," quietly replied Miss Hardisty. "It is so essential that he should understand exactly what I and Henry shall have to say."

CHAPTER XV.

The Double Inquest.

MONDAY morning brought all the bustle of the double inquest. It was held at a public-house in the village. The proceedings in Mr. Louth's case were soon over; and then came on Mr. Janson's. The woman-servant spoke to the finding of the body; the doctors, to the cause of death—the unfortunate blow behind the ear. Mrs. Yorke, looking white as a sheet, trembling inwardly and outwardly, told of Mr. Janson's visit to her that afternoon; and Mr. Yorke's butler was called to prove the hour of his departure from the cottage. It was striking five by the hall clock, he said, as he led Mr. Janson out. At the conclusion of Mrs. Yorke's testimony, she was conducted to her carriage, which was in waiting, and driven home.

Next came Henry Yorke. He had seen the bustle round Mr. Janson's door in passing through the village that night, he said; had heard that Mr. Janson was murdered, and had told the news when he got to Alnwick Cottage. Miss Hardisty corroborated it. She was present with Mr. and Mrs. Yorke, when Henry Yorke entered and mentioned it. Squire Hipgrave observed to Miss Hardisty, that she had not spoken of this the following morning; she had said it was Mr. Yorke who first spoke about Janson. It was not impossible, Miss Hardisty equably answered; what with the double murder, the horror of the affair, and the mixed-up reports, her mind was in a mass of confusion. Mr. Yorke was next called. He confirmed Henry Yorke's assertion as to his bringing the news of Mr. Janson's murder, and added that he supposed it related to the murder spoken of by Crane the gardener. Hence the confusion and mistake.

"Do you know you have greatly relieved all our minds?" cried Squire Hipgrave, linking his arm within Mr. Yorke's as they, and several more gentlemen, came forth at the conclusion of the inquiry. "It was so singular a thing that you, or Crane—whichever it might have been—should know of the murder, in that strange way, without being able to say whence you heard of it. In short, I may say, a suspicious thing."

"The fact is this," said Mr. Yorke confidentially, "though I did not choose to proclaim it before the coroner, I was half-seas over that night, and had a somewhat confused remembrance of what passed. Your good salt beef at luncheon, squire, made me drink like a fish; and, not satisfied with that, I must make my dinner, in the evening, chiefly of drink, for my appetite had gone, but the thirst remained. When I went in, I did not speak of what Crane and his wife had told me,—murder is not a topic to frighten women with,—and after dinner I dropped asleep. Next came in Finch with her tale, which, as the woman truly says, I heard, and did not contradict, and next came in Henry Yorke, with the history of Mr. Janson's murder. What more natural than that I—in the state I was—confounded the one with the other, and assumed that both accounts related to the same—to Janson? Thus it happened. And had it not been for Miss Hardisty and Henry Yorke, who, when you and Crane left on Friday morning, began to think over matters, and strove to set me right, I should have persisted in my own story for ever."

"Well, any way, I am glad it is cleared up."

"That's an intelligent youth, that relation of yours," said Mr. Maskell. "How well he gave his testimony to-day!"

"A superior lad," remarked Mr. Yorke. "Is it quite certain that the murderers of Louth and poor Janson were not the same?"

"I don't see that it was possible. Of the same gang they may have been, but the same individuals, no. A very disagreeable thing for Mrs. Yorke to have been obliged to attend the inquest," added Mr. Maskell. "But, you see, she was the last person, so far as we have heard, who saw Janson alive."

"Yes; no wonder she was nervous. There is some idea afloat of Janson's friends here subscribing together, and offering a reward for the apprehension of the murderers, is there not?" continued Mr. Yorke.

"We were talking of it," replied Squire Hipgrave.

"I should wish to contribute my share," said Mr. Yorke. "The sooner the murderers are discovered, the more satisfactory it will be for the neighbourhood. Shameful so to upset a peaceful community! It has had such an effect upon my household, especially on Mrs. Yorke, that I do not think we shall remain. I tell them that because two men were killed in one night, it is no reason for supposing they are going to be killed; but their fears are aroused, and I can make no impression. However, stop or go, I will be one of the first to join in offering a reward. Mr. Maskell, have the goodness to put my name down for—— What sum are the rest going to contribute?" broke off Mr. Yorke.

"We were thinking of five pounds each. There will be ten of us, or so, which will bring it up to fifty pounds."

"Fifty pounds!" somewhat contemptuously ejaculated Mr. Yorke. "I do not think that sum will do much good."

"Shall I add your name, sir?" asked Mr. Maskell.

"Yes. For a thousand pounds!"

The reply was spoken quietly, but those around were startled at the magnitude of the sum. What had Edward Janson been to Mr. Yorke that he should offer it?

"I would freely give it to bring the murderer to light," resumed Mr. Yorke, as if he had divined their thoughts.

Mr. Yorke went home. Mrs. Yorke was alone in the drawing-room as he entered, and she motioned to him to close the door. "Now," said she, "what is to be your course?"

"My course!" repeated Mr. Yorke, with a keen gaze at her pale, resolute face.

"Spare me from entering into details," she said. "It is enough for me to say, that I know who was the destroyer of Janson."

"You do not," rejoined Mr. Yorke.

"He is known to me, to Olivia Hardisty, and to Henry. Their testimony of this day might prove it to you. I have seen the proofs of the crime."

"The proofs!" repeated Mr. Yorke.

"Yes," she answered, looking down. "The washed-out clothes and the broken gun."

A very angry expression escaped his lips. "Who has dared to become a spy upon me?"

"I have," she replied. "I stove in the back of the bureau. Let it pass; there is no time to waste words. Henceforward I am not your wife, Mr. Yorke; no, nor your friend; but your deadly enemy. But for the name my children bear, I would deliver you up to justice. The same place can no longer hold us both, and you must leave this."

"Not at your bidding," returned Mr. Yorke. "I have business in London, and shall proceed thither to-day."

"Go where you will, stay where you will, so that it be not England," she impetuously rejoined. "You may enjoy the half of your property for your life, the remainder must be secured to me. Without my children, I would not touch a stiver of it; but they must be properly reared."

"Upon my word, Maria, you carry things with a high hand."

"I do," she answered, beginning to tremble. "You have put yourself into my power, and I must make my own terms. If ever you attempt to inhabit the same house with me and your children again, I shall have no resource but to proclaim the truth."

"You talk coolly of separation! Some wives would feel a pang at parting with their husbands."

She burst into tears. Until that dreadful discovery *she* would have felt one. "I cannot help myself," she wailed. "You have made my future a course of abject terror, shame, misery; you have entailed infamy on your children."

"Softly, if you please. I have not done this."

She lifted her hand with a passionate gesture, as if she demanded silence. "Saxonbury must be mine," she said, after a pause. "It is well that my father's grandchildren should be reared in it."

"Quite well. Will you go back to it at once, or wait here until the end of the term that the cottage was taken for?"

She doubted his good faith, he spoke so readily. "I will go back to it," she answered. "But I can make all these arrangements for myself when you have left. You can bid farewell to your children before you start; a farewell that must last you for ever."

"About the 'for ever' we shall see," replied Mr. Yorke, speaking with some irony. "You speak coolly, I say, of separation. Possibly it is what you have been contemplating?"

"Until *now*, the separating from you would have been the greatest grievance that life could have brought," she wailed. "I had grown to love you. Yes, Arthur, let me say it in this our last hour, if our marriage had been productive of nothing else, it had brought out my love for you. No, touch me not," she cried, retreating, as he would have taken her hand. "It is ended, and you have been the one to put a barrier between us. You shall never touch so much as my hand again. Yours is red."

His wife, whom he had so loved! The signs of deep emotion—emotion which she could not understand—arose to Mr. Yorke's countenance. Was he feeling that he had no resource but to become an exile, out of regard to his own hoped-for safety? Had the awful fact already stamped itself on his brain, that a murderer is never safe, go where he will? that the wings of pursuit seem flying after him for ever? But for that wretched, premature avowal, suspicion would not have pointed to him? What madness possessed him to make it?

"I have offered a thousand pounds for the discovery of the murderer," said he, in a cold hard tone to Maria.

She lifted her hands again, as if she would beat these mocking words off. He went up to her.

"One kiss, Maria, before I go."

And, in spite of her resistance, of her shrinking dread of being embraced by one who had become so great a criminal, Mr. Yorke, in his strength, folded her face to his, and kissed it passionately.

He left the house at dusk, to become a fugitive,

as his wife verily believed, on the face of the earth. She fell on a chair after she had watched him away. The excitement which had buoyed her up throughout the day was subsiding now.

The sharers in the fatal secret—Miss Hardisty and Henry—hastened to her. They also had been watching the departure.

"He is gone for ever," she murmured to them. "I pray you let this dreadful thing sink into oblivion. Henry, you are but a boy. Are you sure of yourself?"

"Maria, if I were not sure of myself, I should never have undertaken to save him," whispered the lad. "Rather than betray Yorke, I would say I did the murder myself; for the sake of you and the children."

CHAPTER XVI.

Fever.

MRS. YORKE'S intention had been to leave Alnwick Cottage forthwith for Saxonbury. The very neighbourhood had become hateful to her. If she could have left it the night that witnessed the departure of Mr. Yorke, she would have done so. Preparations, however, had to be made, orders given, notice to people in Offord to send in their accounts, notice to be given to Saxonbury of their arrival. Maria would have left all arrangements undone, have confided to an agent the settling of affairs, but that she feared her hasty removal, following on that of Mr. Yorke's, might excite suspicion. Terrible fears were at work within her.

And, what with the fears to come, and the horror she had passed through; what with the awful ending to her love and her wedded life, for she really had grown to love and esteem her husband; before those preparations were completed, and the day of departure had come, Maria Yorke was stricken with fever. Almost a brain fever.

It was all Olivia Hardisty's care to keep people from the room. She knew not what Maria might give vent to in her ravings. Constituting herself chief nurse, she barred the door to all save the doctors and Finch. Finch had to be admitted occasionally; there was no help for it—the doctors of course. No longer Mr. Janson. He, poor fellow, would never more attend any; never more, never more. The gentleman who had temporarily taken charge of his patients came to Mrs. Yorke, with a physician from a distance. They could not think what could have brought on brain fever.

Neither could Finch. Finch, who was given to talk incessantly, faithful servant though she was, did not cease expressing her wonder to Miss Hardisty. And Finch could make nothing of the ravings.

"She seems to be for ever mixing Mr. Janson and master up together, as if they were having a perpetual quarrel. It's odd that *that* should run in her mind."

"It would be very odd if her thoughts did not run on Mr. Janson, considering the circumstances," returned Miss Hardisty with composure. "Poor Mr. Janson went straight out from her presence to his murder, as may be said, and she had to give evidence that he did. I do wonder whether the thousand pounds' reward, offered by Mr. Yorke, will bring anything to light?"

"It's to be hoped it will," said Finch. "I'd lay another thousand, if I had it, that it was some of the same gang. Wouldn't you, ma'am? They are all returned convicts, it is said."

Miss Hardisty coughed. "Those returned convicts are, many of them, dreadful men, standing at nothing."

"What's the oddest thing to me of it all," cried Finch, "is, that master does not come. A fortnight to-morrow since my mistress was taken ill, and he has never been here!"

"He does not know of it," said Miss Hardisty, in her imperturbable manner. "With his wife in this insensible state, I deemed it useless to write to him. I shall write when she is a little better."

"I should write now if I knew where he was," said Finch, independently. "But I don't. He was not going to Saxonbury when he left here. His things were directed for London."

Maria survived the disease, and began slowly to improve. Olivia Hardisty, when the danger was over, wrote to Mr. Yorke to tell him of her illness, addressing the letter to his banker's in London. Just a few lines, telling of the bare fact—she had been in danger, but was going on to recovery.

Partial recovery came more speedily than they could have hoped. But with the recovery of body, all the distress of mind returned.

"Take me from here," implored the invalid of Miss Hardisty, the first day she sat up. "I cannot bear it. I seem to see the murder in every corner."

"You shall go, my dear, as soon as ever you are strong enough to bear the journey," was the soothing answer.

A few more days, and she was able to move into a sitting-room. Orders were given for their departure on the next day but one.

"It might be to-morrow," pleaded Maria, her wan face, beautiful in its attenuation, looking eagerly up from the pillows of her fauteuil.

"We may not risk a second illness for you, Maria," was the reply of Miss Hardisty. "Thursday will be the very earliest day that you must venture."

Maria sighed. She was feverishly eager to get away from Offord; to get back to Saxonbury; but a conviction every now and then arose in her heart that Saxonbury might prove even less tolerable. Her whole life—and she saw it—must be one of ceaseless terror; there could be no rest anywhere. Lady Saxonbury had been ill herself, and could not come to her in this illness. Maria was glad to be spared her presence: she seemed to turn with a sick feeling of despair from all whom she had ever known.

"Squire Hipgrave's asking for you, ma'am," said Charlotte, putting her head inside the room door and addressing Miss Hardisty. "He is in the drawing-room."

Miss Hardisty rose, folded her work together, and descended, not acknowledging to herself that she felt glad to escape the monotony of the sick-room. Squire Hipgrave was standing at the window, looking out.

"Good morning," said he, turning to shake hands. "Mrs. Yorke's better, I find. Will she be well enough to hear the news? We have caught the murderer of Mr. Janson."

A mist came over Olivia Hardisty's sight. She felt her way to a chair. Did Squire Hipgrave mean the *real* murderer?

"I thought I'd come and tell you the first thing," continued the squire. "There's not a doubt that Yorke's thousand pounds has unearthed the fellow."

Miss Hardisty began to inquire into particulars: but she felt that her voice sounded sharp and shrill.

"It was the man, King, who had been seen with the other two in the afternoon. While the two watched for young Louth, King thought he'd do a little business on his own account, and attacked Mr. Janson. He has been in hiding ever since."

"How is it known?" asked Miss Hardisty, feeling that it was *not* King.

"One of the gang, attracted by the reward, has come forward to betray him. Quite a lad, the informer is, not more than sixteen. He has disclosed both the man's crime and his hiding-place. They are not proof against money, these rogues—would sell their comrades for it, if the bribe 's a high one."

"Was he *seen* to murder him?" inquired Miss Hardisty.

"No. I suppose not. I have heard nothing of that."

"Then, in point of fact, the guilt rests only on the confession of this lad?"

"That's all."

Miss Hardisty shook her head, leaving the squire to infer that she accepted his news, as he rose to depart. She did not say that she knew too much of the guilt of another, to believe him.

Offord was up in arms, when the man, King, was brought in for his examination before the magistrate. That proceeding took place subsequent to Squire Hipgrave's interview with Miss Hardisty.

The informer's testimony was to the following effect. That King had come home one night to the hiding-place of the gang, in a desperate fright. He accounted for it by saying that Cooke and Barnell (the two men taken) had planned an attack on young Louth, and that meanwhile he, King, went back to the village and set on to watch for Janson. He had heard that Janson often carried a good bit of money about him, received as fees. King stole into Janson's garden, and there waited, knowing it was the entrance he often used. In less than a quarter of an hour Janson came in, and he, King, attacked him. He struck him down; he believed that he killed him; and he was in the act of rifling his pockets when somebody came up to interrupt. He, King, attacked the fresh comer; but there he had his match. A scuffle ensued, and the stranger's gun was broken in it; and he, King, finding he was getting the worst, got away, and made the best of his road home, arriving there in his fright. He had not intended to kill Janson, far from it; only to disable him while he eased him of his money. Neither had the other two thought to kill Louth, and that gentleman's powerful resistance had led to the evil.

Such was the testimony given by the approver, and there could be little doubt that such were the facts. Indeed, before that day came to an end, the facts were proved, by the confession of King. Prostrated by his capture, and especially by the treachery of his comrade, he appeared completely to lose heart and spirit. In a reckless, despairing tone, he said to the police that he might as well make a clean breast of it, and he described the circumstances more minutely than the informer had done. He could not make it out he said, how it was that Janson had died so easily; but he knew blows under the left ear had turned out awkward, before now. When asked who it was that came to the interruption, King replied that he did not know. It was a tall, strong man, dressed, so far as he could see for the fog, in a sporting suit; his tongue that of a gentleman.

Olivia Hardisty shook with fear, had shaken ever since the man was captured. That King was the real murderer, she never believed: she had too much cause to attribute the crime to another. But a very confused account of the examination had been carried to Alnwick Cottage.

"Do not acquaint Mrs. Yorke with this unpleasant stir about the murder," Miss Hardisty said to Finch. "She is not in a state for such excitement."

Finch, however, judged differently, and Finch was one who liked to exercise her own will. *She* judged that it would be rather a pleasant divertisement to her mistress, to hear that there was some chance of Mr. Janson's murder being avenged.

CHAPTER XVII.

A Tale for the Christmas Dessert-table.

ON Thursday morning they were up betimes at Alnwick Cottage. Mid-day was to witness their departure from it. Even Mrs. Yorke was in the sitting-room by ten o'clock. It was a room adjoining her bed-room. Finch shook up the pillows of her easy-chair, and drew it near the window. The day was bright for winter, the landscape lovely.

"Is everything packed?" asked Mrs. Yorke.

"All's ready," replied Finch. "I have nothing to do between now and the time we start."

Perhaps it was because she had nothing to do that Finch judged it well to improve the time by telling her mistress of the capture of King, and his confession. "The man is took, and has confessed," she said. "He admits having stopped inside Mr. Janson's garden, and killed him."

Maria held a handkerchief to her face to hide the terror that settled there.

"*Who* is it that is taken?" she gasped.

"The man King, ma'am; one of that dreadful gang. It was thought that he did it from the first."

"Send Miss Hardisty to me," murmured Maria.

Miss Hardisty came. She told Mrs. Yorke the tale, so far as she knew it. Suddenly, in the midst of telling it, she gave a startled shriek: for there stood Mr. Yorke, inside the room door.

He looked as if he had come off a journey. He had a great-coat on his arm, and was unwinding a warm cravat from his neck. Laying them on a chair, he advanced and stood before his wife.

"Are you satisfied now, Maria?"

What was she to believe? Was he guilty or not guilty? She looked up, a strangely yearning look on her white face, her thin hands clasped before her. Miss Hardisty, in her impulsive eagerness, laid hold of the arm of Mr. Yorke.

"Were you *not* guilty?"

"No!" he burst forth, a haughty flush dyeing his forehead. "I was the one who interrupted the wretched murderer at his work—as he has now confessed. Leave me a few minutes alone with my wife, will you, Miss Hardisty?"

Miss Hardisty, walking quite humbly, from her sudden conviction of his truth and their own mistake, crossed the room and descended the stairs. Mr. Yorke, as before, stood in front of his wife, upright, his arms folded, and looking down at her.

"Which is true, Arthur?" she gasped.

"Need you ask?" was his rejoinder, spoken sternly.

"But why did you not tell me at the time?"

"Before I reply to that question, will you answer me one? If I *had* told you, if I had gone so far as to *swear* to my own innocence, would you have believed me?"

No; she felt that she should not, then.

"I saw that all the assertion I could have made on my own part would not dissipate the impression you had taken up," resumed Mr. Yorke. "Therefore, I could but leave it to the elucidation of time. I did what I could. I offered a high reward. I placed the matter in the hands of the London detective police. When I left here, and you so pleasantly consigned me to a perpetual exile, my journey was direct to Scotland Yard. But that circumstances did favour your view, Maria, I might have felt inclined to take you at your word, and render our separation perpetual."

The scales seemed to fall from her eyes. A conviction of his innocence, of his present truth, seated itself within her. She leaned forward in her weakness, and sobbed aloud upon his breast.

Mr. Yorke wound his arm fondly round her, giving her the explanation that he did not give her formerly. He had gone back to the village that evening, inending to beard Janson in his own house; to forbid his visits. He watched for Janson coming home, but he watched the *front* door. Janson meanwhile entered at the garden door, in the side lane, unseen by Mr. Yorke. Standing there quietly, he heard a groan, more than one, and penetrated to the spot whence they apparently came, the garden. The attacker of Mr. Janson turned and attacked him, and in the scuffle the gun was broken. The robber got away, and he, Mr. Yorke, stooped down to examine Janson. He had matches in his pocket, and struck them, and he saw that Janson was indisputably dead. He left him, and made the best of his way home; but he wandered out of the road in the fog, and got into a pool.

"Why did you not give the alarm? why did you not speak of it?" reiterated Mrs. Yorke.

"I can scarcely tell why," replied Mr. Yorke. "My feeling against Janson that night was one of bitter anger. I should not have killed him, as the burglar did; but I am not sure that it was altogether a feeling of grief that crossed my heart, when I saw him lying there—dead."

Maria did not speak. Her face was buried.

"I scrambled out of the pool and came home," continued Mr. Yorke. "As I reached the gate, Crane and his wife were passing; they seemed in distress, in alarm, and I inquired the cause. 'A poor gentleman had just been murdered,' they said. I never supposed, and naturally, that they alluded to any murder but Janson's. I supposed that the body had been found, and the news had spread. Do you remember," he somewhat abruptly added, "that I called to you for a light, when I came in, and asked you to bring it up yourself?"

"Quite well."

"My intention was to tell you of what had happened. Maria, I believe the feeling in my heart was to *taunt* you—that the man whom I had just seen with his hand in yours, was dead and out of the way for ever. In the few moments that elapsed between my calling and your appearance with the light, the mood changed, and I resolved to say nothing. I bundled my clothes, wet with the pool, into the long press, laid the broken gun upon them, and came down to dinner."

"Why did you lay them there, out of the way?"

"As I said before, I can scarcely tell you. In my ill-feeling against Janson, I believe I resolved not to disclose that I had seen anything of the murder; to be entirely silent upon the point. For one thing, Maria—and I have felt ashamed of myself ever since—I was the worse for drink that evening. In my sober senses I should probably have acted very differently throughout; but I was not in my sober senses. I had drunk a good deal at Squire Hipgrave's; he had two or three hard drinkers at his luncheon-table that day, hearty sportsmen, and I drank with the rest. Again, while I was waiting for Janson, near his house, I turned into a public-house and drank more—brandy-and-water You must have seen that I had taken too much."

"Yes," she answered.

"Afterwards there came that unhappy suspicion, through my having mixed up the one murder with the other. That suspicion did attach to me, I could not help seeing, and I was really thankful to Olivia Hardisty, and to Henry Yorke, for helping me to a way out of it. To have tardily confessed, then, to what I had seen, would never have done; it might only have brought suspicion more tangibly upon me. People would have asked what brought *me* in Janson's garden."

"Arthur," she said, raising her white face, "you might have confessed to us at home."

"With what chance of receiving credence?"

It was the old question. An unsatisfactory one now.

"I judged it better to bide my time," said Mr. Yorke. "We will have Henry to spend Christmas with us, and make it a Christmas tale for after dinner. I'll give it them at dessert. I suppose I *may* come home to Saxonbury again?"

She was crying softly and silently, happy tears now. Mr. Yorke held her closer, and bent to kiss them away. "I think you have saved my life, Arthur," she whispered.

"You were going to Saxonbury to-day, were you not?"

"Yes; by the mid-day train."

"But I perceive you are not fit to travel. Shall we stay on here a few days, and see a little more of this strange drama played out?"

"Oh yes, if you please," she readily answered.

"All the places in the world seem glad to me now. I have had brain fever, Arthur."

"I know you have. I had a bulletin up daily of your progress."

"From whom?" she inquired, in surprise.

"From the physician. Had he warned me of danger, I should have hastened to you. He thought I was detained in town by law business, and could not leave. Maria," he more gravely added, "never you doubt my care and love again."

"I have never doubted them," she replied. "I—— Arthur," she broke off, gazing at him earnestly, "it is I who ought to enjoin that. The cloud fell on your mind, not on mine. Has it gone away?"

"It has. I believe I was wrong, Maria. At any rate, it can never now return."

"Thank God!" she murmured. "Quite gone!"

"Quite gone," repeated Mr. Yorke, regarding the remark as a question. "If another thousand pounds would bring Janson back to life, Maria, I would freely give it."

"Shall you speak abroad, now, of what you saw of the murder?"

"No. It would answer no end, for I could not swear to the assailant. I disclosed the whole to one of the head police in London; but there's no necessity to proclaim it further for the benefit of the public. We will keep it as a secret. A less weighty one than that you have been hugging to your heart, Maria."

A sudden pushing open of the room door. Master Leopold flew in boisterously, followed by Finch, grumbling. "Papa! papa!" shouted the boy in his delight. And Mr. Yorke caught him in his arms.

Finch stood transfixed with surprise. "Why, sir, when did you come?"

"Ten minutes ago," said Mr. Yorke. "I am telling your mistress that she will do well to remain on here a little longer, until she shall be more fit to travel."

"You can unpack, Finch," said her mistress.

"Well, that is a bother!" cried Finch, who was in the habit, from long service, of saying pretty well what she pleased. "Have you come to stay too, sir?"

"Yes," said Mr. Yorke.

But they got home to Saxonbury in time for the Christmas dinner. And as to Offord, it has not done talking yet of the tragedy enacted on that foggy night, or of the flight the whole village made to the county town to see the three men executed.

The double murder it is called to this day.

THE END.

MARTYN WARE'S TEMPTATION.

MARTYN WARE'S TEMPTATION.

PART THE FIRST.

CHAPTER I.

The Mother's Grief.

THE somewhat cold and yet wintry sun threw its rays on one of earth's fair and busy scenes in the spring afternoon of a year gone by. By the side of, but not close to, a factory, which was giving forth its tokens of life and work, was a white house, built in the villa style, large enough for a gentleman's residence, pretty enough, with its artistically laid-out grounds and gardens in the midst of which it stood, to attract the attention of travellers on the proximate high road. Other factories might be seen, near and distant, most of them considerably larger than this one, and other houses, surrounded by their grounds, as well as poorer dwellings, cottages, and huts. This place, situated in the heart of England, was called Wexmoor, and the factory first mentioned was known as Wexmoor Factory. Not many years before, this was the only factory in the district, and those larger and better ones had sprung up since. Its owner was a gentleman of the name of Martyn, and the white villa, built by himself some thirty years previously, was the residence of himself and his family.

Those cold thin rays are falling on it, and especially on a young lady who is standing at its entrance-door, between the two pillars, drawing on her gloves. A charming looking girl of twenty-two, with a thoughtful face,—very thoughtful for one so young; and steady, somewhat deeply-set eyes of dark blue. She is attired quite plainly, you see: a violet-coloured merino dress, a warm, grey shawl, and a cottage straw bonnet, trimmed with ribbons to match, straw-coloured. It was long ago, I have told you, before the disfiguring fashions of these later years were invented—the bonnets perched on the top of the head, or surmounting the forehead as a crocodile's mouth; those cottage bonnets of twenty years back made a pretty face look all the prettier.

This was Miss Helen Martyn, the second daughter of the manufacturer. He had four: Elizabeth, Helen, Sophia, and a little one of fourteen, much afflicted, named Amy. He had never had a son, and his wife had died when Amy was born. Elizabeth, the eldest, acted as mistress of the house, and as a sort of mother to the rest, though she was but two years older than Helen.

Helen Martyn drew on her gloves slowly, and then

paused and looked thoughtfully out before her, far into the distance. It almost seemed as if she were hesitating whether to go on, or not. At last she descended the white steps, wound round the broad gravel drive which surrounded the lawn before the house, and passed out at the front gate. In turning to the right she nearly ran against a gentleman, who was about to enter it with a hasty step, on his way from the factory. It was Mr. Martyn; a wiry-built man, with a pale, hard face, and cold grey eyes, bearing not the least resemblance to his daughter.

"Where are you going, Helen?"

"For a walk, papa."

He went on, saying no more. But ere he had well got through the gate, Helen, in her perfect truthfulness, her natural antagonism to anything like deceit, turned and spoke—she was conscious that to take a walk was not the sole object of her leaving home this afternoon. In point of fact, it may almost be said that she was going out in disobedience, for the place she thought to visit, if not positively forbidden in words, had been tacitly interdicted to Mr. Martyn's daughters.

"Papa, I should like to see Mrs. Rutt once more before she leaves on that long voyage. I thought of calling to say good-bye to her."

"You can do as you choose," replied Mr. Martyn.

He did not speak in displeasure, but carelessly, as

if the point were not worth consideration, and he hastened on towards the house as he spoke. Helen, feeling quite a weight removed from her heart, went away with a light step.

Continuing her road past the factory, she soon came to a shady green lane. Nearly half-a-mile down this lane was a low-built cottage, very pretty in summer, with its clematis-covered walls, and its rippling brook purling through its homely garden.

Ah, it was a sad tale, and Helen Martyn's heart sank as she approached the cottage with that feeling the "not liking" to enter it. Robert Rutt had been employed by Mr. Martyn for the past six or eight years. He was one of his first men—a sort of overlooker of the rest—and earned three pounds per week. About four years back he had married a widow lady from a distance. The word "lady" is really not misapplied. It was said she was a lady by birth and education, but had fallen into very poor circumstances. It was said also that she had believed Rutt, who was a well-looking and superior-mannered man, occupied a higher position in Mr. Martyn's works, to what she found he did occupy. Be this as it might, she had shown no disappointment, but had accommodated herself to her position, as the wife of a working-man, from the first hour Rutt brought her to this cottage at Wexmoor. Mr. Martyn's daughters soon made acquaintance with her, and Helen at least grew to like and respect her—to like very much her young son, then a boy of about eleven years.

Things had gone on smoothly until now; or, to speak with strict correctness, until a few months ago. Late in the month of October, the previous autumn, a circumstance had occurred, unpleasant in itself, and grievously disastrous in the results it was to bring forth Robert Rutt, thoroughly well-conducted in general—. otherwise he would never have been retained in his post by Mr. Martyn—was betrayed one day into drinking, and went into the factory in a half mad state. The man was too well aware of the effect drink had upon him, even worse than it has upon some men, and it was so rare he transgressed that his sobriety had grown into a proverb. Still, he had been in this state before—had gone into the factory so—and his master, vexed and angry, had threatened him with dismissal did he ever so forget himself again.

As ill-luck would have it, Mr. Martyn met him on this day as he was rolling in, shouting and singing. Some sharp words ensued. The master ordered him off the premises: Rutt, with some dim idea of proving that he was not incapable, waited his opportunity and stole in afterwards, when Mr. Martyn's back was turned. He attempted to work; he meddled with the machinery, and the result was that a large quantity of work was spoilt and the machinery almost fatally injured. It was a loss that Mr. Martyn could not well bear; his business had decreased of late years, and something like embarrassed circumstances were beginning to show themselves; hence, perhaps, his anger was more implacable than it might otherwise have been. In vain Rutt, when he came to his senses, humbly expressed his contrition, begged to be taken on again, promised that he never would again so forget himself as long as his life should last. Mr. Martyn would not listen. With stinging reproaches, with scornful words, he drove the man from him, declaring that, so far from forgiving him, it was his intention to refuse him a character, and to bring him to public punishment for the damage he had done. Before the moon, then at the full, had quite completed her monthly course, Rutt was dead. In going in search of work to a neighbouring town, it was supposed he came in contact with an infectious disorder: at any rate, he was seized with it, and died in delirium.

His death did not soften the feeling of Mr. Martyn. That gentleman felt the past grievance of his loss as keenly as before, and in this his daughters shared. They sent no sympathising enquiry to the poor wife; they did not vouchsafe her a kind word. It was not perhaps that they did not feel for *her*, but the loss of their father left its bitter sting in their hearts. What with the spoilt machinery, the destroyed goods, the loss of time and incapability to fulfil orders which it entailed, Mr. Martyn's loss could not be estimated at less than a thousand pounds. A formidable sum to the imagination of these young girls, and all the more formidable because of a dim fear, which had been for some time forcing itself upon their suspicions, that their father could not afford it. Helen alone felt deeply for her. In Helen Martyn's strict sense of justice, she asked her sisters how blame could possibly be reflected upon the wife: she pointed out that the poor wife was even more deeply injured than they were. But she did not dare to call and express this: it would have seemed like flying in the face of her father's sense of injury.

Yes, in one sense, the disastrous results fell worst on Mrs. Rutt, for she was left without a living or the means of gaining one. Rutt was a man who had lived up to every shilling of his wages. He liked to see his wife comfortable, to maintain a plentiful home; he was attached to her boy, now a fine lad of fifteen, and had yielded to her wish of keeping him at school, a good day grammar school in the neighbourhood, not yet putting him out to earn anything. It is a fact scarcely to be believed, only that there are unhappily too many such facts in the world, that when Rutt died there was not one penny of ready money in the house. Except the furniture, Mrs. Rutt was left entirely destitute: and the furniture of that small house was not of great value.

Many and many a time did Helen Martyn wonder

what that poor woman would do, and how she was getting on, or would get on. Gossip spreads in a small locality, and the young ladies heard news from time to time of Mrs. Rutt. First, it was said she was living by disposing of the lighter trifles of her household; next, that her son, who had left the school at Christmas, had found a temporary place at the doctor's, to carry out the physic bottles; by which he earned his food and a shilling or two a week. And last, they heard that Mrs. Rutt and her boy were going to America.

This last news, much as it surprised Mr. Martyn's daughters, proved to be correct. Mrs. Rutt had a brother settled near Washington, a farmer; she had written to him on the occurrence of her great misfortune, and after the passing backwards and forwards of two or three letters, he had offered her an asylum with him, and to find some employment for her son in the capital. What was perhaps more to the purpose in her temporary strait, he had offered to send the passage money for one of them, hoping she would be able to find the other herself.

And this, Mrs. Rutt, as it was known, had contrived to do. The very man who had succeeded to her husband's post at the works, made arrangements with her for taking the house off her hands, and as much of the furniture as she could leave in it. That was not much. Her husband had died the first week in November, it was now the end of March, and she had had only that furniture to live upon, parting with it piecemeal. Little wonder, then, that it was with difficulty she could save sufficient money for only her own passage, let alone her boy's. She had no friends in the neighbourhood, no advisers: she had never made a friend or sought an acquaintance since she came into it; and the cause is easily explainable. Her position as Rutt's wife debarred her from associating with the superior inhabitants, and her own previous habits of gentility forbade her placing herself on a level with the wives of such men as her husband. It is true the Miss Martyns had often gone to see her, but only as the wife of one of their father's men, in whom they took an especial interest.

All preliminaries were arranged, and she was to sail from Liverpool at the week's end; was to quit Wexmoor on the morrow. The Miss Martyns heard this; heard that the promised letter from her brother, which was to contain the remittance, had come that very morning; and Helen had determined to run down to bid her good-bye.

To let her go away for ever without a God speed, without a word of kindness to blot out the remembrance of the calamity caused by her husband, and for which *she* was in no way to blame, struck cruelly on the girl's heart. So Helen told her sisters what she should do, and put her things on; and when you saw her hesitating on the steps, she was deliberating whether to go into the factory in passing, and ask her father's consent, or whether she should go first, and confess afterwards that she had been. The meeting him decided it.

Mrs. Rutt in her widow's cap was seated in the parlour when she entered; a pretty room once, but nearly bare now; and Helen started when she saw her. Helen Martyn had seen grief in her lifetime, but scarcely such grief as this. She sat on a low seat, and was swaying herself to and fro in what looked like the extreme of human sorrow, her head bent forward, the tears slowly coursing down her colourless cheeks. It must be confessed that Helen somewhat wondered: Mrs. Rutt was leaving no ties in the place that she should grieve after them, and she had never pretended to be attached to it. She rose from her low seat at sight of Helen, and dried her eyes as well as she could; but the look of anguish remained.

"Oh, Miss Helen! Have you indeed come once again?"

"I could not let you go without saying farewell, and giving you our good wishes," was Helen's gentle answer. "My sisters have not come, but they charged me to say everything that was kind for them. I hope you and Bob will get safely to your journey's end, and find a happy home there."

The words seemed to tell upon her terribly. She

burst into a renewed fit of grief, so violent that Helen was alarmed. In vain she essayed to speak; nothing came forth but sobs. Helen, feeling shy and uncomfortable, knew not what to say: she came to the conclusion that all this must be for the loss of her husband. At length the sobs grew lighter.

"Miss Helen, pray pardon me! You don't know what it is to part with your only child, to leave him alone to the mercy of the world without guide or protector, to go away from him with scarcely a prospect of ever seeing him again on earth. It is like the parting of death; it has seemed nothing less to me."

Helen could not understand. Amidst blinding tears, amidst struggles to suppress the emotion that went well-nigh to choke her, the explanation was given by Mrs. Rutt. The letter had indeed been delivered to her that morning from America, but the promised remittance was not in it. Her brother had expressed his sorrow at being unable to send it; he had a sufficiently abundant home, but ready money was scarce with him; and he hoped she would manage to find it herself.

"It is an impossibility," she gasped. "I have no means of finding it, I have no friend in the world to help me. There will be expenses, too, I hear, in embarking that I had not bargained for, and I shall have to sell some of my clothes to get away myself."

Helen felt shocked and grieved. "What will be done?" she asked.

"All that can be done is, that I must abandon my boy—it seems to me like abandoning him," was the sobbing answer. "I *must* go myself: I ought to have been out of this house on Lady-day, Miss Helen, and now it's the twenty-ninth. I must go; I have not a place to put my head in in the old country, not a bit or sup to support me: and my boy, he must stop behind and get a living as he best can. I'd sacrifice myself for my boy if I knew how to sacrifice myself; I'd almost rather part with life than part with him."

"And how much would it cost to take him?" Helen breathlessly asked.

"I had expected ten pounds," she answered: "it was what my brother said he'd send. We could have made it do, Miss Helen. Of course we go in the cheapest way: it is some years since I could afford to be fastidious. Once on the other side, I should not mind if we had nothing left. We'd find our way on foot to Washington."

It was very natural that Helen Martyn's first impulse was to wish she had the money to give: but in the next moment she remembered how entirely futile was the wish. Ready money had not been very plentiful in their home of late; and what she and her sister Sophia had been able to get from their father, or Elizabeth supply from her housekeeping necessities, had been expended for a specified purpose, of which you will soon hear further. All that she could do was to express her heartfelt sympathy, her regret that she had not the money to give; and she did it with a sincere, low voice, and the tears standing in her eyes.

Mrs. Rutt saw how genuine was the sorrow of that fair young face, how great the pain at heart, and she strove to suppress further signs of her own. But when Helen was taking leave, the sobs burst forth again uncontrolled.

"You'll say a kind word to him now and then, Miss Helen, when you get the opportunity. He'll want it, poor lad, for he'll soon be motherless. I shan't live long, parted from him."

"Does he stop in Wexmoor?" asked Helen.

"Just at present. I went to the doctor this morning, and he'll keep him on for a bit, until something turns up for him."

"What can turn up for him?" wondered Helen.

"Nothing—unless God sends it. And where he'll get a place to sleep, or who'll give him shelter, I don't know. Miss Helen," she continued, in an altered tone, "I'd ask you, if I may dare, when the weddings are to be?"

A soft blush rose to Helen Martyn's cheek.

"In about a month," she answered. "Towards the end of April."

"May Heaven bless you both, and the gentlemen you have chosen!" aspirated Mrs. Rutt, in a low tone.

Helen was walking slowly towards home, thinking upon the poor widow's grief, upon the many sources of sorrow there seemed to be in the world, when a slim, active boy, with a pleasing face and large intelligent dark eyes, came running round the corner of the lane. It was Bob Rutt—as the boy was universally called. He had, of course, no right to the name of Rutt, but he had never been called anything else since he came into the neighbourhood: his Christian name happening to be the same as that of his step-father, Robert, had no doubt contributed to the habit. He raised his cap as he came up to Helen, far more as a gentleman would raise it than a working boy.

"I have been to see your mother, Bob," she said. "This is sad news."

"Was she grieving much, Miss Helen?" he eagerly asked. "I could bear it for myself; but I can't bear it for her."

"But you will be sorry to be separated from her, Bob?"

"Sorry!" he echoed, swallowing down a lump in his throat, and turning his face out of sight of Helen's. "When the letter came this morning, it seemed that I could have moved heaven and earth to go with her, and—and—. But it's of no use talking of it," he added, after a broken pause. "Thank you for your sympathy, Miss Helen."

"Oh, Bob, I *am* sorry! Perhaps you'll get out to her sometime."

"Yes, Miss Helen, perhaps so, if she lives. But she's one to take things dreadfully to heart."

He raised his cap again and went away. And Helen Martyn looked after him with misty eyes through the fading light of the evening sky.

CHAPTER II.

Helen's Knight-errantry.

WHAT we should all do without money it is quite impossible to conceive; but one thing appears indisputable, that, if the world could go on without it, a great many of the crosses and heartburnings we are pleased to make our own, and hug to us as if we liked them, would never occur.

When Helen Martyn entered her home, the drawing-room was lighted and the tea waited on the table. They generally dined in the middle of the day: it suited Mr. Martyn's business habits, and it suited Amy's health. Elizabeth sat before the tea-tray, ready to make it as soon as her father came in. He often kept it waiting, and she generally provided herself with some little trifle of work, not to waste the time, as she had now. She was sewing some lace edging to a strip of thin muslin: it was for a nightcap border for one of her sisters. She looked older than her age considerably: any one might have taken her to be seven or eight and twenty, with her grave manners and her somewhat old-fashioned style of dress. The young girl, Amy, stood by her side, holding her chair: a stranger might have observed with wonder a certain peculiar twitching in this child—in her face, her arms, her whole body. She had had in her life, at long extended periods, three attacks of paralysis, the first having occurred when she was little more than an infant, and its signs never left her—as you may see by these never-ceasing twitches. A great deal of money had been spent upon her: fresh doctors, seaside visits; everything possible to be thought of was tried. She did not get much better; but the medical men thought if she could go over the next two or three years without another attack, she might probably recover.

Seated opposite Elizabeth, her elbow on the table, and her face wearing a discontented look, was Sophia. She resembled Helen much in features, but her eyes had the hard look of her father. Poor Sophia was apt to make a grievance of trifles, and she thought she had a very great grievance to be miserable over just now. Helen also shared in it, and deemed herself as hardly used as Sophy.

To explain this, it must be stated that Helen and Sophia were both engaged to be married. Helen to a gentleman in London, of the name of Ware; Sophia to the Rev. Mr. Gazebrook. You heard Helen tell Mrs. Rutt that the weddings were to be in about a month. All being well, the two sisters would be married on the same day. Neither match was particularly eligible in a pecuniary point of view. Mr. Ware was the secretary to a public company; his salary three hundred a year; and the clergyman was incumbent of a small living in Wales, worth not much more than half that sum. But Mr. Martyn had not deemed it well to refuse his consent. He believed both the gentlemen when they represented that their circumstances would be sure to grow better in time; and he told his daughters that if they chose to risk it, to live quietly until these better circumstances came, they might. Hope is strong in the human heart—very strong in those beginning life. Mr. Gazebrook looked forward to a good fat living; and Edward Ware to at least a doubled salary.

But the weddings, or rather the preparations for them, had brought forth some vexations, and Sophia was dilating upon these as she sat there with her elbow on the tea-table and her chin leaning on her hand. The sum which Mr. Martyn had allowed his two daughters for purchasing what fine people call the *trousseau*, but which I would a great deal rather call the wedding clothes, was miserably small; at least it had proved so in the laying out. When given forth to them—and, not to make a mystery, its amount may as well be stated: thirty pounds each—Elizabeth, somewhat close in her views, pronounced it sufficient; in fact, it was Elizabeth who had suggested its amount to her father, though she did not choose to confess it: sixty pounds for the two would be ample, she said to him. But whether the young ladies had gone randomly to work, and bought too expensive things at the onset, or whether it was really inadequate to their wants, certain it was that the money was gone, and while necessaries had been laid in, most of the finery remained to be bought. Even Elizabeth had come to the conclusion that more money must be had; she helped them a little from her housekeeping allowance, but that did not do much good. They had been permitted to make their own purchases, upon the express condition that every article should be paid for when it was bought.

"We had better not have been married at all, if this is to be it," grumbled Sophia. "I have not got a single new silk dress yet, except the wedding one; neither has Helen."

"You have plenty of old ones," said Elizabeth, who deemed it policy to make the best of affairs to her sisters. "One or two of them have scarcely been worn at all; they are equal to new."

"Old ones! what are old ones?" retorted Sophia, getting crosser and more cross. "Never was such a thing heard of, as going to your new home with a heap of old things, and no new ones. Besides, I must have a lace mantle! How am I to get through the summer without a lace mantle?"

Elizabeth went on with her nightcap border, saying nothing. She had a habit of being silent when found fault with by her sisters. Sophia resumed:

"It's a perfect disgrace! Thirty pounds for girls in our station of life. If mamma had been alive she would represent things fitly to papa, I am sure of it: You ought to, Elizabeth. I can't make it out; papa's not a stingy man."

"Look at papa's losses of late, Sophy; at the one caused by Rutt: and his business has been dwindling down and down through want of capital," urged Elizabeth, in a low tone.

"What are we to do for gloves?" was Sophy's answer. "We can't have less than a dozen altogether, dark and light and white; and we have not got the money for a single pair! I wish you were going to be married yourself, Elizabeth; you'd know what it is."

"You *may* manage with what things you have," was Elizabeth's answer. "I will do what I can in the matter; but if the worst comes to the worst you must—"

"Be quiet, Elizabeth! the worst can't come to the worst. *Can* we be married, Helen, with what we have?"

Helen, who had sat quietly near the fire after taking off her things, looked up with the air of one preoccupied. In comparison with the *real* need of money brought to her notice that afternoon, the present discussion jarred upon the heart as savouring of folly. "What did you say, Sophy?—Have more things? Yes, I suppose we must have them."

"Suppose we must have them! why you know we must," cried Sophy, angrily. "You were nearly crying over it this morning, you know you were."

Quite true. Helen Martyn *had* nearly cried over her wardrobe in the morning, wondering what her husband and his friends would think of it, upon her going amongst them with so scanty a one. Scanty in comparison with the young lady's ideas, you understand.

"Thirty pounds for the wedding outfit of Mr. Martyn's daughters!" repeated Sophy, working herself into a fume. "We ought to have had a hundred at the very least. When Adelaide Gibson was married her things cost two hundred pounds. Helen, we shan't be able to afford a single evening dress."

"And you don't want them," said Elizabeth to this. "Evening dresses you *do not* want: you have enough."

"They have been worn I don't know how many times," shrieked Sophy.

"They *look* good, and they will be new where you

are going. For the matter of that, Sophy, it is not to be expected that you will have much evening visiting in that remote and quiet place. Helen may have more in London. Amy, dear, you are shaking my chair."

"And I shall want dresses for it," said Helen, rousing herself from her recollections. "Oh dear! I wish I was rich!"

"I wish we could have tea!" interposed Sophy, going to another temporary trouble. "I have fifty things to do afterwards, and a long letter to write."

"Talking of letters, did you know that papa heard from Mr. Ware to-day, Helen?" asked Elizabeth.

"No; did he?" cried Helen, eagerly.

"Papa came in for some books he wanted this afternoon, and told me then; he forgot to mention it before. Mr. Ware is coming to-morrow for a day or two."

The pleasure which the information brought to Helen's face soon changed to pain. This embarrassment about the wardrobe seemed all the worse from the near prospect of the presence of Mr. Ware. Elizabeth suddenly inquired whether she had seen Mrs. Rutt.

"Yes," replied Helen. "She was in the greatest trouble; I never saw distress like it before. She has to leave Bob behind her."

"Why?"

Helen explained. Miss Martyn did not seem to

think much of it, and Sophy was too entirely absorbed in her own ill-humour to listen. They did not witness her distress, thought Helen. Just then, Mr. Martyn came in, and tea began. Sophia would touch nothing, and upon her father asking the cause she burst into tears. "Hey-day!" cried he.

"If you would but allow us a little more for our things, papa," she sobbed. "We went over the list to-day, what we have and what we want. We have got nothing, hardly."

"I expect that you have been spending the money foolishly," said Mr. Martyn.

"No, papa. All the things that you would call foolish remain to buy yet. Papa, we ought to leave home a little decent."

He made no reply then, but when he had finished his tea, drew out his pocket-book, took from it two bank-notes, and gave one to Helen and one to Sophy.

"Now, understand me, this is all you will have. Had circumstances been with me as they have been, a score of pounds more or less would be of no moment, but that is not the case now. I am doing all I can to retrieve my position, and I believe I should have gone far to retrieve it by this time, but for the conduct of Rutt. That, with what you have had, will make forty pounds each, and if you can't buy enough finery for a wedding with forty pounds, all I can say is, that you must keep single."

He quitted the room as he spoke, and returned to the factory. Elizabeth took the note out of Helen's hand, and looked at its amount,—10*l*. "I am glad he listened to me," she observed.

"Listened to *you!*" cried Sophy.

"Yes. When papa came for those books this afternoon, I spoke to him: asking him to let you have a little more if he could, as it was difficult to spin out the thirty pounds. You may buy the gloves now, Sophy."

Sophy's eyes were sparkling. Ten pounds certainly would not purchase silk gowns, and evening gowns, and gloves, and lace mantles, and a hundred other things; but it had come unexpectedly, and she was not in the mood just then to make calculations.

And Helen? Helen took a piece of paper and a pencil, and dotted down the things she would like, and their probable cost. Upon adding up the sum total, she found it came to just nine-and-twenty pounds. So she turned the paper to the other side, and put down what she most wanted,—what she thought she could not do without,—and added up that. Fifteen pounds five shillings, this time: and there was nothing for it but to go over it again with fresh subtraction.

While doing this, one sole thought kept presenting itself to her; it worried her brain, it thumped against her conscience. To do without these things would not be a matter of life and death—and that other matter, to which she *might* apply the money, almost was such.

Presently she put the paper and pencil in her pocket, and went up-stairs to her room, and there she sat down seriously to think. Helen Martyn had strong innate consciousness, a powerful sense of the just and the unjust, a keen perception of the precept: Do as you would be done by. Her conscience was aroused, and she could not lull it to rest.

Should she use this money upon herself, or should she divert it from its purpose and give it to Mrs. Rutt? For one thing, she scarcely saw how she was to do without the additional clothes, and it would certainly be a very great smart to her to do without them; for another, she scarcely knew whether it was so entirely her own property that she might give it, or be justified in giving it. On the other hand, there was the performing a good action, the helping that poor woman in her strait of need, there might be the changing of the whole current of the boy's future life. If Bob remained here, unguided, unprotected, who was to foresee what mischief he might fall into? This poor ten pounds might save him from it.

Sorely perplexed—and yet the innate conviction was upon her that she must and should give the money—Helen Martyn bowed her head upon the bed and breathed a word for guidance: she had been taught that wonderful truth, that those who consult God need no other guide. A very few minutes, and she went down-stairs again. Sophy was talking her tongue out about the fresh purchases to be made on the morrow: in that moment all was *couleur de rose* to Sophy Martyn.

"Helen, we must go out the instant breakfast's over, or we shall not be home before Mr. Ware arrives. We may leave the house at nine if we try."

"Yes," replied Helen, but her tone was a somewhat hesitating one.

"Elizabeth, I hope you'll go with us. Your judgment is so good, you know. And without you," added Sophy, ingenuously, "I may be spending nearly all my money in waste."

"I will go if I can," said Elizabeth. "But you had better make a list to-night of the things you require, put down the sum you can afford for each, and not be tempted when in the shop to go beyond it."

"I'll do it now," said Sophy.

Helen meanwhile waited until her father came in. As was nearly sure to be the case (don't we all find it so?), because she wanted him to come in earlier than usual, he was considerably later. The clock had struck nine when she heard him enter, and go into a room that was chiefly used by himself. She ran down to it.

Mr. Martyn was standing with his back to the

door, searching apparently for something in his bureau, the lid of which he held open. Helen advanced and stood near until he had leisure to attend to her. In a minute he turned to her with a questioning glance.

"That ten-pound note that you have given me, papa, may I spend it in any way that I please?"

"To be sure you may," replied Mr. Martyn, with a slight look of surprise.

"I mean, papa, may I lay it out in *any* way?" she repeated. "Suppose I wished to appropriate it to something quite different from clothes—may I consider it entirely mine to do so?"

"You can do what you like with it," he said. "My private opinion is, that the money I previously gave you was sufficient without this. However, you have got it."

Helen went up-stairs, put on her bonnet and shawl, and stole quietly from the house. It was a fine moonlight night, and she had no fear of going alone. She knew that the money, to be of use, must be given that night: Mrs. Rutt had told her that she should be away on her road to Liverpool with morning light. As she was turning into the lane, she met the boy, Bob. He deemed himself perfectly alone, and he was giving vent to his emotion in loud sobs as he walked: loud and distressing they sounded in the still night.

"Bob, is it you?"

Ashamed at being caught so, Bob turned his face away, and pretended to whistle a song. Helen would not appear to have noticed it. "I want to say a few words to your mother, Bob. Is she alone?"

"Yes, she's quite alone. I'll walk with you, Miss Helen."

They went along side by side; Helen steadily, Bob rather noisily. The boy was exercising his legs and his tongue, trying to make appear that such a thing as weeping, for a bold young man like himself, was amongst the physical impossibilities.

Mrs. Rutt was up-stairs, but came down when she heard them. She was not crying, but the settled look of despair upon her face would have wrung Helen Martyn's heart, but for the secret she held within her. She was a shy, timid hand at giving, feeling quite as uncomfortable in it as Bob had felt at being caught weeping, and the explanation was given, and the ten-pound note laid down, more awkwardly than graciously.

But to see Mrs. Rutt's joy!—to see the changed countenance of poor Bob as he stood in a corner, his lips apart, his bright colour fading from his cheeks with emotion! Helen's eyes were wet, as the blessing she had given came home to her heart, and I fear Bob in that moment looked upon her as the most real angel he had ever had conception of.

But Mrs. Rutt had scruples in taking it. She feared

Miss Helen Martyn had procured it at some great sacrifice or inconvenience.

"No, I will tell you the truth about it," said Helen, candidly. "It has been no inconvenience to get it, for papa gave it me unexpectedly this evening; and the parting with it will not entail much sacrifice," she added in a cheerful tone. "It was given me to buy additional things for my marriage, Mrs. Rutt, but I can do without them. It is better that I should be married with a less extensive wardrobe than I had deemed necessary, than that Bob should be left behind you."

She had no time to listen to the heartfelt thanks, to the prayers for her own welfare; she must hasten home again, lest her absence should be discovered, and cause a commotion. Bob Rutt followed her out in silence to see her home.

And in silence they proceeded along the lane. Bob did not speak, his heart was full: and Helen was feeling, as she had never yet felt it in her life, the truth of that golden precept—It is more blessed to give than to receive. She was asking herself in wonder how she could have put, even for a moment, the question of her own finery against this good work. At the end of the lane they were in the bustle and lights of Wexmoor, and Helen stopped.

"You need not come any farther, Bob. I can run on by myself now."

"I'll go with you to your door, Miss Helen."

"No, I would rather go alone. I am all but there. Good by, Bob, I wish you all good wishes."

"Miss Helen," he said, clasping the hand that was offered him between both of his, and struggling hard to subdue all outward emotion, "I shall never forget what you have done this night. I am sure that my mother will repay you as soon—"

"No, no, Bob, I don't want to be repaid," she interrupted; "I shall be going from here almost directly, you know. I hope you will get on in the land you are going to, and that will be my repayment. Fare you well."

She hastened on, leaving the boy looking after her, his heart full, his gratitude shining through his face. Bob's first thought was to wish he was a grown-up man and a gentleman, that he might marry Miss Helen Martyn, instead of Mr. Ware. He deemed it impossible there could be two Helen Martyns in the world.

With the morning, Helen had to tell what she had done. It was quite impossible that she could suddenly decline to make any more purchases, without confessing the cause—that her money was gone; and equally impossible not to be obliged to disclose what had become of it. Elizabeth called her foolish; Sophy opened her cold grey eyes, and wondered whether Helen was mad. "The *whole* of it given!" she reiterated, "why, you can't buy one single thing more! What *will* you do?"

"I shall manage very well with what I have," was Helen's answer. "We had a very good stock of things, you know, Sophy; and I shall contrive sundry changes in my old dresses to make them look like new. I lay awake last night thinking how it could be done."

Yes, it is wonderful how different things look in contrasted aspects of mind. When Helen, like Sophy, had felt angry and mortified over the small sum allowed them, she regarded her stock of clothes with the utmost disparagement; but now that she *wished* to make them do, that she put cheerfully the best face upon the matter, they seemed really good enough and extensive enough for anything she could wish. Ah, my friends, half the worry of life would be soothed, if we could but bring our own rebellious minds into a more accommodating frame.

But Helen had to encounter worse than the reflections of her sisters—the astonished anger of her father. Mr. Martyn was really displeased: perhaps all the more so because *the Rutts* had been the objects of Helen's bounty. But in any case he would have looked upon it in an absurdly ridiculous light: as we look upon some of the feats of chivalry of the old days of romance, and deem them unsuitable to these. He reproached Helen, telling her that money was not so plentiful with him, and that if she had no need of it she should have given it back to him.

"You told me I might use it as I pleased, papa," was Helen's deprecating answer. "I asked you if I might."

But the reminder only made Mr. Martyn more angry. In point of fact, he had not given much thought to the matter when Helen applied to him, carelessly supposing that if she did not wish to spend it upon clothes, it was only because she had set her heart upon some other sort of superfluity. Helen felt thankful that the Rutts were really gone, lest in his displeasure he might be for ordering her to reclaim the money from them.

Mr. Ware arrived in the course of the day, and the story was told to him. Without openly casting blame to her, Helen could see that he condemned her at heart, looking upon it in the same light as her father; and there was a tone of ridicule in his voice when he spoke of her "knight-errantry," which made her cheeks burn. Poor Helen shut herself in her chamber, and sobbed aloud. In that bitter moment she felt tempted to wish she had not given away the money.

PART THE SECOND.

CHAPTER I.

Mr. Vavasour's Promise.

THE sultry summer's day was drawing to its close, and the cooler air and slight breeze which came up with twilight was inexpressibly refreshing. On some of these London suburbs the heat of the crowded and close metropolis seems to reflect its rays, rendering them hotter than country places.

In a small but very pretty drawing-room, whose windows looked over the lawn to the high road, sat two ladies on this sultry evening. One of them was not doing anything; unless anxiously watching every omnibus which came past laden with its freight of gentlemen returning home from their labours in the city, could be called anything. She is a very pleasing looking woman, graceful and ladylike; and her countenance would be even more pleasing but for the almost painfully anxious look which it wears just now. You would guess her to be perhaps eight-and-thirty: in reality she is several years more, but Time has passed lightly over her. On these fair, calm, serene countenances he does not leave his mark as he does on more stormy ones. Do you recognise her? Her eyes are dark blue, and her silky brown hair is abundant yet. She wears a pretty muslin dress, with a white collar of lace, matching the hanging lace to her open sleeves. It is Helen Martyn: or rather Helen Ware; for she has been Mr. Ware's wife ever since you saw her last in those old days.

The lady opposite to her is little and thin, with quite a grey complexion, and a cap shading her remnant of scanty hair. She looks as much older than her age as Helen looks younger; in fact, any one would take her to be the older of the two. Only note the contrast in their hands! Helen's are small, young, delicate hands yet; those others are prematurely old and wrinkled. It is Amy Martyn. She has partially recovered the affliction of her childhood, but it has aged her before her time.

Time had wrought its changes. When Mr. Martyn died, and died an impoverished man, leaving nothing behind him, a grave question arose of what was to become of Amy. Elizabeth had died long before, and there was only Amy left. "She must come to us," Helen had said to her husband. "Yes," he replied, "I suppose she must: poor Sophy, with her cares and her children, cannot be burdened with her."

Poor Sophy, indeed! Those fond hopes of future greatness. cherished, as you may remember, by the two bridegrooms elect, had turned out but delusive ones. They often do so turn out in common life. The Reverend Mr. Gazebrook had never been remembered in his remote Welsh living, but lived there still; and poor Sophy, in her small parsonage home, with her nine children, had had her temper irretrievably soured in the struggle to bring them up, and to make both ends meet as she did it. It was clear that she could not give a refuge to Amy. Mr. Ware had not risen, either: he held the same situation at the same salary; the board would have been glad to raise it, as they told him every Christmas when they made him a present, but they could not afford it, for the company was not a rich one, and though it did not retrograde, it did not advance. Still, with Helen's good management they were tolerably at ease; in luxury, as compared to Sophy; and Amy was welcomed by them. Amy made herself as useful as she could; her hands were pretty steady, and she could manage plain sewing: she is at present, you see, hemming one of a dozen white handkerchiefs which lie neatly folded before her, and which are already marked with ink in full—"Martyn Ware."

The orange tinge of the sun in the western sky fell on Helen's features, on the smile of hope which hovered on her parted lips, parted just then with the eagerness of expectation. A city omnibus had drawn up close to the gate, and a gentleman, whom she could not yet see, was getting down from the other side of the roof.

"Here he is, Amy."

Amy Martyn glanced up by way of answer, in time to catch the bitterness of disappointment which fell like a dark cloud on her sister's face. The gentleman had come in view, and proved to be not him for whom she was looking.

"Is it not Martyn?" asked Amy.

"No. It is Mr. Ware."

But do not mistake her. Not because it was her husband who had alighted did her voice fall to faintness, her heart turn to sickness, but because she had expected some one else: some one whom she feared she *could not trust* to remain late in town as she could her husband.

A great fear had recently fallen upon Helen Ware. They had never had but one child, a son, named Martyn after his grandfather; and how she loved him no tongue could tell. It is not well; it is not well for a woman to have one only son, for he is all too apt to become her idol. I am not saying this with special reference to Mrs. Ware. She did love her boy, none save God knew how much; but she had never spoiled him, and she was more anxious for his eternal than for his temporal welfare. Only of late had the fear fallen upon her that he was in some way going wrong.

A fear that had taken hold of her very being. She dared not breathe it to others, to her husband, to Amy; she scarcely dared breathe it to her own heart. *How* Martyn was going wrong, or in what particular manner he was transgressing, she could not think, did not know; but the living fear was there.

Mr. Ware came in: a tall man, with grey hair and quiet manners. Helen rose. "I thought you expected to be very late to-night, Edward?"

"Yes; but the meeting was put off to another day. Is Martyn home?"

Helen answered quite carelessly, as she turned to ring the bell, "Not yet; I dare say he won't be long."

"It will be a difference, then, from what it has been lately," was the remark of Mr. Ware as he turned to leave the room.

Tea came in, and they sat down to it, Helen making it as usual. It had grown dusk then, and the lamp was lighted. Afterwards Mr. Ware paid a visit to a friend who lived close by, a gentleman addicted to scientific pursuits, to experiments, and Mr. Ware was fond of joining in them. But for these frequent evening absences, he might have known more of the general irregularity of Martyn's return.

Helen threw a shawl upon her shoulders, and went

out to the lawn. Hot as the day had been, a damp had arisen now. Nobody saw her in the dark night, and she laid her head gently upon the iron spikes of the low gate, her breath hushed to listen for the omnibuses in the distance. With the appearance of each one her heart beat with renewed hope. All in vain. They passed; they passed in succession, one after the other. Weary and sick, she turned in as the clock struck eleven.

Amy had gone to bed; she scarcely ever sat up later than ten; her husband, she knew, would not be long, for eleven was the signal for his quitting his friend. But not of her husband, not of Amy, did Helen think; they were in safety. She threw herself into a chair with a sobbing sigh.

Just then the roll of another omnibus was heard, and she started up. "No," she said, heart-sick with the past hour and what it brought, "I will not go, it will only be another disappointment;" and she sank down again.

But it came on slowly and more slowly, and at length stopped. Mrs. Ware went to the door then, and looked from it. Yes! it was her son at last.

He came in at the gate, a gentlemanly young man of twenty-one, with a pale and somewhat gentle face, very much like what hers had used to be. Helen waited. "Martyn," she whispered, "you are late again."

"Not very late, mother. It is only eleven."

"Where did you stay?"

"I went home with Vavasour, and somehow the time slipped on."

"Martyn! you always say that!"

Martyn laughed. "Yes, I think I do very often go home with him."

Ready as the replies had been, there was a nameless something in the tone which grated on Helen's ear; a sort of evasion—as if he were not telling the whole truth. The miserable conviction was upon her —had been upon her for some time now—that he did not tell her the whole truth; that there was something to be concealed. In vain she strove to draw more and more from him, she never succeeded, she could come at nothing certain, but she did fear Martyn was going wrong. She might never have suspected it at all, but for the picking up of a bit of paper, a torn note in Martyn's handwriting: it appeared to be an urgent appeal to somebody about money, some money which somebody ought to have furnished, and it stated there was nothing before him but ruin, unless the somebody "came down" with it. So much she managed to make out of the torn writing. She showed it to Martyn; but he laughed it off, and said it only concerned some fellows in their house. Mrs. Ware was tolerably satisfied at the time: but the fear and the suspicion had grown upon her ever since.

"Will you take anything?" she asked him to-night.

"No, thank you. I suppose everybody's in bed."

He sat down at the table as he spoke, carelessly opening a book that was on it: and at that moment Mr. Ware's step was heard outside.

Seeing his son seated there, a book before him, it is probable Mr. Ware supposed he had been home some time. He began describing the fine experiments at which he had been assisting; he was always full of them after these evening visits. Helen listened mechanically: she heard the words, "condensed air," "syphon," "electric phenomena," and many others, without the least power of connecting them. Her attention was fixed on Martyn. At first he had responded to his father, made every show of listening eagerly, of being powerfully interested: but now a vacant look had fallen on his face, a dim scale seemed to rest on his eyes; his thoughts were lost in themselves, and it looked very much as if those thoughts were troublous ones.

A very desirable situation, as was supposed, had been found for Martyn Ware in the house of Hill and Aukland, West India merchants; and he had now been there four years. The first two years he earned nothing, the third year they had given him thirty pounds; this year he was to have sixty; the next year one hundred. In short, his prospects were sufficiently good, and there seemed no reason why he should not in a few years be gaining his five hundred a-year salary: other clerks were doing it. The firm lived in Mincing Lane—that is, their house of business was there. Mr. Hill was the partner in England; Mr. Aukland resided in Jamaica, where they had a corresponding house. A great portion of Martyn's particular duties lay at the custom-house, passing entries for goods, and such like—but this won't interest the reader.

After breakfast on the following morning, Martyn and his father went to town together, as was their general custom: they had to be at business at the same hour, ten o'clock. It was striking as Martyn entered the house in Mincing Lane; he was always punctual, always attentive to his duties. The head clerk of the room in which Martyn sat was already at his desk, and he looked over his spectacles to see which of the three under him, attached to that room, was coming in.

"I thought it was you, Mr. Ware. Don't take your hat off. This entry must be passed the first thing."

"Very well," replied Martyn. And it may as well be remarked that his civility, gentlemanly manners, and punctuality, had rendered him of good report in the house.

He stood for a moment, looking at the paper the

head clerk handed him, and some one else came in. Quite a notable person this last, resplendently grand. He stood six feet high, was of very dark complexion, and might have been pronounced remarkably well dressed, but that his ornaments were profuse and shone too much. His clothes were of the best and newest, well made, entirely such as a gentleman might wear. A light kid glove was on one hand, and two rings were on the other; his cable chain crossing his waistcoat was a double one, several trinkets dangled from it, and a great diamond pin glittered in his blue stock.

"Good morning, Mr. Mann," said he, raising his hat in a somewhat affected manner.

"Good morning," replied the clerk. "Be so good as to step round to the post office, Mr. Vavasour, and see if the letters are ready. The mail is in."

Mr. Vavasour looked thunderstruck at the order; a little supercilious.

"*I* step to the post office?" he repeated.

"If you please," said the clerk, with quiet authority. "Young Jones is not here yet this morning; he is ill: and Mr. Ware must go at once to the custom house."

Mr. Vavasour put on his hat and went out. Martyn, who had preceded him, was waiting at the entrance-door, looking round with an eager, questioning glance.

"The West India Mail's in, Vavasour," he whispered.

"So Mann says," was the reply; and the careless, drawling, indifferent tone with which Vavasour spoke bore a marked contrast to the anxiety of Martyn's—an anxiety that amounted to pain.

"You have not your letters yet?"

"Is it likely? I shall get them, I suppose, in the course of the day."

"Vavasour, I am quite sick with the suspense," was the impassioned rejoinder of Martyn Ware. "I am not fit to go about my business."

Mr. Vavasour laughed heartily.

"I can't help it, Ware," he said, in a tone of half apology. "You are such a fidget! Never was your equal, I should think, under the sun."

"Think of the stake," said Martyn.

"Stake be ignored!" cried Mr. Vavasour, pleasantly. "My good fellow, it will be all right. Such 'stakes' are risked and got over every day."

They had been walking on together; but now their roads lay in different directions. Martyn stayed to say another word.

"Will your letters be directed to Mincing Lane this time, or to your rooms?"

"As if I could tell! To Mincing Lane, most probably."

"Well, put me out of suspense, Vavasour, as soon as you can."

Vavasour nodded: and the two clerks parted.

But it is very probable that Mr. Vavasour would fire with indignation did he hear himself called a clerk. The son of a wealthy West India planter, he had been sent to Europe for his education, and had received a comprehensive one, though it may be questioned if he profited by it as greatly as he might have done. A private clergyman's first, King's College next, Germany afterwards. Then he was placed in the house of Hill and Aukland, by the desire of his father; not with any view of his continuing in it, but simply because Mr. Vavasour the elder deemed it expedient that he should acquire some notion of business before his return to Jamaica. No salary was paid to him, and he was not looked upon in the light of a common clerk, but he had to do what was required of him.

He had entered the house the previous summer, rather more now than twelve months ago. His fame had preceded him. A rich young West Indian, coming into the house as a gentleman, not as a clerk! No wonder a commotion of expectation was excited among the regular employés; and the commotion was not lessened when he arrived. His tall and really fine person, his very dark skin, his purple-black hair and whiskers, shining with Rowland's oil, his expensive style of dress, his ever-perpetual new gloves of the lightest tints, and his glittering ornaments! Of the clerks, some laughed at him, and called him a fop; some envied him; all stared at him. There are young men in this London world who believe that a ring displayed on their own finger is the grandest sight in life: when Mr. Vavasour appeared amongst them with *two* their admiration knew no bounds. They envied him for something else — his apparently unlimited command of money. That he was supplied with money in a reprehensible degree—reprehensible considering that he was thrown on the world without control—was undoubted.

Take him for all-in-all, he was an affable, pleasant sort of man. He made himself agreeable enough to the clerks of the house, assuming no airs over them; but the only one with whom he formed an intimacy was Martyn Ware. Martyn was essentially a gentleman, and it was in Martyn's room that a place was assigned to Mr. Vavasour: hence, perhaps, the inducing causes to the close friendship that sprung up between them.

Is the word "friendship" a fit one in such a case? Scarcely: as it seems to me. That word ought to imply an intercourse, good, thoughtful, almost holy: but the intercourse of Mr. Vavasour and Martyn Ware was rather evil than good. Until Martyn met with him, he had been of unquestionably steady conduct: one of those sons for whom a mother's heart will glow in thankfulness to God, who has kept them from the temptations of the world. Not so after the intimacy was formed. The word fast—so disagreeable a word to my ears, that I can't bear to write it—might be applied in its worst signification to the manner in which Mr. Vavasour spent his evenings, sometimes his nights; and that terribly contagious thing, example, drew Martyn into the vortex.

How he hated himself! Gambling, and money spending, and singing rooms, and supper eating, may be very delightful recreations at the moment, but they *do* leave their sting upon the conscience to those who have been trained as was Martyn Ware. They leave something else generally — debt. Debt; embarrassment; despair: and they had left all these on Martyn. If Mr. Vavasour with his large allowance could not keep out of debt—and he did not—how was it possible for Martyn Ware to do so, sharing in the same amusements?

Mrs. Ware suspected, as you have seen, that all was not as it should be; she feared that Martyn was spending more than was justifiable; more, in fact, than he had to spend. She feared the habits he might be falling into; she feared the debt. Trifling debt, it may be, that her thoughts strayed to, but yet too great for Martyn and his limited means: what would she have done had she known the reality? A hundred pounds—no, nor a good deal added to it—would not clear Martyn.

Nothing weighs down a sensitive mind like debt; and when the hourly dread of exposure is added to it, the incubus is almost greater than can be borne. With parched lips and fevered brain, Martyn Ware proceeded to the custom house; scarcely capable, as he had confessed to Vavasour, of transacting his work. Vavasour, who was good-natured in the main, had promised to help him out of his difficulties. He wrote home to his father to advance him money in excess of his allowance, and for the last three mails had been expecting the order for it. Some of it was for his own debts, but he intended honourably to keep his promise and help Martyn. Another mail was now in, and Martyn, with a sick longing, anticipated the news it had brought.

When he returned to the office, which was not until past mid-day, for he had to go to the docks, he threw his fevered eyes around the room, but Vavasour was not in it. Mr. Mann had gone to his dinner, and the junior clerk, Jones, who had now come, but looked pale and ill, was alone. "Is Vavasour out?" asked Martyn.

"He is gone," replied Jones.

"Gone!" repeated Martyn, not understanding. "Gone already?"

"Gone for good, I mean," said the junior clerk. "He has left: but I suppose he'll come to see us again before sailing. A letter came in for him by the mail, and another to the governor. I don't quite know about it, but Preston thinks Vavasour has been dipping in deep, and his father has stopped the supplies. The upshot is, that Vavasour has peremptory orders to go home by the first packet, and the governor had him up in his room, and gave him a precious good talking to, and then told him he might be off and see to his preparations.

Martyn wondered whether he was in a dream. The words "his father has stopped the supplies," fell upon him with a cruel shock, causing his brain to reel. His heart pulses stopped, only to bound on with a rush; his sight partially left him. Young Jones held out a paper.

"Mr. Mann told me to give you this if you came in before he did. You'll see what it is. He said you had better go at once to your dinner, and then come back and go over the accounts it refers to. They must be sent off by the evening's post."

What Martyn answered he never knew; something to the effect that he did not want dinner. He took the paper, and sat down in his place and put it before him on the desk, and cast his eyes upon it. All mechanically; mechanically as a machine works: utterly incapable was he just then of seeing or hearing anything. Young Jones was scratching away busily with a pen and did not observe him.

"When does Vavasour sail?" asked Martyn, when the silence had lasted some five minutes.

"Well, the mail's in before its time, and the other does not go out for three days. The governor told him if he chose he might get away by that one. Oh, Ware—I forgot to tell you! Mr. Aukland's come."

"Ah," said Martyn, with indifference. "He was expected last time, somebody said."

"He is up-stairs now with the governor. I have not seen him. Preston says he———"

The clerk dropped his words. Coming down the stairs then, nay at the very door of their room through which they must pass for egress, were Mr. Aukland and Mr. Hill, who in the house was irreverently styled "the governor." The junior partner had arrived in town that morning from Southampton, having travelled from Jamaica by the packet which had brought the mails. It was the first visit he had made to it since his connection with the house: a report was afloat in it that he would remain for good, partially superseding Mr. Hill, who was growing old and rich, and that another partner would be taken in to reside in Jamaica.

Young Jones lifted his eyes with some curiosity. Martyn would have done the same but for the awful news just told to him, touching Vavasour. Mr. Hill came in first, a bald-headed man, very fat. Mr. Aukland next; a tall, thin, gentlemanly man of seven or eight and thirty, with dark eyes and a pleasant look. Mr. Hill halted when he reached the room, and began explaining to his partner the peculiar duties connected with it.

"Where's Mr. Mann?" he asked.

"Gone to dinner, sir," said young Jones.

"Oh—ay. What accounts are those, Mr. Ware?"

As Mr. Hill put the question he approached Martyn. The stranger followed him, and they stood close to the desk. "They are Mauresby's, sir," was Martyn's answer—and he thought himself lucky to be collected enough to answer it.

"Mauresby's? They ought to have been sent off yesterday. How was it they were not?"

Had it been to save Martyn's life, he could not have told why. A dim recollection arose to him that some particular cause hindered it, but memory seemed to fail him. The swinging open of the door saved him an answer. It was the postman who entered. He walked straight up to Martyn's desk and laid down a letter. Mr. Hill had stretched out his hand for it, but the man spoke out its address aloud:

"Mr. Martyn Ware."

More reeling of the brain for Martyn; more heart-sickness. He thrust it into his pocket, trying to conceal his whitened countenance from the notice of his master. Too well he guessed what were the contents

—a peremptory demand for money, which he had not to give.

Mr. Hill suspected nothing—saw nothing: he went out with his partner, and Martyn contrived to drag through the day and its duties. The moment he was released he tore up to Westminster in a hansom cab to Vavasour's lodgings.

It was all too true. Vavasour, in his good-nature, had waited in for Martyn, who he knew would be sure to come. But he could not disguise the facts, however he might wish to soften them. No money had come for him. Mr. Aukland, a friend of his father's, had arrived armed with credentials to see Vavasour off without delay, to see his debts paid: but not a penny-piece, save for unavoidable personal expenses, was he to give Vavasour. Old Mr. Vavasour had grown frightened and cautious.

"If some one has not been writing a confounded long yarn to him about me, I'm not here!" exclaimed young Vavasour. "My asking him for a paltry three hundred extra, never could have brought forth this row. Besides, I put it upon back German expenses."

"What am I to do?" gasped Martyn, sinking in a chair.

"Do? Well, the first thing is to come along with me and have a rattling good dinner. I have had nothing all day. I shan't dislike the change for home,

Ware. I have been getting tired lately of this fast London."

How sick, how tired of it Martyn had long been, he alone could tell.

"Oh, if I were but clear of it—if I were but emancipated from this horror!" had been his inward cry, day and night. Once released, not even Vavasour could have dragged him into the vortex again. But release, it seemed, was not to come, and Vavasour's light tone drove him nearly mad.

"Don't, Vavasour, for Heaven's sake! Have you no pity for me? The ruin is at hand, and I can't escape. I'd rather throw myself into the nearest pond than live to face it."

"Ware, look here!" answered Vavasour, with more impulsive feeling than he had been ever known to speak. "We are both in the same hole, and perhaps you'd never have got into it but for me. I am being helped out of it, and I swear that you shall be. The return mail that goes out of Jamaica first, after my landing in it, shall bring you the money. You may trust me, old fellow, for I swear it."

And Martyn, believing in the good faith of Vavasour, did trust him.

CHAPTER II.

The Fall.

It was a fiery temptation. It was a temptation that I trust you, my readers, will never be exposed to, in conjunction with its exciting cause, the grievous *need* of yielding; and Martyn Ware, honourable though he was by nature, honestly as he had been reared, succumbed to it.

The fraud seemed so easy, and the difficulty he was in so great! Nearly a month after Vavasour sailed, that difficulty reached its climax, and the unhappy young man knew that, ere the morrow's sun should have run its course, all would be known. To be arrested for the debt was inevitable; he could not *hide* himself as some can; he must be at his post whether or no, and the sheriff's officer could choose his own hour for taking him, all leisurely and comfortably. To fall into this disgrace; to forfeit his place in the house of Hill and Aukland—for that would be the inevitable result; to prove to his good and dearly-loved mother what a worthless, deceitful scoundrel he had been— the thought of all this nearly turned the brain of Martyn Ware.

Oh, if the good ship, then bearing the help to him which Vavasour had promised, could but skim, swift as a bird, over the waters! He reposed the blindest trust in the promised help of Vavasour; he never for a moment would allow himself to think that it could fail him; or, if the thought did dart across him, he sprang up from it and plunged into some vortex of daily business, escaping as it were from himself, for it was a contingency too frightful to think of.

Oh, if the fair ship could but make an impossible voyage and come in before her time! A week yet; two weeks yet—how did he know?—ere she could be in and bring to him salvation. In vain he tossed on his uneasy bed at night; in vain he flung himself from it, praying that some miracle might save him. The ship *could not* come in before she was due, and those relentless creditors were merciless. Only a week— two weeks it might be—to wait, and all would be smooth, and he not sacrificed! If he could but run away and hide himself in some cavern for the intervening time; if he could but drop into a prolonged sleep, as the people do in the magic tales, and wake up at the moment that the sure ship was touching land, he need not be sacrificed! But he could not; he could not! He had to deal with the hard realities of every-day life, not with imaginative fiction.

Let us give Martyn Ware his due? He dreaded the shock to his mother far more than the consequences to himself. He loved and reverenced his mother as I believe only those children *can* love and reverence her who have been brought up arightly. From his earliest years she had striven to lead him to his duty; earnestly, gently, untiringly, had she shown how God loved him, and how he might live so as to deserve this love; she had made the good path to him a pleasant path. My friends, rely upon it, it is only such mothers as these, who are loved by their children with a fond love: who are reverenced by them more than anything else on earth ever can be reverenced.

Yes, it was the thought of his mother that made the worst trouble to Martyn Ware. If he could but keep the knowledge from her! if he could but stave over this short week or two, and get the money, and relieve himself from his embarrassments, she would never know what a vile, ungrateful cast-away he had been. From henceforth he should return to good ways, to sober evenings, to rational pleasures; and it was no shallow or transient resolve, this, but the firm, fixed purpose of Martyn's mind. He had had enough of folly and sin; he had had enough of deceit; but to leap over the intervening weeks, or to soften the hearts of those who had his fate in their hands, was alike impossible.

It was at this critical juncture that the temptation came. Its precise details I would rather not relate, and you will probably deem the reserve an expedient one; it is sufficient to say that a large sum of money, 92*l.*, belonging to the firm, fell into Martyn Ware's hands. It was encompassed about with all the apparent immunity from danger that these temptations often are encompassed with. The circumstances under which it was paid in were peculiar; the circumstances altogether attending it were unusual; and it seemed all but an impossibility that discovery could supervene before Martyn had the opportunity of replacing it by the arrival of the mail. For one thing, Mr. Hill was absent. He was taking a holiday; and until his return, which would not be until after the coming in of the mail,—unless the mail foundered at sea,—there would be really little chance of discovery. Any one else would have said so as well as Martyn.

And so—and so—Martyn Ware yielded to the temptation.

But do you think it brought him the relief he sought? Do you think such yielded-to temptations *ever* bring relief? Ah, no. From the very hour of his taking the money, a horrible fear, like unto nothing he had in his life experienced, seized hold of him. By night and by day a yawning gulf seemed before him, he on its very brink; ready to fall into it; to be annihilated for ever. He almost wished he *could* be annihilated for ever, as a less terrible fate than this living agony.

What had been the pains and perils he had escaped from, compared to those that he had invoked now? The very worst position that *debt* could have placed him in, was as nothing, as *nothing*, by the side of the consequences that might be drawn on his head by *crime*. With the proceeds of the order (for in point of fact it was not actual money he took, but an order for it: the same thing when cashed) he set himself free from debt; at least, from pressing debt; but he had increased his peril, his perplexity, his remorse, a thousand-fold. Martyn Ware had not been constituted by nature for the commission of crime: he was endowed with a strict love of justice, with lively conscientiousness; and such, should they unhappily succumb, cannot *live* under the burden it entails upon them. How willingly, oh how willingly would he have undone his work, and gone back to the lighter embarrassment from which he had been so eager to escape! To be taken by a sheriff's officer, and civilly marshalled to one of the debtors' houses, would have been enough for his mother to bear; but to be taken by a different sort of official and confined without hope or sympathy within the strong walls of a criminal prison——!

A groan escaped him as the vision rose before his mind; rose, as it seemed, with the prevision of fatality. He could not undo his work; the money was spent, and there were no possible means of recalling it. The wonder to him now was, *how* he ever could have been so mad and wicked as to have used it. Wicked he knew he had been, but he did believe that he must have been mad, or he never would have done it. Worse than all, with the taking of the money his confident hope changed, and he began to doubt the faith of Vavasour as surely as he had believed in it. He tried to hope still; he tried to do battle with his poor sinking heart; and thus he lived on as he best could until the West Indian mail came in.

It came in, that packet; and you scarcely need to be told, I should think, that it did *not* bring the relief expected; for this kind of dependence, of expectation, proves so almost invariably a failure, that it seems superfluous to record it in this additional instance. The mail brought a letter from Vavasour, but it brought no money. He had found it difficult to appease his father, he wrote, who accused him of having been doing what he could to "go to the bad," and he found it impossible to draw money from him yet. He would try hard to get it by the departure of the next packet, and he hoped Ware would continue to "rub on" until then. Of one thing he might rest assured: that the money *should* come to him earlier or later, for he would be faithful to his promise.

Martyn Ware sat at his desk, staring at the letter. He tried to read it again deliberately, after his first rapid glance at it, but he could not: the characters were dancing before his eyes, sparkling and gleaming as if they were living fire. Discovery was inevitable: long before the next mail was in (but he had no hope now in *that*), Mr. Hill would be home, and he would find it out the first day. As he sat thus, his brain throbbing, his pulses beating, his spirit ebbing with a sick faintness, Mr. Aukland passed through the room on his way up stairs, and turned his head to Martyn.

"I want you, Mr. Ware."

He crushed the letter in his hand, and followed that gentleman to his room. Mr. Aukland, his hat off, was already seated at his desk. The clerks scarcely knew whether they liked Mr. Aukland or not. He was kindly and genial in his manner to them, but so imperative in matters of business, so entirely a man of business himself, and so uncompromising in exacting that their duties should be performed, to the letter, that quite a revolution had taken place in the house. Mr. Hill, easy and lenient, rather addicted to dropping asleep at his desk after his early city dinner, had allowed things to go very much as they pleased, and the clerks to have an easy life of it; but all that was changed, now that Mr. Aukland reigned.

Mr. Aukland bent his dark eyes on Martyn. "I hear that Lovibond's account has been received and cashed, Mr. Ware. It was paid, I find, to you, but I don't see it entered."

Every drop of blood forsook Martyn's face. His heart stopped still, and then leaped onwards with a bound of agony. This was the money he had received and kept. He strove to answer, any excuse that came uppermost, something to the effect that he "would look," "would see about it;" but the words came forth in gasps from his trembling and ashy lips. It was utterly impossible but that Mr. Aukland should detect that something was wrong.

What questions he would have asked, it was impossible to say, but Martyn was spared for the moment. One of the clerks came up showing in a stranger, and Mr. Aukland nodded to Martyn to go down.

He did not know how he got down. He did not know whether his head was on his shoulders or whether it was off; it seemed not to be himself, but somebody else—as we may have experienced ourselves in illness, in the attack of a fever-dream. He heard Mr. Mann address him as he was about to sit down to his desk, telling him there were those samples of sugar to be got from the docks, and just time enough left to do it before the gates closed, if he made haste. And Martyn put on his hat and went out.

As he walked along amidst London's bustle, steering his course mechanically, he put his hand into his pocket for the letter: he had but superficially read it before; had mastered only its broad facts, not its details. But the letter was not there.

He wondered where he had dropped it. He looked back along the narrow and crowded pavement, but could see no sign of it, and a dread came over him that he had dropped it in the office. Dread? Why, if he had; if the letter had been read by Mr. Aukland and every clerk in the place, it could not tell them half as much as must be known in a few hours' time from one end of it to the other.

He got home from the docks just before the office closed. The resident porter stood at the door, and Martyn asked him if he had seen or picked up a West Indian letter; he had lost one: but the man said he had not seen any.

"Is Mr. Aukland gone yet?" asked Martyn, as he walked in, putting the question as indifferently as he could.

"Yes, sir."

Mr. Mann was yet at his desk, and he spoke for some little time with Martyn about business matters, quite in his usual tone. It was evident that he had not seen the letter. Martyn looked about for it, but could find no trace of it, and he came to the conclusion that it had been lost in the street. What mattered it where? Ere the setting of to-morrow's sun, the whole world would know the guilty fool he had been.

He went home, and that night all was told to Helen. Believing himself alone, heavy groans had burst from him, which his mother happened to overhear. She stole to him; she sat down by him; she confessed what grievous fears had long been upon her; she prayed him to have love and confidence in her, his mother: and with her arms entwined about his neck, and his cheek drawn against hers, Martyn told her all.

What a night it was for her! She retired to rest as usual, not to excite observation; but how she lay through it, how she *bore* to lie through it, her unconscious husband sleeping by her side, none can tell. Her son, whom she had been striving to train for heaven; her darling son, of fair report in the sight of the world, to have ended thus! How fully she trusted him, how truly she knew that she might trust him, when he said that, could this pitfall have been escaped from, he would, with God's help, never fall into another!

There appeared to be one little loophole of a chance—that Mr. Aukland would listen to her prayer for mercy, and forgive him. *Her* prayer; Helen's: who else was there to offer one up? Much as she should dislike the office, sensitively as she should shrink from it, she must, nevertheless, go through it. She must present herself before that great and dreaded man (great as her son's master, dreaded as his injured accuser), and beseech him to spare that erring son— to conceal his offence in consideration of his strong temptation, his bitter repentance, his inexperienced youth—not to blight his prospects at the very threshold of life. She would beseech it in mercy to herself; she would pray to be allowed to repay the money: and though she had it not, she would find it, even if she had to sell her clothes.

With this fixed resolution in her mind, Helen rose. She went to Martyn's room and told him. It would be productive of no good, he despairingly said; but she persisted in trying. It was necessary that she should be at the office in time to catch Mr. Aukland on his arrival, and she had to invent some plausible excuse of shopping, of wishing to get the shopping over before the heat of the day came on, for going up to town in the omnibus at the same time as her husband. Mr. Ware talked half the way up to town about Martyn's unusual dilatoriness that morning in not being ready for the omnibus. If he had but known that the dilatoriness was but assumed; that he dared not go!

Mr. Aukland was already there. With the West India mail in the previous day, and its load of business for them, he was not a man to be tardy at his post. A whole heap of papers, of letters, were before him on his desk, when a card and a message—that the lady asked to see him upon urgent business—were carried to him. He glanced at the former: "Mrs. Edward Ware."

"Desire the lady to walk up," he said in answer.

She came up the stairs. She closed the door, and threw back her veil, and disclosed a face white with an agitation it was utterly beyond her to suppress. Mr. Aukland had risen to receive her, and he courteously, with every manifestation of respect, handed her a chair.

But she was too agitated to avail herself of it. In fact it may be questioned if she so much as saw the movement in her agony of emotion, in the sick feeling of suspense that threatened to overwhelm her. She stood up and grasped the railings of the desk with one hand, and entered upon her prayer.

With a rapidity of emotion that gave him no chance of interrupting, with a wailing tone that betrayed too well the pent-up anguish, she told her tale She told what she had come for—to beseech pardon for one who was a guilty sinner, but dear to her.

"It is the turning point in his life, sir; the crisis of the years that have passed, of those that are to come," she breathed, hardly conscious in her trembling vehemence what she did say. "Upon your mercy depends his well-being here; perhaps that hereafter. I *know* that he will never transgress again, and if you will but allow me to refund the money privately to you, it—it—"

She could not go on: she broke down with a sound between a sob and a shriek. Mr. Aukland, still with every token of respect, took her hands in his; he smiled at her with his pleasant lips, with his friendly eyes.

"Do let me speak, Mrs. Ware. Can you suppose that *I* should betray *your* son? Don't you know me?"

Know him? She looked up at him in surprise. She knew him by hearsay; she had never seen him. What did he mean? Her silence spoke her bewilderment, and Mr. Aukland smiled.

"Have you forgotten Bob Rutt? I am he. Look at me, and see if you do not trace my old features. *Yours* have not altered."

Bob Rutt! Robert Aukland, that influential West India merchant, the poor Bob Rutt of the days gone by? It was even so: and she knew, she felt, that Martyn's peril was over In her revulsion of feeling she sank down on the chair and burst into loud sobbing tears.

At that moment there came a knock at the room door. Mr. Aukland drew it open about an inch. Some one wanted him on business, and young Jones had come up to say so.

"I am engaged," was Mr. Aukland's short answer, delivered in so sharp, so imperative a tone, that Mr. Jones shot down the stairs again in consternation. But the interruption did more towards recalling Mrs. Ware to herself than anything else could have done.

"I did not even know that your name was Aukland," she said, wiping her pale face. "Or—yes, I suppose I did know it in the old days, but I had completely forgotten it: you were so universally called Rutt. Certainly I never once thought to connect you with Mr. Aukland of this house. I can hardly believe it now. I see the likeness, I recognise your face, and yet—it appears incredible."

"I did not stay long in Washington," he observed. "About a year and a half, I think; and then an opening was found for me in Jamaica, in this firm, which at that time—as perhaps you may know—was Sewell and Hill. I had been in it fifteen years, when Mr. Sewell died, and I then succeeded to a share in it. On the whole I have been very prosperous, Mrs. Ware."

"Oh yes," sobbed Helen. "And Mrs. Rutt? Is she alive?"

"She died six months ago," he answered, glancing involuntarily at the crape on his hat. "I was able to make her a good home in Jamaica: happier, I believe, than she had ever enjoyed before. I wrote once to Wexmoor for news of you: but did not obtain it. The answer received was, that Mr. Martyn was dead, and his family had dispersed. The very first day of my arrival here I recognised your son; the name 'Martyn Ware' attracted my attention to him, and I traced in his features the strongest possible resemblance to yours. Yours," he significantly added, "had not faded from my recollection."

"And—you—will not refuse to save him?" she said, in a timid whisper.

"Refuse to save him! Him! Mrs. Ware, do you forget all I owe to you?" he rejoined, his own tones trembling with the earnestness of their emotion. "But for the sacrifice you made for me, I might be a poor working man now, instead of what I am: and my dear mother, wanting a home, might have sunk into the grave before her time. Were the whole of my savings —and I have saved something—necessary to extricate Martyn Ware, he should have them."

He spoke with quiet deliberation. Helen, wondering whether mercy so great had ever been shown to anybody before, asked a few questions.

"I can understand how it was," he said, "that he was seduced into the trouble and extravagance by young Vavasour. It came to my knowledge yesterday that Martyn had received this order for money and obtained the cash upon it—not obtained the cash in the regular dealings of the house, but in an irregular way. It awoke my suspicion instantly. I called him into this room, intending to get the truth from him, but before I had barely put a question we were interrupted, and he went down. In going out of the room he dropped a crumpled piece of paper, which I found to be a letter just received from Vavasour. It told me all. That with the remittances this letter was to have brought—and did not—he meant to replace the ninety-two pounds taken. Mrs. Ware," he continued, smiling at her, "I made it all right myself yesterday afternoon—at the bankers' and in the books here. It would not have been expedient for Mr. Hill to come home and find it out—and he is coming back to-day."

"How shall I ever thank you!" she murmured. "How can I ever repay you?"

"Nay—I have been saying that to myself this many a year—'How can I ever repay Miss Helen Martyn?' My mother has echoed it in my hearing many a time."

"You will—do you intend to allow him to come back here?" she questioned with great hesitation through her tears.

"Indeed yes. Send him up as soon as you get back. I have no fear of such a thing as this being repeated: it will serve as a lesson to him for life. And I will try and push Martyn on in the world, as your benevolence, my dear lady, was the means of pushing me. I should have come down to your house to see you ere this, but since my landing I have had so much to do, Mr. Hill being away. You will allow me to do so?"

Allow him to come to see her! Helen's tears fell faster, and she held his hands in her grateful clasp. The great Robert Aukland, poor Bob Rutt of the former days, who had only presumed to address her as "Miss" Helen.

"I shall tell my husband now, and he will welcome

and thank you, Mr. Aukland. I had not dared to tell him before; he would have been so implacable with Martyn. He has a perfect abhorrence of anything that savours of dishonesty: and if he had known — that Martyn——May Heaven bless you, Mr. Aukland, always and always!"

Mrs. Ware returned home. It happened that she took the same omnibus which had brought her. The same conductor stood on the foot-board; the self-same advertisements, pasted up inside, stared her in the face. With what a sick sensation of despair had her eyes rested on those advertisements in going! But now, in her changed feeling, it almost seemed as though she had been suddenly lifted into Paradise.

Martyn was not to be found when she got home. Nobody knew where he was. Amy had a faint recollection of having heard the front door slam about an hour before, and she supposed he must have gone out. Helen waited: waited with restless, joyous impatience for his return.

But he did not come in. Hour after hour passed away, afternoon after morning. Helen grew sick and uneasy with an undefined dread. Still he did not come in, and the day drew to its close. She stood at the window, stealthily watching, and could have counted the beating of her own heart. Suppose — in his despair — he —

A wild rush of terror overpowered her and drove

away all consecutive thought. The inert suspense grew unbearable, and she threw on a bonnet and shawl and went out in the dusky night, some faint idea upon her of looking for Martyn, however hopeless the search appeared to be.

But it did not prove hopeless. She had bent her steps instinctively to the most lonely walk near their residence, one running alongside the canal: and there, as she came in sight of it, she saw Martyn looking down at the water. His shoes were dusty, as if he had spent the day in walking.

Was he about to do an ill deed?—one that could never be redeemed? Let us give him the benefit of the doubt. Did his mother fear it? Who can say? She gave a great cry as she sprang to him, and, clasping her arms about his neck, sobbed aloud.

"Don't, mother; don't! Your trouble is the worst of all. I can bear anything better than that."

"Martyn! Martyn! They are tears of joy, not of grief. I—I—was fearing I should never find you," she sobbed. "Martyn, I have seen Mr. Aukland. He is the Bob Rutt of my girlhood's days, a dear friend from henceforth. He will be your friend through life and will push you on. He paid the money into the bank yesterday and made it all right in the office. He knew you, and never meant to let it fall upon you. Oh Martyn, my darling, it is true! it is true!"

Martyn grasped hold of a post near him, as if for

support: he felt sick with suspense lest it should *not* be true. But not long could he doubt the joy that shone in the wet eyes of his mother: and a yearning cry went up to heaven: to that heaven which had surely intervened to save him. "Lord, be with me from henceforth! keep me, keep me from temptation!"

And Helen knew that her boy was her own once more. She linked her arm within his and they walked on in silence towards home, the home that would be again a happy one, as it had been before the ill-omened shadow of Vavasour fell on Martyn's path. Not a word was spoken. Helen's thoughts were buried in the past, and her face was turned upwards to the faint crimson light which yet lingered in the western sky. Very, very present to her in that moment were the ways of God and His wonderful dealings. That little sacrifice which she had made so many, many years ago; the poor ten-pound note she had given away from her necessities, her superfluities if you will, had brought forth *this*. Long and long had the recompense been smouldering—a recompense for which she had never looked or thought of looking—and now it had come, and come a thousand-fold.

Never had that beautiful promise, which you have all read as often perhaps as Helen Ware, been more directly exemplified: never had it come home with such force to her heart: "Cast thy bread upon the waters: for thou shalt find it after many days."

THE END.

THE

NIGHT-WALK OVER THE MILL STREAM.

THE NIGHT-WALK OVER THE MILL STREAM.

CHAPTER I.

The Lady Katherine's Wish.

THE red light of the setting sun shone full on the windows of a farm-house, standing amidst its own lands; shone into a chamber which faced the west. On the bed lay the mistress of the house, suffering from some sudden attack, which caused intense inward agony.

A woman-servant, who had been standing at the window, turned round, her face brightening with satisfaction. "There, there, don't take on so, missis! He is coming in at the gate. It will be all right now."

The moans from the bed ceased; but, nevertheless, a more troubled expression arose to the face, lying there. It was as though the bodily pain had given place to mental.

The servant left the room. A couple of minutes, and she returned, showing in a gentleman. A tall, fine, gentlemanly man of thirty years, with a pleasing countenance. His large, earnest grey eyes were bent with sympathy on the bed, as he advanced to it, and took the patient's hand.

"Nancy says you have been ill these several days past, Mrs. Key," he said. "Why did you not send for me before?"

"I was ashamed to send for you now," she murmured. "I feel ashamed to see you, Mr. Olliver. Indeed it has not been our fault. We would have found the money to pay you if it had been in our power."

His lips parted with a sweet smile, reassuring in its brightness. Her husband, who was a hard-working farmer, had fallen into misfortunes; had been obliged to wipe off his debts with a sponge. A heavy account, long due to Mr. Olliver for medicine and attendance, had been thus cancelled. They were not willing debtors, and Mrs. Key felt it keenly; felt, as she had thus expressed it, ashamed to see him once more at her bedside.

"Were I never paid in any coin but money," he said in a gentle tone, "I should deem myself poorly remunerated. The pleasure of alleviating suffering, looking for no recompense, is one of the green spots in the desert of a doctor's life. And now tell me what is the matter," he continued, drawing a chair to the bedside. "It is the old enemy in the side, I presume?"

"Yes; but worse than I have ever experienced it.

I never had an attack such as this. As Nancy has told you, I have been suffering for some days past; but this morning the pain grew into agony. I thought I should have died with it."

"You have been fretting lately, I fear," observed Mr. Olliver.

"True," she answered. "How am I to help it?"

How, indeed! The surgeon knew, as well as she did, that for the suffering brought on by trouble there is no help. Half the world have a daily fight with it. He prescribed his remedies, said he would send some medicine immediately, and sat chatting soothingly for a few minutes. None, save the sick, know the comfort a sympathizing doctor brings to the bedside. By the time he rose to go, Mrs. Key felt better.

"I shall not be able to see you to-morrow, or for a week or ten days subsequent to it. You know why," he added, a smile illumining his features. "But you will receive every attention from Mr. Hill. And I will come up again this evening."

"No, sir, not again. Do not take the trouble to come again. I could not think of it. I shall do well now."

"We will see," he answered, leaving it an open question, as he shook her hand to depart.

The sun had sunk beneath the horizon when he quitted the house, but clouds of purple and crimson lingered in the sky. It was a fine, clear evening at the end of October; clearer and finer than they had had it latterly. Before him at a short distance lay the village of Hilton-Coombe, and Mr. Olliver hesitated which way he should return to it. By the roadway, bearing to the right, it would take him about twenty minutes to get to his own residence in it; if he cut across the fields opposite to him, and crossed the mill stream, he might gain it in little more than ten. But it was the crossing of this mill stream which caused him to hesitate, for the floods had been out lately—as the phraseology ran in the neighbourhood—and the path might be dangerous.

Being pressed for time, he turned to it. A stream, narrow in that part, and only to be crossed by an unprotected wooden bridge. It was little more, in fact, than a plank, and two persons could not stand abreast on it. Mr. Olliver found the water very high, nearly reaching to it; but he had a steady eye and step, and traversed it in safety. Immediately before him, at only a field's distance, was the church of Hilton-Coombe, its large graveyard surrounding it, and its spire stretching up against the sky. As he gazed at it, a soft colour flushed his face, akin to that in the crimson sky; a quicker motion arose in his beating heart; for in that church on the morrow, the last day of October, he would receive the hand of one who was dearer to him than his own life. It would be his wedding-day.

The field path took him direct to the little gate of the churchyard. Passing through it, he crossed the path which wound round by the church door, and emerged on the high road. The village lay on his right, and he turned to it. It was a large village, containing a great many gentlemen's houses, and but a small proportion of poor.

The first house he came to was the rectory. It was not close to the church; one side of the churchyard, and a field in which the rector kept his cows, intervened. A low house it was, old-fashioned and commodious, built of greystone, lying back from the road, and half-hidden from the gaze of passers-by, by the trees crowding its garden. Mr. Olliver cast an eager glance to it in spite of the trees: it might be, that he should catch a glimpse of a beloved face at one of its windows, many of which were bright with firelight. The only daughter of that rectory, Annis Dudley, was she who would become on the morrow Annis Olliver.

He did not see her, and he walked on with a fleet foot. Under an engagement to dine there that evening, he was hastening home first to despatch medicines to Mrs. Key, and to make some slight alteration in his dress. A carriage passed him and drew up to the rectory gate. He turned and looked after it, for he had no doubt it contained Miss Bellassys.

It did contain Miss Bellassys, a little lady with

grey hair, who walked lame as she traversed the winding path through the garden to the rectory door. A fair girl came hastening into the hall to meet her; one with a gentle face and a soft dark eye. She wore a shaded silk dress of a delicate colour, quiet and ladylike as she was.

"Can this be Annis?" asked the visitor. "My dear child, you have grown into a woman!"

Annis blushed and smiled. "It is six years since you saw me, Aunt Ruth, and I am twenty-one."

"Ay, time flies. I wish I could come to you less rarely, but you know how I am chained to home. I put off coming now until the last moment. My dear Katherine!"

The servant had thrown open the door of a drawing-room on the right of the hall, and the last words were addressed to a lady who was sitting by its fire. She was middle-aged now, but must have been handsome in her day; she would have been more so now, but for the coldness of her blue eyes, and the haughty cast of her aquiline features. She wore a rich dress of blue watered silk, and gold ornaments.

"Mamma, it is Aunt Ruth."

The two ladies met and clasped hands. They were first cousins. The rector's wife was the first to speak. "Never to come to us until this evening, Ruth! You might almost as well not have come at all. Jacob, where is your master?"

The servant, who had been closing the door, opened it again. "I think he is in his room, my lady."

"Inform him that Miss Bellassys is here."

But before Jacob could depart, he found himself put aside by his master, the Reverend William Dudley, a man of simple manners, and a calm, good face. A stranger need not have been told that he and Annis were father and daughter; the likeness between them would have proclaimed it.

"And so you are going to lose Annis!" exclaimed Miss Bellassys, sadness mingling with her tone.

A strangely frigid expression settled on the face of Lady Katherine Dudley. She made no rejoinder; it appeared that she would not make one.

"Not quite to lose her," said the rector cheerfully, a happy light shining in his soft dark eyes, so like his daughter's. "It might have been worse, Ruth; she goes away from us but a stone's-throw."

"But is it a desirable connexion for Annis?" doubtingly resumed Miss Bellassys.

"Wait until you see him," said Mr. Dudley. But the Lady Katherine formed her lips into a "No," and lifted her head with a defiant gesture.

For the approaching union with Mr. Olliver did not give pleasure to Lady Katherine Dudley. She had married the rector of Hilton-Coombe in early life, when she was plain Miss Bellassys, plain in station, poor in pocket, and she had deemed it an excellent settlement. But through the death of several intervening heirs, her father succeeded to an earldom and she to a title, and then she began to find the quiet rectory of Hilton-Coombe, with its five hundred a year, all told, somewhat unsuited to her degree. For herself, she could not change it; no money had accrued to her with her title; she must continue to live the quiet life, and not escape from it, and she was content enough to do so, but she began to cherish dreams of ambition for her only child. Annis should marry well; should soar into the rank to which, as her daughter, she was entitled; should become noble and wealthy. Great dreams! cherished by many a mother, and by many found to be vain ones: as they were so found by Lady Katherine Dudley. For Annis marred the whole scheme by falling in love with the plain village surgeon, Thomas Olliver.

It may be a question, though, whether Mr. Olliver did not fall first in love with her. However it may have been, the mischief was done. The rector viewed it favourably. He knew the man's worth. He knew that his practice was a lucrative one; that he could keep Annis just as comfortably as she had been kept; and dreams of greatness for her did not trouble him. He gave his consent heartily to the marriage. Lady Katherine did not refuse hers, but she made it into a grievance, and very much enjoyed dilating upon it.

She had been given all her life to make things into grievances and dilate upon them; so much so, that the effect upon the rector's mind had worn away. To use a familiar phrase, her grumblings went in at one ear and out at the other; but she sometimes said things in her hasty spirit for which even she would be sorry afterwards. She despised Annis's want of taste almost as much as she deplored it. That dashing young officer of dragoons, and her relative, the Honourable Captain Bellassys, had come on a visit to Hilton-Coombe rectory, and before he left it he laid himself and his two thousand a year patrimony at the feet of Annis. Annis only shook her head at him: he was not Thomas Olliver. Little wonder that my lady was put out by a taste so plebeian!

"Child!" said Miss Bellassys, as she stood in the bedroom to which she had been shown, and clasped the hands of Annis in hers, "do you love him, this Thomas Olliver?"

The hot crimson rushed to Annis's cheeks, and the tears glistened on her eyelashes. But, save a smile which hovered on her lips, there came no other answer. It was not needed.

"I see," said Miss Bellassys. "And your father says he is good,—worthy,—noble. May God bless the union!"

Mr. Olliver was in the drawing-room when they returned to it. He had but then entered, and was bending over Lady Katherine, whose hand he had taken in greeting. Lady Katherine had a pleasanter look upon her face as it was raised to him. In spite of her prejudices against his position, she liked the *man;* and could she have forgotten that outer, far-away, high-sounding place, called the great world, she might have been fully content with Thomas Olliver.

Miss Bellassys scanned him keenly. She was a reader of character in the human countenance. He turned to her with a frank smile, and her heart went bounding out to him, for Annis's sake. A good, noble face; one that could not belie itself. Had Annis been her daughter, she would have given her to him fearlessly, although all the honourables in the peerage had been arrayed against it.

The dinner was announced. The rector crossed the hall with Miss Bellassys, Mr. Olliver took Lady Katherine. Annis walked alone, and Mr. Olliver whispered something to her as they sat down, which called forth a smile. They were dining alone, but several friends were expected to drop in later in the evening. The conversation naturally fell upon the wedding and its preparations, and an allusion was made to the decorating of the church, which Miss Bellassys did not understand. She said she did not.

"Nor anybody else," cried the rector, half crossly, half lovingly, as he glanced at Annis. "Perhaps that young lady will explain it to you, Ruth."

She lifted her bright cheeks to her father. "Papa, it is not my fault. It was not my proposal that it should be done."

"Of course not," said Mr. Dudley. "It was nobody's fault, was it? The fact is, Ruth,"—turning to his guest,—"they have wormed a consent out of me to allow the church to be set off with evergreens for this grand ceremony to-morrow."

"Set off in what manner?" asked Miss Bellassys.

"Oh, you must ask them about that. They are to be strewn up the path, I believe, that my young lady's shoes, there, may not come in contact with the stones. Are you afraid of your boots, Mr. Olliver?"

"No, sir."

"The placing evergreens in the church has my *full approbation*," spoke Lady Katherine with emphasis, from her seat at the table's head. "As Annis *is* to be married, I deem it well that the attendant circumstances should be of distinctive mark: as befits her position as my daughter. The evergreens will not hurt the church, Mr. Dudley."

"My dear, I did not say they would. They can be there if you like: I conclude they will be there. I only think they will look a little foolish. Mr. Olliver I believe to be perfectly innocent in the matter; but for Annis—she no doubt considers the branches and boughs indispensable adjuncts to the binding of the ceremony."

Annis laughed, and slightly shook her head as she glanced at Mr. Dudley. In point of fact, the evergreens had been settled without her knowledge. Some young ladies of Hilton-Coombe (who would have the pleasure of walking over the evergreens themselves as bridesmaids) had suggested it to Lady Katherine, and she had caught at it.

"They are to be placed in the church this evening, Aunt Ruth," said Annis. "We are going down presently, a good many of us; and old John will be there with a truck load."

"Who is old John?" asked Miss Bellassys.

"Papa's clerk. Have you forgotten him? He will be seventy-seven next January, but is hale and hearty as ever."

"And old John is like a child with a new toy over this evergreen business," returned the rector. "He has been stripping the best shrubs in my garden this afternoon before my face. 'You'll spoil them, John,' I said to him. 'Eh, sir, what of that?' said he. 'It is for Miss Annis's wedding.' You are in his good books," added Mr. Dudley, looking at the surgeon.

Mr. Olliver laughed. "Am I, sir? I am glad to hear it. Better be in people's good books than in their bad ones."

"Pray, are you going to assist at this rush strewing?"

"Oh, papa! *rush* strewing!" interposed Annis. But

she looked at Mr. Olliver somewhat anxiously for his answer.

"I cannot," he replied to the rector. "I have to go as far as the Brook farm. Mrs. Key is very ill."

Annis glanced round at him timidly, and a shade of disappointment was perceptible in her voice as she spoke. "You will be in again this evening?"

"Of course. I have but to go to the Brook farm. By the time your party returns from the church, I daresay I shall be home again."

"How are the Keys doing now?" inquired Lady Katherine of Mr. Olliver.

"Not very great things, I fear," he replied. "I am sure it is anxiety that makes her ill. It brings on the old complaint in her side."

Barely was the cloth removed when Mr. Olliver asked if they would excuse him. He would prefer to go to Mrs. Key's at once: he might have medicine to send down after his return, he said, possibly some few other things to do at home, and the sooner he got off, the sooner he should be at liberty to come back to the rectory. Mr. Dudley rose at the same time. He wished to call on a parishioner at the other end of the village, and would walk so far with him.

They went out. Lady Katherine turned to the fire with a pettish movement. "You see what you must expect, Annis, in this marriage. A doctor cannot sit even to his meals."

"How much I like him!" warmly exclaimed Miss Bellassys. "If he cannot boast of rank, Katherine, he can boast of something better. He is a true gentleman."

"Annis! Annis!" impulsively interrupted Lady Katherine. "Do run after your papa. Ask him if he will call in at Jones's. It will save my sending, and the servants are so busy to-night."

Annis ran off as impulsively as her mother spoke. She caught them in the dark winding path, midway between the house and the gate.

"Call at Jones's?" repeated the rector, as she delivered the message. "What for?"

"To remind them to send in time, I suppose, papa," replied Annis. "I don't know what else mamma means."

"I had better ask and make sure," said he to himself. "Wait an instant for me, Mr. Olliver."

Annis did not turn to the house with her papa; she walked slowly by Mr. Olliver's side to the entrance-gate, and they stood there together. The moon was very bright, showing out the features of the landscape all clear and distinct; the tinkling of a sheep-bell, near, was heard on the quiet air. Mr. Olliver drew Annis to his side, and stood with his arm round her.

"How beautiful the night is!" she exclaimed. "So calm and peaceful."

"May it be an earnest of the peace of our future,

Annis," he earnestly said. And her heart responded, Amen.

The steps of the rector were heard leaving the house again. Mr. Olliver bent his face upon hers.

"I will say good-bye to you now, my darling."

"Not good-bye! not good-bye!" she hastily answered, some feeling, which she could not account for, then or afterwards, seeming to rise up against the words. Could it be a foreshadowing of evil? "It sounds as if you were never coming back again."

"What am I to say?" he rejoined in a laughing mood. "Borrow a phrase from our continental neighbours, and say *au revoir?*"

Annis appeared unusually serious. "Are you *obliged* to go to Mrs. Key's to-night, Thomas?"

"Not perhaps obliged; but I wish to do so. I shall soon be back again."

No, not obliged. But the very fact of his not having been paid by Mrs. Key, rendered the surgeon more anxious to give her every attention. Of a benevolent, generous nature, refined and considerate, he would rather have slighted all his rich patients put together than poor Mrs. Key. He had not been paid for his past attendance; he did not suppose he should be paid for the present; but in his creed that was no reason why he should refuse his services.

Mr. Dudley linked his arm within his, and they walked through the village together. About midway in it was situated the house of the surgeon; a handsome residence, the surgery being detached. "I must call in for one moment," said Mr. Olliver, as they came to it.

The rector entered with him. Mr. Olliver's business was to ascertain whether any message had come for him, demanding him professionally. Mr. Hill, his qualified assistant, who was in the surgery, replied that there had been none.

"I shall soon be back, then," he observed to the rector, as they continued their way towards the end of the village. There they parted; and Mr. Olliver branched off on the road leading to the Brook farm.

Meanwhile, Annis had re-entered the dining-room. And she found her mother's mood changed. When in the actual company of Mr. Olliver, whom she really liked, Lady Katherine was apt to forget her prejudices: it was as though the presence of the man imparted its own charm. But no sooner had he departed than the charm was broken, and up came the prejudices again.

It happened that Miss Bellassys had laid on the table a copy of the *Morning Post* newspaper for that day, and Lady Katherine took it up. The first paragraph her eye rested on was a glowing account of a "Marriage in high life," the young lady being a connexion of the Bellassys family. It was quite enough for Lady Katherine Dudley.

She flung the newspaper on the table as Annis

entered, and turned to her angrily: "You might have done as well had you chosen," she cried in a bitter tone.

Annis was surprised. "Dear mamma, what is the matter?" she asked, wonderingly.

"The matter! Read that."

She pushed the journal towards Annis, and the latter ran her eyes over the indicated part. Then she looked up brightly, a smile upon her face.

"I am very glad not to do as well as that, mamma. I should make a poor wife for a nobleman. Better as it is."

"Yes, better," added Miss Bellassys emphatically. "A man whose days are spent in the fulfilment of duties, in the benefiting his fellow-creatures, is more to be honoured than one who leads a useless life. You may wish now, Katherine, that Annis had married differently, but you will not wish it long. As we draw nearer to the other world, the great truth impresses itself more and more forcibly upon us, that it is not what we are in the scale of rank that will help us on the road to heaven; but what we do with the time, the talents, the opportunities bestowed upon us by God. The day will come, rely upon it, when you will have no other wish than that she had chosen Mr. Olliver."

"I wish he was dead!" was the intemperate rejoinder of Lady Katherine.

Annis glanced up with a shiver. Accustomed, though she was, to her mother's thoughtless remarks; knowing, as she did, that they meant nothing, and that Lady Katherine was generally the first to feel sorry for them, the words yet seemed to strike on her heart with a chill.

CHAPTER II.

Decorating the Church.

Merry tongues, merry laughter resounded on the night air. A gay party, most of them gleeful girls, stood in the porch of the church. The clerk, old John, had forgotten to get the keys from the rectory, and he was now gone for them. A load of evergreens in a truck rested outside, and the bright leaves of the laurel quite shone in the moonlight.

Two of the young ladies, Georgina and Mary Balme, were more impatient than the rest. Intimate at the rectory almost as Annis herself was, loving her much, this wedding was a great event to them. They might not have entered into its preparations so blithely, had they been going to lose Annis; had she chosen to marry that young dragoon officer, for instance, and thereby have abandoned Hilton-Coombe for a distant home. But she was going to remain amongst them, to be their friend as she had been, and they aided the wedding on with all their hearts.

One of them went beyond the porch to watch for the clerk's return. It was Georgina. "Annis, don't you think old John's getting beyond his work?" she asked.

"Not at all," replied Annis. "Papa was saying only to-day how strong and well he kept."

"At any rate, one would think his memory was failing. It must be very stupid of him to forget the keys."

"He may have thought that I should bring them," returned Annis. "In fact, I ought to have done so. The forgetfulness lies with me."

"Here he is," interrupted Mary Balme. "I can hear his footsteps. Now, who will do the most work?"

Old John came up, opened the doors, and went forward to light one or two of the lamps in the church. To do this, he had to get a match from near the vestry. The outer door of the edifice opened to a somewhat large vestibule—if the word may be applied to a consecrated building. It was square, and paved with stone. On the right hand, a door in the wall led to the belfry; on the left, a similar door opened to a small room, little better in fact than a passage, which, in its turn, opened to the vestry. The folding-doors opposite the entrance led at once into the church. It was an old-fashioned, low church, with high windows, and a smell of damp.

They were not long over their work. The boughs had been prepared beforehand, only small branches, fit for strewing on the floor, having been brought into the church. "I *wish* we might decorate it elaborately, as we do for Christmas," earnestly exclaimed Mary Balme.

"Mr. Dudley said he would not agree to it," returned Georgina. "I asked him."

"I know. He calls this nonsense that we are doing now. Annis, what a nice lady that is in your drawing-room!"

"It is Miss Bellassys, mamma's cousin. You have heard me talk of my Aunt Ruth?"

"Is she your aunt?"

"No. But I learned to call her Aunt Ruth when I was a little girl, and I shall never leave it off now. She is so good, so kind. Her days are spent nursing a relative, who is a confirmed invalid. Indeed, Aunt Ruth is little better than an invalid herself. She suffers from some chronic complaint, which causes her to walk lame."

"Old John, shall we put some laurustinus round your desk?"

"Better not, Miss Georgina; I should only have to take it off afore the rector saw it."

Georgina Balme laughed. They rather liked to tease old John. But he was used to them.

"I wonder if we may go up into the organ-loft and play a psalm?"

"Can't," responded John. "It's locked, and I haven't brought the key."

"Just like you, old John!" said Mary Balme. "I cannot think, for my part, why you keep the places inside the church locked up so! Are you afraid of thieves getting in?"

"There'd not be much to steal if they did get in," was old John's reply. "It's my habit to keep the places locked, Miss; it's better that they should be kept so. When I am gone, and the rector gets a new clerk in my place, he may do as he likes—the new one may; but *I* am not a-going to leave them open. I suppose I can take out the barrow now?"

As the work was finished, there was no reason why he should not take it out. Throwing into it a few stray evergreens that remained over, he wheeled it outside, and left it at the churchyard gate. Then he returned to the church, and waited their departure.

But they were in no hurry to depart; and old John got tired, and sat down on a chair in the side aisle. Full of light-hearted happiness, this night visit to the church bore charms for them from its very novelty, and they forgot old John.

"We must go," said Annis at length. "Remember we have friends with us to-night."

They turned to depart. Georgina Balme was the first to go through the green baize doors. But she turned speedily back again; she had remembered old

John. "Oh, there he is!" she said. "I thought perhaps he had gone to sleep."

Old John was putting out the lights, and when he came forth, they were standing in a cluster in the space I have called the vestibule, between the belfry and the vestry doors. One of the young ladies was proposing, amid some laughter, that they should hang a chain of evergreens from one door to the other. Of course, she spoke it only in joke, but it served to detain them again. Old John went forward, and stood with the outer door in his hand, ready to lock it as soon as they should come forth, which they speedily did in a body; and he turned the keys, and took them out of the lock.

"I will carry them home for you, John," said Annis, as they hastened down the path. "You need not come on purpose to the rectory."

"The master told me I was to stop for supper to-night, Miss Annis, when I took in the keys."

"Oh, that is all right, then," returned Annis, gladly. And they made the best of their way to the rectory, while old John threw the keys into the truck and followed them, wheeling it along.

Annis cast her glance round the drawing-room when they entered it: but she did not see Mr. Olliver. In point of fact, she had scarcely expected to see him; for, had he returned, he would be sure to have come to the church to meet her; but, nevertheless, the not seeing him called up a feeling of disappointment. Colonel Balme was talking to the rector; Mrs. Balme sat near Miss Bellassys; and Lady Katherine stood apart, reading a note which had just been delivered to her. The note contained an apology from a family who were to have joined them for the evening; very old friends; the Lawrensons. One of the daughters had been poorly all day with cold and fever, and appeared to be growing so much worse, that they did not like to quit her. A line of request was added that Mr. Olliver would call in to see her at once: they evidently took it for granted that he was at the rectory.

"I wondered what caused them to be so late," exclaimed Lady Katherine, as she turned to the room, and made known the news. "Is Mr. Olliver back?"

"Not yet," said the rector. "I thought he would have been here before this. He has not been with you, I suppose?" he added, turning to the group just arrived from the church.

No, he had not been with them.

The evening went on; went on so long without any appearance of Mr. Olliver, that Annis's heart sunk within her. It would soon be too late for him to come; the time was drawing on for their guests to depart, for the rectory to close its doors on visitors; and then she should not see him again that night! No very great disappointment, you may think, considering that on the morrow they would be joined together beyond fear of separation; but it may be that you cannot understand the feelings of one, who loves as did Annis Dudley. She supposed he had heard in some way of Miss Lawrenson's illness, had gone to see her, and was detained.

At the moment that this supposition was running through her mind, the door opened, and Mr. Lawrenson appeared at it. He was a man of good property, residing a little beyond the church. He stood looking into the room, but did not attempt to enter. The rector saw him, and went forward.

"No, thank you, Mr. Dudley; I am not fit to come in. Look at my dress. I only want Olliver. Janey gets worse and worse; we cannot think what can be the matter with her. It is too bad of Olliver not to come up. Of course we know what night it is, and can make allowances for him; but he might just come and give her a look."

"He is not here," said the rector.

"Not here! Is he out anywhere, then?"

"I am much surprised that he is not here," answered Mr. Dudley. "He went to see Mrs. Key, but that is some hours ago; I thought he would have been back long and long before this. I conclude he has been called out somewhere."

"I'll go down to his house, then. Many thanks, Lady Katherine; I can't stay. Janey? Well, we begin to think now that it is an attack of inflammation on the chest. Mrs. Lawrenson was very sorry not to come, but she could not leave her. I am looking after—"

"If you please, sir, Mr. Hill is asking to see you."

The interruption came from Jacob, a many-years' servant in the rectory. He was not accustomed to stand upon ceremony, and had bustled up to his master with the message, paying little heed to the courtesy due to his master's guests.

"Mr. Hill?" repeated the rector.

"Yes, sir. He asked for Mr. Olliver. I told him Mr. Olliver had not been here since he went out with you after dinner, and then he said he would see you. He—"

"I beg your pardon, Mr. Dudley—only one word," interposed Mr. Hill, coming forward. "Can you inform me where I shall find Mr. Olliver? I thought he was here."

"The very question; the very request I have been just making, Hill," observed Mr. Lawrenson, as he shook hands with the doctor. "I want to find Olliver on my own score."

They both looked at Mr. Dudley. "Olliver has not been back here," he said. "I parted with him just after we left the surgery," added the rector to Mr. Hill. "He went on down to the Brook Farm, and I have not seen him since."

Mr. Hill looked puzzled. "I cannot think where

he can be," he presently said. "Mr. Key is waiting at the surgery for certain medicinal remedies, which Mr. Olliver was to have sent down, and did not. Mrs. Key is worse to-night."

"Perhaps Mr. Olliver is staying there?" cried the rector.

"No; you do not understand," dissented Mr. Hill. "Mr. Olliver, when he got there to-night, found her so much worse, that he remained some time. He said—so Key tells me—that he would have remained longer, but that he wished to hasten home to send down some medicines which might prove a relief. But he never did come home. And Key, finding the things did not arrive, came up for them. I thought to be sure Mr. Olliver was here."

"He would not neglect the sending out of remedies to one in need of them, even to come here," remarked Mr. Dudley.

"Very true," answered the surgeon. "It would not be like him to do it. But what could I think! Where can he be?"

"I'm sure I don't know where he can be. It is very strange. Annis"—calling out to his daughter—"did Mr. Olliver—"

The rector's words died away. Leaning her head round the drawing-room door, was Annis, with a face so scared, so white, that it startled her father. She came forward into the hall, and stood with them.

"There's nothing to be alarmed at, child," said the clergyman, placing his hand kindly on her shoulder. "Why do you look so frightened? I was about to ask you if you know of any place where Mr. Olliver is likely to have gone?"

"No," said Annis; "no. He was going to Mrs. Key's only, and he told me he should be back very shortly."

She put her handkerchief up to her face, as if she would hide its excessive pallor. A strange dread had taken possession of her; a dread as yet vague and undefined, pointing to nothing tangible.

"He must have called in upon some other patient," remarked the rector.

"I do not think so," said Mr. Hill. "By Key's account, his wife must be dangerously sick, and the medicines which Mr. Olliver was to send were of vital importance to her. Rely upon it, he would have come straight home the first thing, and sent them, whoever else may have wanted him."

"Then what can have become of him?" cried Mr. Dudley.

"That's what I am thinking of," was the assistant-surgeon's rejoinder.

"What I am thinking of is, what are the patients to do who are wanting him?" interposed Mr. Lawrenson. A somewhat choleric man, he thought Mr. Olliver was doing a very unjustifiable thing in stopping away, wherever it might be that he was stopping. "You must come up to Janey, Hill; that's all."

"Certainly. I will attend with pleasure after I have been to Mrs. Key's," was the surgeon's reply. "I must go there first."

"But why?" asked Mr. Lawrenson, some sharpness in his tone.

"From what Key says, I gather that his wife must be in danger. I cannot tell what to prescribe, unless I see her, and I fear there's no time to be lost. There we have been in the surgery, I and Key, waiting and waiting for Mr. Olliver to come in. It is so much good time lost."

"Well, you will come up as soon as you have been there, then?" rejoined Mr. Lawrenson, feeling that he could not, with propriety, hold out for the first visit.

"Instantly. I can cut across the fields from the Brook Farm. It will not take me many minutes to get to you that way. It may be, that I shall find Mr. Olliver in the surgery now, as I go back; in which case he will no doubt attend. As I suppose you would prefer him to do."

"I don't much mind," replied Mr. Lawrenson. "Only, I hope, whichever of you it is, will be as quick as possible. I think I will walk with you as far as Olliver's."

"I will go, too," said Mr. Dudley. "The fact is,

I want to see Mr. Olliver. There are one or two little matters connected with to-morrow's arrangements which remain yet unsettled. They were left until to-night."

The conversation had attracted most of them into the hall. Colonel and Mrs. Balme and Lady Katherine stood in a sort of wonder: of wonder that any fuss should be made about so simple a matter as the absence of Mr. Olliver. The not entering when expected, must be looked for in a medical man. One thing must be said for them: they had not a sick child waiting for Mr. Olliver's attendance.

"The affair is easily explainable," remarked the Colonel, in a slighting tone, as if in reproof of the commotion. "Mr. Olliver must have met a messenger on his return from Key's, bringing him word of urgent need of his services somewhere. He will turn up presently."

This view was taken up and adopted. They appeared to forget that Mr. Hill, who might be supposed to know best, had given his decided opinion against it.

Adopted by all but Annis. The vague dread, she knew not of what, remained upon her, and the colour would not come into her face, or the light to her eye. Mr. Dudley drew her aside.

"Child! why are you looking like this?"

"Papa, I don't know," she answered, with a shiver;

"I feel frightened, but I cannot tell at what. It is so *strange* where he can be."

"Not very strange, Annis. Remember how many times Mr. Olliver has been detained out before, when we have been expecting him. Detained for hours."

"Yes, I know, papa," she said, trying to hide the trembling of her lips. "I am sorry to be so foolish, but I cannot help it."

"You little goose!" he said, bending to kiss her. "What would you have done, pray, had your mamma's wishes been followed, and we had given Mr. Olliver his *congé?*"

A half smile flitted over her lips, and the tears glistened on her eyelashes as she lifted them. Mr. Dudley laughed at her; and followed Mr. Hill and Mr. Lawrenson, who were half-way down the garden.

Mr. Olliver's house reached, they found he had not arrived. The farmer was still sitting in the surgery. They questioned him as to the precise time that Mr. Olliver had quitted his house, but he could not tell; he had not been home until afterwards.

Nothing could be done, except that Mr. Hill should proceed at once on the visit to Mrs. Key. He took with him the medicines which he thought might prove efficacious, though he could not be sure until he saw her. Mr. Lawrenson said he would walk with him; it may be, that he deemed himself surer of securing the visit to his daughter, did he keep in the surgeon's company. The rector went also; he could not bear to carry home uncertainty to Annis.

"There goes eleven!" exclaimed Mr. Key, as the church clock struck the hour, and its echoes came borne on the air in the still night. "And I left home before nine. I wonder how the wife is!"

They rang at the gate when they reached the Brook Farm, and Nancy came out with her key to unlock it. Her mistress was not worse, she said; a little better, in fact; but impatient for the medicines. Mr. Hill and the farmer hastened in; the rector and Mr. Lawrenson, declining the invitation to enter, preferred to wait outside. Mr. Dudley detained the servant to question her.

Mr. Olliver had found her mistress worse, she said; in dreadful pain. It was the old complaint in her side, but a very bad attack, and he seemed to think there was danger. He stopped at the house the best part of an hour, she thought, and put on the hot fomentations himself. They seemed to relieve her mistress a very little, but not so much as Mr. Olliver thought they ought, and he then said he would hasten home and send down some other remedies.

"And I suppose he came off towards home?" observed Mr. Lawrenson; a doubt crossing him whether the doctor might not have had some other visit to pay farther on.

"That he did," was Nancy's answer. "I came here

to lock the gate after him, sir, and I watched him away. A sharp pace he stepped out at, too. Did master say, sir, that he had not got home yet?"

"No, he has not got home," testily returned Mr. Lawrenson. "And there are patients waiting for him; half a hundred for all I know."

A pause ensued. Nancy was leaning on the gate. "Sure he can't have gone and fell into the mill stream!" she exclaimed.

"The mill stream!" repeated Mr. Dudley. "Did he go *that* way?"

"Yes, he did," said Nancy. "He crossed the road, sir, and got over the stile. I thought to myself it was a nasty way to take at night, with the waters so high as they have been, and that unsafe bridge: but I supposed he was in a hurry to get down the things for my missis."

Had any foreshadowing of evil crossed hitherto the clergyman's mind, as it had that of Annis? Perhaps not. But the dread rose up tumultuously now. He said a word to Mr. Lawrenson.

"It can't be," replied that gentleman. "It's impossible. Such a thing was never heard of."

Mr. Hill was not very long before he came out, and they crossed the road and the stile; the way taken, according to Nancy, by Mr. Olliver. Not that *they* had any intention of attempting the unsafe way. A detour to the left, before they came to the bridge, would take them to a lane which led close to Mr. Lawrenson's house. As if by common consent, however, they bore on towards the bridge. Clear and cold looked the water in the moonlight, as it coursed on towards the mill-dam. Everything around was perfectly still; and there was certainly no trace of Mr. Olliver having fallen into it. But what trace would there be, allowing that such a calamity had happened? The ground rose on the other side above this wretched bridge, and the banks were muddy.

"Pshaw!" cried Mr. Lawrenson, who was the first to speak as they were taking their survey. "An active, sure-stepping man, as Olliver is, would not be likely to lose his footing by night any more than by day. For the matter of that, the night's nearly as light as day," he added, glancing up at the bright moon.

Mr. Dudley extended his hand, and pointed to the bank on the other side. "Does it not look as though somebody had slipped there?" he said. "To my eyes —but they are not so young as they were—it seems that two feet, or two knees, had been sliding downwards."

"It looks exactly like it," said Mr. Hill, bending his face forward. "Some one evidently has slipped. I should say, in attempting to step up the bank after crossing the bridge, must have slipped backwards."

"But they'd not slip into the water; they'd slip on

to the bridge," observed Mr. Lawrenson. "There'd be no danger in that."

"True. And it is not obliged to have been Mr. Olliver. The only danger in crossing this bridge lies in its unprotected sides," added the doctor. "And I know none with a steadier eye and foot than Mr. Olliver. Who's this?"

Footsteps were approaching, and they turned to the sound. It proved to be the miller's servant-boy, Ben, who was returning to the mill from some errand on which he had been sent. He looked considerably surprised to see those gentlemen there, watching, as it seemed, the water.

"Is anything the matter?" he asked, touching his cap to Mr. Dudley.

"Not exactly, Ben," replied Mr. Dudley. "At least, we hope not. You have heard no commotion here to-night, I suppose, as if— as if— anybody had fallen into the water?"

But, in truth, the rector almost blushed when he had put the question. It seemed so improbable a fear when spoken openly; almost an absurd fear; not unlike a far-fetched incident in some wild romance. Ben, the boy, met it unromantically enough.

"Who *has* fell in?" asked he.

"The fact is, Ben, we were looking for Mr. Olliver," interposed Mr. Lawrenson, somewhat bluntly. "He came over this bridge, as is supposed, from the

Brook Farm to-night, and nobody has seen him since. But he is not likely to have fallen in."

Ben advanced to the very edge of the bank, and stood looking into the water; for what purpose, he alone knew. "Not he," cried he presently; "Dr. Olliver could cross over there with his eyes shut, he could. He goes over it often enough. Why, I saw him cross over it this afternoon with my own eyes, I did. I couldn't do it safer nor he."

There was nothing to be gained by lingering, and they turned on their road, saying good-night to Ben. Leaving the church and churchyard on the right, they gained the high road of Hilton-Coombe. There they shook hands and separated. Mr. Lawrenson and the doctor turned to the left, Mr. Dudley to the right.

A short way, and he passed the church and churchyard, the gravestones looking white and cold in the moonlight. Would that proposed ceremony take place in it on the morrow?—or *had* anything happened to him, who was to hold—it may be said—the most prominent part in it? If so—poor Annis! poor Annis!

She—Annis—came forward to meet him in the hall as he entered, eager inquiry in her eye—not on her lip: her agitation was too great. The question on Mr. Dudley's tongue had been, "Has he come in yet?" But somehow he could not put it.

"They think he must have been called suddenly to see some other patient on his return from Mrs.

Key's, Annis," said the rector, quietly. He knew not what better to say.

"Then, you have not found him?" And the words seemed to come forth with a burst—the burst of pent-up emotion.

"Not yet, child. We might find him if we knew where to look for him."

"Oh, papa!" she uttered, raising her streaming eyes to his, "perhaps he will never be found again!"

"A good thing that she can cry," thought the rector. "My dear," he said, gravely and kindly, as he laid his hand upon her head, "we are told not to anticipate evil."

"I cannot help it," she murmured; "I wish I could. I never felt as I am feeling to-night."

"It is nervousness, child; nothing else. Try and shake it off."

Their guests were gone then, and Lady Katherine and Miss Bellassys were in the drawing-room alone. They could not by any means admit the fear; they could not see cause for any fear. Lady Katherine was not of excitable mind; she was particularly unimaginative. Mr. Olliver was detained out with some patient, was all she said. Neither could Miss Bellassys view the thing in an apprehensive light. It must be remembered that they knew nothing of his having crossed the stream; in fact, Miss Bellassys, nearly a stranger to the locality, was not aware of there being any stream to cross.

"You must be tired, Ruth," said Lady Katherine. "It is past bed-time. Are the candles there, Annis?"

"Oh, mamma, we cannot go to bed yet!" exclaimed Annis, clasping her hands. "Pray sit up a little longer!"

Lady Katherine, who had a book in her hand, turning over its leaves, put it down and stared at her. "What can you possibly mean, Annis? Do you know that you are making yourself highly ridiculous?"

Annis gave no reply. She was seated at the back of the room, but they could see that her lips were twitching, and her fingers trembling on her lap.

Miss Bellassys turned to her, and spoke. "You cannot *really* be fearing that any untoward thing has happened to Mr. Olliver, Annis?"

"It is nervousness, I tell her," said Mr. Dudley. "She is feeling nervous to-night; naturally, perhaps. I suppose she cannot help it."

"But—good gracious! I never heard of such a thing!" remonstrated Lady Katherine. "Why, if anything had happened to Mr. Olliver—in the light you seem to insinuate, Annis—there could be no wedding! What would become of all the preparations?—the servants will be up half the night yet. What would become of the breakfast?"

Very pertinent questions. The breakfast and the

preparations were clearly good reasons why the bridegroom should appear. Poor Annis lifted her white face.

"But where can he be?" she could only reiterate.

"Where?" angrily rejoined Lady Katherine, "where should he be, but with his sick? I hope *now* you see the disadvantages of marrying a doctor."

Mr. Dudley rose. It cannot be denied that he was growing uneasy himself: but the feeling may have been caught from Annis. He went through the hall, out at the porch, and walked towards the gate; some idea of watching for Mr. Hill on his road home from Mr. Lawrenson's, inducing the movement. It might be a relief further to discuss the probabilities and the improbabilities with the assistant-surgeon.

He was barely in time. Mr. Hill was striding past with long steps. The rector arrested him.

"Miss Lawrenson is not very ill," cried he. "It is a violent cold on the chest, nothing more. Is Mr. Olliver back yet?"

"No, he is not," replied the rector. "Do you know, I am beginning to—"

The rector stopped. Some one had come stealing up behind him. It was Annis, unable in her restlessness to be still. "Papa, why have you come out?" she asked. And then she saw Mr. Hill standing there.

"This foolish child is fearful that something may

have happened," said the rector. "Lady Katherine argues that he can only be with his sick patients."

"There is no real fear, Miss Dudley," observed Mr. Hill to her in a kind tone. "It is strange where he can be, I do not deny it; but, depend upon it, it will turn out all right."

With a hasty farewell he walked on. Mr. Dudley remained at the gate a few minutes, and then turned slowly up the garden path, his arm round his daughter. Not a word was spoken between them. Annis felt sick with suspense; and Mr. Dudley probably deemed that any attempt to cheer her would but be a mockery.

Scarcely had Annis gained the drawing-room, and Mr. Dudley was yet in the middle of the hall; when there arose a sound as of hasty footsteps outside; and a gentle knocking—a knocking as if the knock did not want to make itself heard too much—came to the door. The rector turned and opened it. There stood Mr. Hill, and with him the miller's boy, Ben. The rector's eyes fell on the latter, and a rush of dread came bounding to his heart.

They were holding out a cane. A small cane with a silver top, which belonged to Mr. Olliver: he had carried it with him when he went forth that night. Both began to speak at once, in a subdued tone; but the words reached Annis's ears in the distance, and seemed to blister them.

There could no longer be any doubt of Mr. Olliver's fate—that he was drowned in the stream. The miller's son had picked up the cane floating on it, some hours before. It had gone floating down towards the mill just about the time that he must have attempted to cross the bridge.

"What do they say?—*what?*" uttered Lady Katherine, who caught but imperfectly the sounds of the commotion. "What is that, about Mr. Olliver?"

Annis turned to her; her livid face a sight in its rigid stillness. Now that the blow had fallen, she was unnaturally calm; but it seemed the calm of a broken heart.

"He is dead, mamma," she quietly said. "You have got your wish."

And the Lady Katherine Dudley, as she gathered-in the full sense of the words, shrieked out aloud and fell backward. For the first time in her life she had fainted away.

CHAPTER III.

Old John's Fright.

"Oh, my dear child, I did not mean it, I did not mean it! Forgive me, Annis! forgive me!"

What a night it had been! How she had got through it, Annis knew not. Not a soul in the house had been to bed. Lady Katherine had been kept in her chamber by sedatives; and now she had come forth from it to throw herself at the feet of her daughter.

Annis leaned forward and kissed her; she strove to raise her. The same unnatural calm was still in her white face, in her bearing, the same meek stillness in her quiet voice. Lady Katherine would not be raised.

"Annis, I loved him; I did indeed. It was all my folly, my temper, speaking against him. At the time I spoke it, I knew it was false, for I *did* like him."

"Yes, yes, dear mamma. *Pray* get up."

"I did not mean what I said," she shuddered. "If I did say I wished him dead, it—it—could not have brought the death upon him. I did not really wish it. I said it in my fractious spirit. Annis, love, I would give all I am worth to bring him back to life. Why, why did he attempt to cross that dangerous stream?"

Give all she was worth to bring him back to life? How many of us pour forth the same unavailing wish, for evil done, or said, or rendered, to those who are gone! And we can only prostrate ourselves in the dust, as Lady Katherine did, and wail out our repentance in vain.

All was arrested. The preparations, which had been so much thought of, were stopped midway, and the servants stood in dismay over the half-laid tables; uncertain whether to finish them, or to remove what was already on them, or to leave them incomplete. What was to become of the wedding breakfast? the meats, the fowls, the game, the sweets? What was to become of the grand wedding-cake? Trivial doubts and dilemmas, you will say, by the side of that awful news which had come; but they concerned the servants, and were by them indulged in.

"What comfort can I speak to you, my poor child?" asked Miss Bellassys, getting Annis to herself, and sheltering her aching head upon her bosom.

"None just yet, Aunt Ruth," was the subdued answer. "I do not know that I could bear it."

"But, my dear child, this apathy, this absence of emotion is unnatural," urged Miss Bellassys, who was fearing from it she knew not what of consequences. "Better that you should give way, and weep."

"I can't," said Annis: "my eyes burn so."

Was she going out of her mind? Miss Bellassys felt her own pulses quicken at the fear. "My dear," she gravely said, "you must bear up for your father and mother's sake. You are all they have."

"Oh, yes! I shall bear up. I shall not die. I may get better, Aunt Ruth, when the years have gone on."

"The *years!*" ejaculated Miss Bellassys, aghast at the word.

"It will take me a long while," she simply answered. "You cannot tell what he was to me."

Miss Bellassys leaned her head upon her hand, and looked at Annis, her eyes, her tone full of solemn meaning. "Do you know, Annis, that I believe there arises in all our lives some one especial period, above all others, when we have most need of God?—when, but for God's sheltering hand, we might lie down under our grievous weight of sorrow, and die? Such a time is this, for you."

"Yes," answered Annis, speaking with somewhat less of apathy.

"But God *is* with us, my child. He is with you, be assured, and will bear you up through this dreadful trial. Put your whole trust in Him."

"I will, I will," she said, with energy, a revulsion of feeling coming over her. And she burst into a flood of distressing tears.

Miss Bellassys left her. She thought it might be better that the grief should have full vent. Outside the door stood Lady Katherine, listening to the sounds of distress.

"Oh, Ruth, what shall I do?" she cried, in anguish. "We cannot comfort her. We cannot bring him back to life! That wicked wish will haunt me to my dying day."

"Your consolation must be that you did not mean it," murmured Miss Bellassys, knowing not what else to say. "It was spoken impulsively; without thought: we are all too apt so to speak."

"No, I did not mean it, I did not mean it," bewailed Lady Katherine, wringing her hands. "God knows I did not. And yet—how shall I dare ask forgiveness of Him?"

If any lingering doubt, suggesting a glimmer of hope, had remained in the mind of the rector during the night, the morning dispelled it. A hundred times during those long hours had the argument presented itself to his reason: Mr. Olliver might have dropped this cane, might have gone off afterwards to see some patient, and would be home again in the morning. But the morning broke, and brought him not. With the first glimmer of dawn Hilton-Coombe was astir, for the calamity touched its inhabitants in no measured degree. Apart from the distressing character of the accident,—and it would have been distressing happening no matter to whom,—Mr. Olliver was a favourite with all. In himself, as in his professional capacity, he enjoyed the esteem, the respect, it may be said the admiration of Hilton-Coombe. The banks of the stream were crowded. People flocked down thither, seeking traces of the accident. The marks, discerned by Mr. Dudley the previous night, imparting the idea that some one had slipped, in stepping up the bank after crossing the bridge, and had slid back again, were examined with anxious curiosity. The marks were quite deep in the mud, but sufficiently clear: in fact, the mud seemed much disturbed, as though some one had completely fallen there. The miller's son told the tale of his finding the cane over and over again; no sooner had one set of listeners heard it, than they were replaced by another. He had gone on the stream in his punt, in pursuance of something required in his business, when he saw the cane come floating down towards him. He picked it up, and when he went indoors, carried it with him. Some hours afterwards, when Ben entered, he mentioned that Mr. Olliver was supposed to be missing, and it then flashed over the mind of both that this was Mr. Olliver's cane; they recognised it, now the clue was given. "You had better run with it at once to the rectory," the young man said to Ben. All this gossip was retailed over again and again; and preparations were made for dragging the stream.

The morning went on. At ten o'clock old John came to the rectory for the church keys. Mr. Dudley went out to him, looking pale and ill. The loss of Mr. Olliver, whom he so greatly liked and esteemed, and the rending of his daughter's happiness, were indeed heavy trials to him.

"What do you want the keys for, John?" he asked.

"The church was to be opened at ten o'clock, ready for the wedding," was old John's sapient response.

"But there can be no wedding. What are you thinking of?"

Old John deliberated. "And them green things that we put in the church last night? I might as well go and clear 'em away, sir."

A strangely keen pang shot across Mr. Dudley's heart. The evergreens which had been placed there for so different a purpose, to be swept away ignominiously now! Somehow he could not bear to order it.

"Not just yet, John; not just yet. There's plenty of time."

"Very well, sir. But he is certain to be dead, poor gentleman. If he was in life, he'd be here fast enough for his own wedding."

"I know he is dead—that there is no hope," wailed the rector. "But—don't sweep the boughs away yet. These windows overlook the churchyard, and it will bring the calamity all the more forcibly home to—to Lady Katherine."

The clerk took his departure. Presently a crowd came up from the stream and sought the rector. The drags had been plied, but they had brought forth nothing. Still there could not be a doubt of Mr. Olliver's fate: his non-appearance to fulfil the contract of his marriage proved it. Would Mr. Dudley order the death-bell to be tolled for him?

Oh, no! not then. How could they, the rectory's inmates, bear the sound of the death-bell, ringing out at the very hour that, if all had gone right, those other bells, the joyous ones, would have rung out? "My daughter could not bear it," he said to them.

"True, true," they answered, struck with compunction for their want of thought. "Poor Miss Dudley! What a wedding-day! what a wedding-day!"

The day dragged itself on, and the shades of evening began to fall. The rectory that day had been like a fair, people tramping in and out of it. Hilton-Coombe made the calamity its own, and pressed its friendly sympathy, its lamentings on the rectory in person. Had testimony been needed by Mr. Dudley and Lady Katherine of the worth of their intended son-in-law, of the estimation in which he was held, that day would have supplied it. Many a case of benevolence, exercised in his professional capacity, of considerate kindness to the poor, which otherwise would never have been held up to the light, was poured forth then. "What a good man we have lost," breathed Lady Katherine, as she wiped the dews of remorse from her troubled face.

"How do you feel, my child?" whispered the rector, approaching the sofa where Annis sat so still and quiet, her head bent in the dusk of the evening.

She turned and laid it upon his arm, not speaking.

"Remember our Father's promise," he continued, bending his lips on her cold cheek. "As thy day is, so shall thy strength be."

"Yes, yes, papa," she breathed. "It is His strength which is keeping me up, not mine."

That troublesome old John again! The rector was called out to him. "Them boughs, sir? *Be* they not to be got out of the church to-night? It'll never do to let 'em stop in for service to-morrow. The folks would do nothing but stare at 'em."

"For service to-morrow?" mechanically repeated Mr. Dudley.

"It will be the 1st of November, sir; All Saints' Day."

In his great trouble, the rector had positively forgotten the fact. For once in his life the coming day, marked in the Church calendar, had slipped his memory. "To be sure, to be sure," he cried. "Clear the evergreens out at once, John. It is dusk now, and you may escape spectators."

Old John took the keys, and made the best of his way to the church. He had barely entered it, when a sharp knocking came sounding right in his face, inside the vestry door.

"Lawk a mercy!" ejaculated he, startled half out of his senses.

The knocking came again, sharper than before. It may be that a thought of ghosts crossed John's mind, causing him to hesitate; to doubt whether he should not run out of the church, bellowing, and alarm the neighbourhood. But ghosts don't knock, or speak either; and this one was calling out, in unmistakably stentorian tones, "Let me out! Open the door!"

The vestry door—it has, however, been explained, that though called the vestry door, it was only the door of a small place leading to the vestry—opened from the outside alone. The clerk turned the latch, and—saw Mr. Olliver.

"Heaven be good to us!" he repeated. "Then—are—you—not at the bottom of the mill-stream, sir?"

"I hope not," replied Mr. Olliver. "Am I supposed to be there, John?"

"Well, yes," said John. "The drags have been at work all day; but they haven't fished you up yet."

He sat down on a gravestone to overget his astonishment, and stared at Mr. Olliver. That gentleman did not present a very reputable appearance, inasmuch as the front of his black evening suit was a mass of mud, which had dried on.

"Have you been in there all this time, sir?"

"Yes, I have; since you quitted the church last night, after decorating it."

The story was soon told. It was a very simple one. In passing over the bridge the previous night, Mr. Olliver by some means let fall his cane. Making a spring to catch it, he fell down upon the muddy bank, hands and knees and clothes, and slid downwards in the slippery mud. The cane went floating along the stream, and Mr. Olliver was a sight to be seen in his state of mud. There was no time to look after the cane; poor Mrs. Key was in urgent need of her medicines, and he hastened on by the path leading through the churchyard. The lights and voices in the church attracted him to enter; he knew what they were doing, that merry group, and he intended to treat himself to a secret peep. But, at the same moment, the inner doors opened; Georgina Balme came forth; and Mr. Olliver, not caring to be seen in his muddy attire, slipped inside the open door, of the vestry passage. There he waited until the coast should be clear again; and there he got—shut in. Old John closed the door in passing it; and it was only by the silence that supervened that Mr. Olliver awoke at length to the unpleasant fact that he was fast, and the church empty. He tried the vestry door, but that was also fast—thanks to the clerk's habit of locking every place up; he shouted and knocked, but without much hope of being heard. In fact, there was no probability that he could be heard; the passage was an inner passage, and any noise made in it would not be likely to penetrate outside. And there he had remained, with the best patience he could call up.

"I should think you are hungry, sir," cried John,

unromantically. "What a blessed sight you'll be for Miss Annis!"

She—Annis—was still sitting on the sofa as her father had left her, alone in the room. Mr. Olliver went in quietly; he had gone straight up from the church, in spite of his muddy clothes.

"Annis!"

She started up at the voice, her eyes staring fitfully. Did she think it his ghost,—as perhaps old John had thought? But there was no time to give way to fear, for Mr. Olliver caught her to him, and sheltered her on his bosom.

"I am not dead, my darling. I hear you have been fearing it." And Annis burst into delicious tears.

The news spread through the house, and everybody in it came flocking in. Mr. Olliver thought his hand would have been shaken off. Lady Katherine seized hold of him, and—gave him a hearty kiss.

"This past night and day have taught me to appreciate you, Mr. Olliver, if I never did before. I shall give her to you with all my whole heart."

He laughed with pleasure, and grasped Lady Katherine's hand in his. "Does anybody know how Mrs. Key is?" he inquired.

"Better. She—"

A joyous peal of ringing bells burst out from the church, hard by. The clerk, on his own responsibility, had set some ringers to work. But he had not remained with them, for there was his happy old face peeping into the room, and singling out the rector.

"About them evergreens, sir? Be they to be cleared out now, or to be left for to-morrow morning?"

Mr. Dudley turned his eyes on Mr. Olliver, on his daughter's blushing face, and read the signs.

"You may as well let them be, John," said he. "I suppose a marriage celebrated on All Saints' Day will stand good?"

"I expect it will," replied John. And he went to help the ringers.

"How merciful has God been to *me* this night!" was the concluding thought of Lady Katherine Dudley.

THE END.

PRINTING OFFICE OF THE PUBLISHER.

Printed in Great Britain by
Amazon.co.uk, Ltd.,
Marston Gate.